Praise for *Love Child*

THE INN AT VERDE SPRINGS TRILOGY
BOOK TWO

LOVE CHILD

Wendy Cohan

LUCID
HOUSE
PUBLISHING

LU(ID
HOUSE
PUBLISHING

Published in the United States of America by Lucid House Publishing, LLC
www.LucidHousePublishing.com
©Copyright 2023 by Wendy Cohan
This title is available in print and as an e-book via Lucid House Publishing, LLC.
Cover and interior design: The Design Lab Atlanta, Inc.
Author photo: Sarah McIntyre Photography, Albuquerque, NM
All rights reserved. First edition of *The Inn at Verde Springs Series* Book 2.

Love Child is a work of fiction and the events described are not biographical in nature. All characters and events in the book are wholly derived from the author's imagination and life experience, and any resemblance to real people or events is coincidental. Some geographical and business locations are mentioned by name to orient the reader. However, the setting of the novel, Verde Springs, is purely fictional and intended to evoke small-town life in the American Southwest. Please do not rely on any of the medical advice suggested in this novel. For all health concerns, please see a qualified physician.

Library of Congress Cataloguing-in-Publication Data
Name: Cohan, Wendy 1960–
Love Child/Wendy Cohan
Description: First Edition. Book 2, the Inn at Verde Springs Trilogy/Marietta, Georgia: Lucid House Publishing, 2023
Identifiers: Library of Congress Control Number: TK
ISBN: 978-1950495436 (paperback)
ISBN: 978-1950495443 (e-book)
Subjects: 1) Contemporary Romance 2) Sisters Fiction 3) Divorce Fiction
4) Women's Fiction 5) New Mexico volcanic action 6) Traumatic accident
7) Unexpected inheritance 8) Custody battle 9) Northern New Mexico 10) Single mother
11) High-risk pregnancy 12) Estranged family 13) Wedding planner 14) Tech entrepreneur
FIC027020
FIC027100
FIC027340
FIC027110

Love Child is dedicated to my own two precious babies,

Bridger Cohan and Bryce Cohan,

all grown up and experiencing life and love on their own.

No mama could be prouder or more delighted.

"Getting over a painful experience is much like crossing monkey bars.

You have to let go at some point in order to move forward."

– C.S. Lewis

"Realize deeply that the present moment is all you ever have."

– Eckhart Tolle

PROLOGUE

Late October

"*I*'m late," Paige Crawley said, holding her Google Pixel to her ear.

Late for what? A business meeting? A coach made out of a pumpkin? A very important date? her sister, Harper, asked.

"You know, LATE. As in…"

Oh, gotcha. So…nothing's happened there since a certain night spent making whoopee with the Lord of the Renaissance Ball?

Paige nodded, chewing on her lower lip. "Ed Barrett. It's okay to call him by his name, Harper. I've been known to skip a few weeks when I'm under a lot of stress, but I'm not usually *this* late. Even though I turned thirty-eight last month, I haven't had any other signs of early menopause, and this would be, like, *precocious* menopause. Besides, I've been throwing up every morning like clockwork."

That sounds awful, Paige. What are you going to do?

"I'll be home in a few more days. Then, I guess I'll be making a trip to the pharmacy. I really don't want to find out when I'm alone in a generic hotel room. That would be a sad story to tell my future child."

No kidding," Harper said. *Don't worry too much. I'll be here, and we'll find out together. Until then, drink a lot of ginger tea and try to stay hydrated.*

Paige flew home after spending a week co-hosting a conference for Virginia's Chamber of Commerce leadership. After eliminating the university's business department and any chance she'd had at making tenure, her former provost had thrown her a bone, and the money had been hard to pass up. But she *hadn't* expected to be suddenly struck down with what she was almost sure was morning sickness. After catching the red-eye from Virginia, she transferred in Denver and arrived in Santa Fe at the crack of dawn. But her early-bird sister wouldn't mind the two-hour round-trip to pick her up.

Fatigue struck her hard as she prepared to exit the plane. Uncharacteristically, she felt fuzzy in the noggin and weak in the knees. Between having to use the bathroom annoyingly often, and throwing up twice, she probably hadn't had enough to drink to stay properly hydrated. If the next few months were going to be this miserable, she was going to be one unhappy camper.

"Well, *you* look a little green around the gills. I hope you held onto your motion sickness bag from the flight—you might need it," Harper greeted her in arrivals. "Here, let me take your carry-on before I have to mop you up off the floor."

Not for the first time, Paige wished for a kinder, gentler sister. When it came to having her back, Harper never let her down—and still feeling woozy, she was grateful for her sister's strong arm linked with hers. She just wished Harper came with a mute button. "Thanks for picking me up. We just need to swing by baggage claim and we'll be out of here." As they navigated the small rustic airport, tiny black dots swam in front of her eyes.

Once they reached the baggage carousel, Paige slumped into a seat, leaned back, and closed her eyes. "I hope it doesn't take long, or else I'll have to use the bathroom again."

"Oh, I brought you this," Harper said, handing her a bottle of lemon-ginger tea. "I thought it couldn't hurt."

"Thanks, that's really sweet," she said, twisting open the lid. When she heard the carousel start up, she asked, "I think I need a minute—could you please look out for my bag? It's the big Luis Vuitton."

"Not a problem. You just stay here and rest."

Paige breathed slowly through pursed lips. *If she could just postpone her queasiness long enough to take in some fluids…*

Harper returned momentarily with her suitcase, but when Paige leaned forward to stand up, her wobbly legs wouldn't support her and she crumpled back into the chair.

"Easy, there. You're white as a sheet! Breathe in, breathe out—breathe in, breathe out," Harper coached, pursing her lips.

"I'm not in labor, Harper, I'm just a little light-headed. Give me a minute—better yet, go find a wheelchair, please." She had to admit, focusing on her breathing helped a little, and when she could open her eyes without seeing spots, she sipped on the lemon-ginger tea and attempted to rally. Verde Springs was less than an hour away. Assuming she'd make it back to the ranch, she planned to take the rest of the day off. Then, a new thought entered her foggy brain: *What if she wasn't pregnant? What if she'd contracted some horrid contagious illness, and by now, she'd probably infected everyone on the plane—and her sister, to boot? In these days of unrestricted international travel, anything could, and did, happen...*

Harper showed up with the requested wheelchair, interrupting Paige's swirling thoughts, and she climbed in like a person of very advanced age. "Thanks. I owe you one."

"De nada," Harper said, quietly, steering the wheelchair out the airport door and toward the car.

On the drive home, her sister caught her up on life at the ranch, which was winding down after their busy summer. Then she drove them into Verde Springs and found a parking spot near the pharmacy. As usual, the town felt peaceful and welcoming, and Paige felt her nerves begin to settle a little.

"I'll come in with you—but first, I'm buying you a pre-emptive breakfast at Maggie's. No one should have to pee on a stick with an empty stomach," Harper said, no more brusquely than usual.

"Thank you for your support. I appreciate it. But do you think this morning you could be a little less, well, *you?*" Paige asked, as they exited 'Ethel,' the luxury SUV Harper had inherited from their late Aunt Sabina. Her sister had sold the car in the spring to help with expenses—but Ethel had mysteriously returned to them last summer when Paige had the chance to buy her back. They didn't call New Mexico the Land of Enchantment for nothing.

"You get what you get," her sister responded, "especially before I've eaten breakfast. I'm getting *chilaquiles* and a smoothie. I'm still in the mood to reward myself for my incredible patience with Caleb through an entire summer. It may have taken a while for the two of us to get together—but, my gosh, does that man know how to deliver!"

"If Caleb's so good at delivering, you might find yourself peeing on your *own* stick, soon," Paige replied.

"Not gonna happen. Kevin *really* didn't want kids, so I've had the implant for a couple of years, now," Harper said, tapping her toned upper arm.

Even with her summer tan fading, her sister already looked like a New Mexico outdoors-woman, while a glance in the car's visor mirror confirmed that she looked ghostly pale—which pretty much matched the way she felt.

"Well, thank God Kevin's out of your life, permanently. But if you and Caleb want to make a little brother or sister for Ellie anytime soon, you'll have to do something about that," Paige advised.

"Whoa, Nellie—one step at a time! We're happily engaged and sleeping together, frequently, which is something we both greatly enjoy. Mariah seems to have accepted that Caleb has moved on, and Ellie seems to be totally cool with all of it—I swear, she could give lessons to other kids with divorced parents. But enough about *me*—let's focus on *your* situation."

The cheerful marigold-yellow of Maggie's diner came into view. She'd recently repainted the stucco, touched up the bold green trim, and oiled the double doors. The harsh sunlight of northern New Mexico required frequent maintenance. Inside, they found their favorite booth empty, and after they'd placed their orders, Harper asked, "So, when are you planning to tell Ed? You know, if there's a reason to?"

Paige drained the last of her lemon-ginger tea and set the empty bottle aside. "I haven't even let myself think about that, because it's not a decision I ever thought I'd have to make. I'm gonna need a minute."

"I'm sorry—that just popped out. It's your decision, and you know I'll support you no matter what you decide to do."

"Look, there's really no 'big decision' to make, which is probably why I've waited this long to deal with whatever's in the cards. I'll *always* believe in a woman's right to choose, at any age. But I'm capable of supporting myself—well, historically—and I'm approaching forty. So, if there *is* a baby, there will be a baby. Got it?"

Harper nodded. "Yep, got it. I'm going to just shut up now and wait for our food to arrive," she said, turning her attention to the view of the quiet town square lined with cottonwoods and elms glowing with glorious autumn color.

Their heaping breakfast plates arrived, which effectively dealt with any hangry feelings for the Crawley sisters. And as usual, they both walked away happy after a meal at Maggie's, their home away from home.

Griegos's Pharmacy had pregnancy test kits, and Paige bought two. Twenty minutes later, back at the ranch, her sister sat on the edge of their big claw-foot tub while Paige peed on a plastic stick. She'd set her cellphone timer for three minutes, and all they needed to do was press "start."

She buttoned herself back up and flushed, taking her good old time, while Harper drummed her fingers on the enameled cast iron. Finally, Paige laid the stick on the counter and blew out a breath,

Harper pressed "start," and they waited. Three tense minutes later, the timer went off, and Paige bent over to take a look. Pursing her lips, she nodded: in a little over seven months, give or take, she'd be bringing a baby home to her Aunt Sabina's old chicken ranch, now lovingly reimagined as The Inn at Verde Springs, their sole source of income for the foreseeable future. Glancing at her sister, she thanked her lucky stars that she wouldn't be doing this all on her own.

CHAPTER ONE

The Inn at Verde Springs had enjoyed its decent first season, with a successful Renaissance Faire, a handful of autumn weddings, workshops, and retreats—but they couldn't rest on their laurels just yet.

"We need to talk about how we're going to get through our last two weddings," Paige said, taking mini-sips of the pregnancy tea she'd ordered from Amazon.

"Okay, I'll do whatever I can. But I'm not exactly wedding-planner material," Harper said, "especially when I'm spending most of my free time planning my own."

"Well, the Williams-Lujan couple is bringing their own event planner, and if I'm upright, I'll coordinate everything on the day of the wedding. You'll just need to be on stand-by. I promise I'll only force you to put on a dress and behave like a civilized human if there's really no alternative."

"Okay, I guess I can do that. What about the other couple?"

"The Figuero-Schulberg wedding is very small, with family only, and I said I'd handle all the arrangements. It's in 'the book,'" Paige said, indicating the magical three-ring binder currently taking up a good chunk of their rustic farmhouse table. "Everybody just needs to do their part."

"And then?" Harper asked.

"What, then? There's nothing else on the books that I can think of," Paige said, glancing at her sister for confirmation.

"I'm talking about giving the father of your love child a heads up that he's going to be a daddy," Harper said.

"Oh." Paige remained silent for a long moment. Between fatigue, nausea, and trying to keep what she ate down, she was running on empty. "Well, right now, the thought of *that* conversation makes me want to head straight for the bathroom and let it rip." She sipped her tea and grimaced. *Flavorful, it was not—but without it, the severe nausea never let up.* "Besides, Ed sent me a text a few weeks ago. He'll be in Europe on business until after Thanksgiving. And this isn't something I can tell him over the phone—it'll be hard enough to do face-to-face. I just have to get through my first trimester, then the nausea should let up. At least that's what my nurse practitioner said when she confirmed the pregnancy last week."

Harper sighed and shook her head. "I sure hope you know what you're doing."

Paige stared out the window, breathing in—breathing out, trying to keep her rising queasiness at bay. "I was *so* looking forward to these last two weddings, and I hope we can pull them off without a hitch. Thank goodness, I was still feeling okay for most of September—of course, I had no idea I was pregnant then. The nausea only hit me hard until about the sixth or seventh week—but since then, it's been like a tsunami." She finished her tea and set the cup on its saucer. "I think

I'll head into town and see if I can find anything that will help me feel a little better."

"Ah…not by yourself, you're not. What if you fainted while you were driving? I'm coming with you, and you'll be relaxing in the passenger seat." Harper picked up her keys, leaned against the kitchen counter, and crossed her arms across her flannel-clad chest. "But you might want to change."

"Oh, yeah," Paige muttered, glancing down at her most comfortable pajamas, pale blue flannel with pink-and-white cabbage roses, complete with a stain of unknown origin on one side of her chest. *But she could hazard a guess.* Like Alice, she'd fallen down a rabbit-hole in the high desert of New Mexico last summer. Somehow, she had to find a way to adapt to all of the sudden changes in her life—and go shopping for comfy-yet-stylish maternity clothes. But with the sluggish lethargy that had taken over her formerly sharpish brain, she just couldn't summon the energy.

Paige sat down with Mel Griegos, Verde Springs' only pharmacist, who looked uncannily like actor Edward James Olmos. He suggested that she purchase a case of fruit-punch-flavored Pedialyte, and some Sea Bands—the wrist bands that Midwesterners wear on cruise ships to alleviate sea sickness. Mel helped her find the pressure point for reducing nausea, which was located in the mid-point of her inner wrist. In lieu of keeping her finger planted there permanently, the Sea Bands would have to do.

"Listen, if these don't do the trick, call me. I may have a name for you," Mel said.

"A name?" Paige asked.

He shrugged. "You might want to try the alternative route. Some people say meditation can help—and if you can't find someone in Santa Fe to help you meditate, you must not be looking very hard. But I know someone good, and she's a hypnotist, too. So, you could try something out-of-the-box like that, if you wanted."

"Okay. Well...maybe. I'll think about it. First, I'll listen to some meditation videos on YouTube, and I'll give the bands a try, too. Thanks, Mel. Can you not, you know, spread the word that I'm in the family way? At least, not yet."

"Mums the word," Mel said, smiling at his dad joke. "But, no, seriously, I'm a healthcare professional, bound by HIPAA. No worries, at all."

"Thanks, Mel, I really appreciate it."

"Do you want to stop at Maggie's for a bite?" Harper asked, when they reached the car.

"Mm...not this time. I think I need to get horizontal. And, Maggie's is where the Verde Springs grapevine seems to be rooted, not that I blame any person in particular. I'm pretty sure it's a community effort. Let me duck into the car while you go get us our bi-weekly supply of carbs and sugar."

"Gotcha," Harper said, unlocking the door for her sister. "I'll do my best. See you in a few."

Harper loaded up on all of Paige's favorites and some of her own. Maggie's lunch special was vegetable beef soup, so she got a quart to go and cornbread for each of them. Then she hurried back to the car, stowed everything in the cargo-hold, and sat down in the driver's seat. "I've got us covered for days, and we'll be home in twenty minutes," she said. "Am I the best sister, or what?"

When her sister didn't respond, she glanced at Paige, fully reclined in the passenger seat. Her sister was white as a sheet, and when Harper touched her forehead, it was cool and clammy. When she shook her hard, she only moaned. *Not good.* Instead of heading home, Harper immediately drove around the square to the small emergency clinic. Not for the first time, she was glad that Verde Springs' business district was roughly the size of a high school football field.

"Listen, I'm going to run inside and get the doctor. You stay right here, and—just, stay right here," she said, not entirely sure whether Paige was alert enough to hear her.

"Paige, you're severely dehydrated, and your blood pressure is low. Have you fainted before today?" the doctor asked. "And have you been having any other symptoms, like headaches?"

"Um, no. Just the nausea, which never goes away, entirely. I just picked up a case of Pedialyte and some Sea Bands at the pharmacy. And I've been drinking ginger tea at home. I *do* try to keep up my fluids. But, today…I'm not sure what happened."

"Well, I'm assuming you fainted because your blood pressure is low, due to dehydration. I'll get an electrolyte panel, today, too. Do you know how far along are you?"

"A little over nine weeks. Why?"

"Severe morning sickness usually begins to subside around the twelve-week mark. If it doesn't, you might have a condition called hyperemesis gravidarum, or HG. It's a more serious form of morning sickness, causing severe, persistent nausea and vomiting, which can often lead to dehydration. It's manageable, but even so, there may be times when you need intravenous fluids and even medications. The two liters of IV fluids I'm giving you today should help to get you back on track—but if not, you should definitely speak to your OB/GYN about your symptoms," the doctor said. "Meanwhile, you need a lot of rest, and zero stress. Just take it easy, and when you're feeling better, you're going to need to focus on your nutrition. Have you been able to keep anything down?"

Paige grimaced. "Not much. Some simple carbs, like crackers, and applesauce. Broth. Sometimes. I nibble on ice chips when nothing else wants to stay down. I've been pretty worried about the baby."

He nodded. "I understand it might be scary, but, as far as we know, there isn't a significantly higher risk of miscarriage with HG. Your doctor might want to keep a closer eye on you, though."

Paige closed her eyes, too exhausted to explain that she had only recently started seeing a certified-nurse-midwife, and that Janice Romero was also a licensed nurse practitioner, not a doctor. "I'm starting to feel better—a little less like I'm going to keel over. You mentioned medications? Is there anything I can take that would be safe for the baby?"

"I'm not an expert in HG, and I'm not even an OB/GYN. It's best that you speak to your doctor. When you're feeling a bit better, you should call and make an appointment, soon."

When they got back to the ranch, Paige crawled into her bed and curled up into a ball, and Harper covered her with a warm down comforter.

"Just rest," she said. "I'll give you an hour, then I'm going to heat up some soup from Maggie's and try to get you to eat something, alright?"

"Yep. Sounds peachy. Thanks."

Miraculously, the Williams-Lujan wedding, scheduled the following weekend, went off without a hitch—largely due to the couple's excellent wedding planner, Rebecca Perez. She'd been very understanding about the situation, and took charge of everything. While Paige was feeling too ill to leave her bed, Harper followed Rebecca's lead and made herself available when needed.

The following Tuesday, Paige had her second appointment with her certified-nurse-midwife.

"You're quickly nearing the end of your first trimester, Paige, and you really should start feeling better soon," Janice Romero said. "If not, then it's possible that you *do* have HG. But let's cross that bridge when we come to it. Meanwhile, just stick with rest and hydration, and keep your stress levels low. Believe it or not, the safest 'medication' we can try isn't a medication at all: it's pyridoxine, or vitamin B6, which has a good safety record. It can improve nausea, and it has minimal side effects, so we usually begin with pyridoxine as the initial treatment. I'll write the dosage on your discharge instructions, and you can pick it up over-the-counter at any pharmacy."

"Thanks, I'll give that a try. Meanwhile, I'll try to get as much rest as I can. We'll host our last wedding this weekend, but it's very small. After that, we'll be in our slow winter season for a few months. Thank you, God."

"That's great timing, and I'm happy to hear it. But if your symptoms persist, or start to worry you, don't hesitate to call and make an emergency appointment. Night or day, we always have a nurse-midwife on call," Janice said, handing Paige her discharge instructions. "So, call us."

On the drive home, Paige reclined her seat and practiced the breathing exercises she'd been learning online. "Would you mind driving like a little old lady on the way home?" she asked.

"Your wish is my command. What music do you want to listen to?" Harper asked, reaching for the car's stereo.

"Unless you know of a musical genre that specifically reduces nausea, I'd prefer silence."

"For a variety of reasons, I am really, really hoping you're coming to the end of your ordeal, Paige."

CHAPTER TWO

Six weeks later…

"We're going in, Harper, and you're going to try on whatever I hang over the door. You are *not* buying a vintage wedding dress from an online retailer in Pagosa Springs, and I don't want to hear any more about it. If I can face looking in a mirror, so can you," Paige said, as the two of them drove toward Santa Fe on the recently plowed and cindered highway. She wasn't a fan of their recent frigid weather. For some reason, she'd thought the winters here would be milder than winters in Virginia—after all, New Mexico seemed to be a lot farther south on the map. *She hadn't been remotely prepared.*

"But you look adorable with your tiny baby bump. While I look like shi—somebody who was shoveling chicken poop an hour ago and then had to hurry through a three-minute shower because of the drought."

Harper was learning to navigate the world without cursing, because her fiancé's five-year-old daughter had recently started kindergarten. Both she and Caleb wanted Ellie to make a good impression, and not get sent to the principal's office for a potty mouth on a regular basis.

"It's your wedding—don't you want Caleb to be knocked off his feet when he sees you? Besides, haven't you ever been to a museum? People used to be *tiny* a long time ago—you wouldn't even fit into a vintage, size-four wedding gown."

"I'm only agreeing to try on dresses if you promise to take me out for an early dinner, somewhere nice. Having a quick bite to eat seems like a thing we should probably do after shopping for my bridal gown, even if it is the second time around."

"Are you kidding? I'm nervous enough spending time in Santa Fe, without parading myself around town. Ed's *home*, now. What if he *sees* me? He's not stupid. Ed's probably a certifiable genius, and he won't have much trouble putting three-and-a-half months and a regretful amount of mead together in his head." The longer Paige had put off telling Ed, the harder it had become. Actually, that was an understatement the size of their neighbor, Texas.

"Well, it's your choice. I can always buy the vintage dress online."

"Alright, we'll find you something to eat. Then we're heading straight back to the ranch. I need a nap," she snapped, before reclining her seat and closing her eyes.

Giving up the battle, Harper shrugged and moved on. "So, I hate to bring up a sensitive subject, but when, exactly, did you conceive your love child?"

"Why?" asked Paige.

"I want to do the math in my head," Harper said.

Paige shook her head, "I have my due date marked on my calendar in bright red Sharpie: The baby is due April twenty-sixth."

"And Caleb and I are getting married the second weekend in April, which is as close as we could get to the one-year anniversary of the day we met," Harper reminded her. "According to the websites I'm obsessed with, first babies can sometimes be a little late, but you can't really count on that. So, in case you weren't aware, you'll be roughly eight-and-a-half months pregnant, with the clock ticking."

"You couldn't have picked a better time to get married?" Paige grumbled. "Like, the second weekend in June? I don't think they'd let anyone stay pregnant for *ten* months."

"Well, not another date that has personal significance to us, and that will work with both of our schedules. The second weekend in April is right before the beginning of Caleb's busy construction season, but it's still in the lull between spring break and the start of our summer season at the Inn. And we'll need at least two weeks for our honeymoon. I'm sorry, but it's really the only possibility, and we're not changing it. You can hardly blame *us* for not anticipating whatever's going on in there," she said, waving vaguely in the direction of Paige's sizeable baby bump. "Let's just hope this kid's on-time, or overdue. An early bird would really mess things up."

"So…I guess I'll just be the one wearing a circus tent," said Paige. "So, what specific color of circus tent should I be looking for? Have you decided?"

Ignoring her, Harper continued, "So, *maybe,* we should spend a little more time shopping for the perfect matron of honor dress for you, and a little less time shopping for the perfect wedding dress for me. *Mine* will be a lot easier."

After navigating the maze of narrow streets in Santa Fe's hip business district, she skillfully parked the car against the curb a few spaces from the bridal shop, and they both headed out into the frigid December weather.

Harper began to walk toward the bridal shop, then turned on her heel and headed back toward the car.

"*Now*, where are you going?" Paige asked.

"To get the pillows out of the back. We're going to need a ton of padding if we're going for a realistic effect," Harper said.

"But Birdy and Sunny sleep on those pillows and they're covered in dog hair," Paige protested. "What if I pick up a tick or something? I don't think Lyme disease would be good for my love child."

"It's not tick season yet—that comes in the spring," Harper said, sighing. "Haven't I taught you anything?" She shrugged, putting the dog pillows back in Ethel and closing the car door. And without further argument they made their way into the bridal shop.

Paige found a selection of gowns for Harper to try on, which, in her mind, was today's priority. After a few minutes, Harper came out and modeled two gowns that really suited her. The first one had a halter top and a back that dipped low, which looked fabulous on Harper's toned body. *But, early spring in New Mexico?* The chances of snow were pretty darn high. As a former resident of bucolic Richmond, Virginia, Paige found Northern New Mexico's climate appalling; the temperature swings, alone, were mind-boggling—from the low twenties to the high fifties on a daily basis.

The second gown Harper tried on was a simple tea-length sheath with three-quarter-length sleeves, tiny buttons running up the back, and a loose drapey neckline. The ivory tone set off her sister's fair skin and tawny brown hair. She'd let it grow out over the past few months, until it loosely brushed her shoulders. Harper liked to pull it back into a pony-tail when she was working. And since she was no longer married to Kevin, an up-and-coming architect who favored the big city, she'd completely ditched her former pixie-chic haircut and all-black ensembles. Whatever she was doing was working—she'd never looked happier or more beautiful.

"So, what do you think?" Harper asked.

"If it were a summer wedding on a really warm day, I'd go for the halter top. But early April in northern New Mexico? I'd hate for you to get hypothermia on your wedding day. The dress you have on now is perfect—but if you want to keep looking, we have time. You don't need to decide today."

Harper scrunched her face in the mirror. "I like this dress a lot, but I might need a few days to think about it. I think I'll put this one on hold. Now, you," she said.

"No way. I looked around while you were in there dreaming about your spring wedding, and I didn't see any maternity dresses that would suit me. Besides, I can't seem to make my mind up about anything, right now." Paige said, battling shopping fatigue. She'd much prefer to go home, curl up in her warm cozy bed, crawl under her down comforter, and sleep until the baby started kicking.

"Well, maybe women who are going to be close to full-term don't have such great options—just pick something you'll be comfortable in," Harper advised, talking through the dressing-room door. She came out dressed again in her usual jeans, t-shirt, and long-sleeved flannel. Then she politely thanked the sales person, arranged for the dress she liked to be held, and they both headed toward the door. "Is it too early for dinner?" Harper asked. "Maybe I should have tried on a few more gowns."

"It's only a little early, and the tiny human wants to eat, pronto. Take me somewhere and feed me. As requested, I'll treat you, but you know this town a lot better than I do," Paige said.

"The Inn at Verde Springs is close to being in the black, and Caleb's now on-board as a working partner, so let's splurge. I'd like to try that place that Ed took you to last summer, the one with the fountains," Harper said. "As I recall, you raved about your mezze plate until I had to tell you to shut up."

"It's winter. The fountains won't even be turned on," Paige said. She remembered every detail of her last meeting there with Ed, only weeks before she'd discovered her surprise pregnancy. *How strange that it seemed like several lifetimes ago.* "Okay—the tiny human wants to try hummus and pita."

When Paige and her sister stepped out onto the sidewalk, they were met with Santa Fe's brisk December wind. At least she had some ballast now, she thought, holding onto her expanding middle. Only a few weeks into her second trimester, her waist was already looking a bit "thick," like a New Mexico pit bull—an opinion she'd be keeping to herself.

When they were settled in the car, Harper's hands remained motionless on the wheel. "Before we drive to the restaurant, there's something I need to say: You *have* to talk to Ed. He needs to know, and he deserves to know. You've been feeling a little better over the last couple of weeks, and I know you can do this, Paige. Besides, if you don't stay out of the kitchen and stop 'procrasti-baking,' I'll never fit into my wedding dress."

"I *know* I have to tell him, and I don't know *why* I'm having such a hard time with this, or, to be honest, making any decisions at all.

My brain is in a fog most of the time, and all I want to do is sleep twelve hours a day. I'm happy to be pregnant, but who knew building a human could be this hard?"

Harper sighed. "Focus on the bright side—at least you're not throwing up much anymore. Just…let go of any emotion or expectation. Give Ed a call and state the plain facts. If you need to tell him in person, meet him for coffee. Then, share the good news, and we'll take it from there. He *has* to know, and *you* have to be the one to tell him. There's no point in waiting any longer—you're already starting to show!"

It was probably all of the procrasti-baking. "Thanks for pointing *that* out," Paige sniffed, catching the tears that spilled over with a brush of her hand. *Damn it, she wasn't a crier!* This constant surge of hormones was turning her into someone far removed from the sensible, direct person she knew herself to be. But her sister had made one valid point: at least she'd finally stopped throwing up.

Twenty minutes later, they sat in a small interior room—the elegant restaurant having traded burbling outdoor fountains for cozy indoor fireplaces. The warm, inviting space and its glowing fireplace embers were definitely a mood booster. Feeling like a pro, Paige ordered the mezze plate to share with her sister, and since it was nearing the dinner hour, she suggested they each order an entrée as well. In her experience, Mediterranean food made excellent leftovers, which would come in handy for late-night pregnancy snacks. After a number of weeks in which she could hardly keep anything down, she was making up for it with the appetite of a professional endurance athlete.

Twenty minutes later, the mezze plate arrived with a flourish, and the assorted appetizers were every bit as good as Paige remembered. After that, she made quick work of her Mediterranean chicken, while Harper savored every bite of her medium-rare lamb. Paige ordered another round of hot tea, and then decided to make a pre-emptive trip to the ladies' room.

Before she'd taken ten steps, she glimpsed a burly, bearded gentleman walking toward her across the crowded restaurant. *Good God— where was a potted palm when she needed one?*

"Paige? What are *you* doing here?" Ed Barrett asked, in his distinct baritone.

"Um, I'm having an early dinner with my sister. Harper and Caleb are planning a spring wedding, and we came into town to do a little dress shopping," she said, wishing the ground would open up and swallow her.

"It's…been a while," Ed said, meeting her eyes expectantly.

"Yes, it has. Um, it's good to see you, Ed," Paige said, after an awkward silence, as her heart beat out a staccato rhythm. A single microsecond later, the great hammer of justice hovering above her suddenly dropped right on her head—and after weeks of paralyzing delay, she was seized by the uncontrollable urge to blurt out the truth.

"Please, come with me," she said, grasping his arm and leading him to an alcove out of the way of the other restaurant patrons. "Ed, there's no easy way to say this, and I *know* this isn't the place. But, it's *definitely* time. I'm pregnant."

His deer-in-the-headlights look lasted a few seconds before he recovered his power of speech. "Oh, wow! Congratulations!" Ed said. "Who's the lucky guy? Is it someone you knew back in Virginia?"

For once in her nearly four decades of life, Paige was completely speechless. The moment stretched between them, long and uncomfortable, while Ed did the math in his head. All of the color left his ruddy face, then returned in full force.

"Paige, is there something you haven't told me?" he asked, in a low voice. "I assumed, since *you* initiated what happened between us, you were protected, too," he said in a low voice. "We used a condom, but they aren't always fool-proof."

"I…hadn't been with anyone since my divorce, so I stopped using anything. I know it's a shock, but I just really needed to tell you in person, Ed. It's…been a big adjustment for me," Paige said, stumbling over her words. "I was back East for a few weeks, before I knew for sure. Then, you were in Europe, and I had about eight weeks of terrible morning sickness, all while we were busy with the last of our weddings. I know I absolutely should have found a way to tell you the minute I found out. I'm *so* sorry that…I didn't."

"I've been back in town for a few weeks, now, which you would have known if you'd bothered to check your messages. What kind of man do you think I am? If I've fathered a child, with anyone, I would absolutely want to know, and I *deserve* to know. And especially from *you*, Paige. I thought we were friends, at the very least."

"I'm so sorry, Ed, I really am." The dreadful feeling in the pit of her stomach was the culmination of all the nausea she'd felt for the past few months, and then some.

He opened his wallet and handed her a crisp business card. "Obviously, we're going to need to talk about this…but I'm gonna need a minute. Call me—when it's convenient for you." Then he turned and strode out of the restaurant without a backward glance.

Paige stood in shock, her legs shaking. She couldn't move until she felt her sister's arm around her waist, guiding her back to their table. In a gentle voice, Harper said, "Well, *that* could have gone better. It's almost like I manifested the big guy to appear, but I swear, I didn't. I'm *so* sorry. This was a really bad idea—I never should've insisted we come here."

Paige shook her head. "He's right. I had plenty of time, and I should have found a way to tell him. I've made a ridiculous mistake, and I wouldn't blame Ed if he never spoke to me again." She brushed away her tears and looked at her sister. "Just, please don't say 'I told you so.'"

CHAPTER THREE

$\mathcal{E}$d Barrett sat in front of the fire savoring a tumbler half full of single-malt Scotch, but its pleasant burn didn't dull the sting from Paige Crawley's startling revelation. On the magical August night that he could still remember so clearly, he'd conceived a child with a woman he'd *really* connected with—*the kind of woman he'd been searching for and thought he'd finally found.* And, as it turned out, a woman who hadn't thought enough of him to tell him he'd become a father, for more than three months, going on four.

He took another sip of Scotch and thought about the massive impact tonight's news would have on the rest of his life. He wasn't unhappy—he'd always wanted to be a father. He'd just never thought it would happen the way it apparently had. But he'd make damn sure that he played an equal role in his child's life from day one, and he didn't care what Paige Crawley had to say about it. He'd get an agreement on paper, and he'd see that his parental rights were clad in stone. For once, he was happy to have the resources to make things happen—but he'd never in his wildest dreams imagined a scenario like the one he now found himself facing.

He picked up his cell phone to leave a message for his attorney, whom he kept on retainer: "Tom. It's Ed. I'd like to set up a meeting as soon as possible, preferably this week. It's not business-related, it's personal. Call me as soon as you can."

He stared into the flames, wondering who the child would look like. *Would the baby have his brown eyes, or Paige's green? Would it be a boy or girl? Did Paige already know?* Maybe that was just one more thing she'd left him in the dark about.

He sighed, realizing that if his own father, Reginald Edward Barrett II, ever found out, he'd be livid. Barretts did not have children out of wedlock. Barretts had carefully thought-out courtships, appropriately long engagements, and lasting marriages—all within the appropriate West-Coast social strata. Any children would be carefully planned and conceived, and before they learned to walk, or talk, their places would be reserved in all the best schools. *It's the way things were done.*

The thought of his narrowly prescribed family background caused his throat to constrict. Ed had made a decision to walk away and live an independent life years ago—and that decision had left him, as it turned out, living a life alone. He'd chosen to part ways with *his* family of origin—but he'd made that conscious choice as an adult. Deep down, he believed that a child needed two parents. Since he was fifty percent of this new equation, the best-case scenario would be to find a way to make cordial co-parenting work. But considering his emotional state tonight, that possibility was going to take some getting used to…

Possessing a strong sense of empathy, Ed tried, for a moment, to put himself in Paige's shoes. *Yes,* having a child was unplanned, and it sounded like she'd been really ill for quite a few weeks. Still, why would she *not* tell the man who'd fathered her child about her pregnancy?

Was it too much to expect that they'd handle the decision to become parents together, like mature adults? *No, it was not.* Swallowing the remaining Scotch, he set the glass down on the Mission-style side table. What Paige had done, or rather, *not* done, was unforgivable.

"What am I going to do? I've made such a terrible mess of everything!" Paige sat with her sister at their big farmhouse table in the sunny breakfast room, mulling over the afternoon's events. At least the view from the window was pleasant—Harper's creative, low-water gardens were truly a showpiece in their autumn glory, highlighting the warm natural tones of the Inn's one-hundred-year-old adobe walls. Her sister had a gift.

"Blame it on baby brain? I've been reading up, and it seems to be a real condition for some women," Harper said. "Like, maybe something got scrambled in your pre-fontal cortex, which temporarily affected your executive function? Or, maybe you had an electrolyte imbalance from throwing up so much? Low sodium impairs cognition—I think I read an article about that in *Science Daily*."

Paige shook her head. "For quite a few weeks, I was pretty sick. But after that, I was just an idiot! *You* were the one who kept telling me to talk to Ed, and *I* was the one who kept putting it off. It's true that the first trimester wasn't a walk in the park for me—and Ed and I weren't even on the same continent for over a month. By the time I was feeling better and Ed was finally back in New Mexico, so much time had gone by. I got stuck, I think, wondering if Ed would *believe* me or even accept that the baby was his."

Harper was silent for a moment, before she offered a concrete suggestion: "I know it's early days, but I think you should speak to a family attorney and find out your legal position; the custody laws could be different here than they are in Virginia. It can't hurt to check, Paige, and I still have Cherie Gonzalez's number. She's the only family lawyer I know around here."

Paige sighed. "That's not a bad idea. Can you text me her number? If Cherie can fit me in, I'll make an appointment."

"Sure thing," said Harper. "Okay, that's done. Anything else I can help you with?"

"The tiny human says she's hungry again. How do you feel about making us a midnight snack?"

"No problem. Caleb left some pizza pockets in the freezer for Ellie—she loves those. I can heat us up a couple."

"Okay. That sounds good. And do we have any of that strawberry ice cream left?" Paige asked, happy to be taken care of. Pizza pockets and strawberry ice cream sounded like the perfect combination, and for once, she didn't even mind eating processed food. She'd get back on the pregnancy health train tomorrow: *lean protein, kale, and prenatal vitamins…*

Tom Price came out to greet Ed, and waved him back into his office overlooking the snow-dusted Sangre de Cristo mountains. Winter came early in New Mexico's higher elevations, and it often stuck around until spring.

"Thanks for meeting me on short notice," Ed said, taking a seat in a leather chair.

"Of course! Your message has me a little worried, though. It's personal, you said?" Tom asked, motioning for Ed to take a seat across from him.

"Yes. Personal and confidential. I'm going to be a father," Ed said, without preamble.

"Well, congratulations! So, when do I get to meet the lovely lady?" Tom asked.

"Ah…it's a bit complicated, which is why I'm here. I spent some time with a friend and business associate over the summer. I liked her quite a bit, enough that I thought there might be something between us. And I hoped there *would* be. We ended up hooking up one night in August, which is when we apparently conceived a child together."

"Apparently?" Tom asked, arching one bushy eyebrow.

"Well, she's definitely pregnant, and gauging from her reaction to my seeing her, I'm sure the baby is mine. She's a professional, roughly my age. Although I'd been wanting to ask her out, our hookup was spontaneous, and I don't think either of us were expecting to have sex that night. But I *did* use a condom. I guess that's why they say they're only 98% effective—and Paige happens to be one of the two women out of a hundred that get pregnant." *And since he'd discovered he was going to be a father, his mind hadn't stopped spinning.*

"Wow! Those are some odds. August was quite a while ago, though. When did she let you know about the pregnancy?" Tom asked.

"That's just it—she nearly didn't. I happened to run into her Saturday night, here in town. She seemed just as surprised to see me as I was to see her. That's when she basically blurted out the truth—but I believe her."

"So…what would you like to do now?" Tom asked.

"I want to know what rights I have as the father of a child conceived out of wedlock. I'm almost forty, and I don't have children of my own. I've always wanted to be a dad, but it's never happened. Until now. And, even though I'm angry at Paige for not telling me a whole lot sooner, I'm excited to have the chance to be a dad. I'm asking you to make sure my rights are protected. When this baby is born, I want partial physical custody, right from the get-go. I want my child to know me from the very beginning—none of this every-other-weekend nonsense that fathers so often have to settle for."

"I'll see what I can do," Tom said. "Family law isn't my specialty, so I'll put out some feelers and find someone good to represent you. But we have some time: you won't have any real parental rights until the child is born. Oh, and Congratulations, Ed! Despite the circumstances, this will be a whole new chapter in your life. I have a feeling you're going to enjoy it."

"Paige, it's Ed." He came straight to the point over the phone. "Look, I know this situation is awkward for both of us, but I am this baby's father. I know you don't want me involved, but I'm *going* to be. I hope you understand. Can we come to an agreement on this?"

It's not that I don't want you to be involved, Ed, it's that I wanted to speak to you in person, and I wanted to wait until you'd returned from Europe. Besides dealing with severe morning sickness, which lasted all day long for at least six straight weeks, Harper and I were ridiculously busy with the last of our fall weddings, and I was focused on seeing them through. Yes, I should have told you much, much sooner, and I don't know exactly why I didn't. I know I owe you a huge apology: I'm truly sorry you found out the way you did. Frankly, I'm embarrassed, and…I realize that my not telling you right away was really hurtful, Paige said.

"Well, I'm glad you're feeling better now. Get some rest, Paige." He hung up before she had time to say anything else. She'd had *months* to tell him they'd conceived a child, including the two-and-a-half weeks since he'd returned to New Mexico. Frankly, Paige Crawley didn't have a leg to stand on.

CHAPTER FOUR

$\mathcal{P}$aige craved chocolate in the worst way, and the tiny human she was gestating agreed. Now that her cautious sister had finally cleared her to be back behind the wheel, Paige drove Ethel up to the ranch's Coop Studios, where Harper was working on a project with Caleb, helping to make their guests' stays as comfortable as possible Or, *not* working on a project and snuggled up somewhere enjoying some afternoon delight with her sweet fiancé. The two of them had been going at it like a couple of desert cottontails. When Caleb wasn't out on a contracting job, he and Harper were usually joined at the hip—or possibly, by some other body part.

Paige stepped cautiously onto the newly built porch. "Hey, I'm making a run into Maggie's. Do you want me to bring anything back for you?" she asked, from behind the firmly closed door.

"Yep. Whipped cream," Caleb yelled. This was followed by an outburst of juvenile giggling from Harper. Paige frowned in a way she hoped wouldn't become permanent. Unwed pregnant ladies who found themselves knocked up by a Renaissance Faire musician after drinking too much mead had to sit some time-out in the spontaneous hookup department—*and* the online dating department—*and* the meet-cute department. It was even quite possible that, as a working single mother, she'd be alone for the foreseeable future. At thirty-eight, that was a very disturbing thought.

"I'll bring you both back something—but if you make a mess in there, clean it up," Paige yelled. "We're holding a wreath-making workshop in the studios next weekend."

Paige headed into town and parked in front of the diner. The tables and booths were packed with locals at this time of the year, mostly long-time farmers and ranchers, and a few younger couples with small children. In the cold weather they'd been having, everyone wanted to be inside somewhere warm and cozy, and Maggie's definitely fit the bill. Paige smiled at Miguel Rodriguez, who lived on a neighboring ranch with his wandering rooster, *Capitán*, and received a nod and the local four-fingered wave in return.

"Hey, Paige, what can I get you?" Mariah Johansson asked. "We have a lot to choose from today." She gestured at the long glass display case, which held antique cake plates piled high with brownies, crumble-top pies, and chocolate-swirl cheesecake. On top of the display case, two large glass cookie jars held a variety of seasonal cookies. Sniffing appreciatively, Paige felt her stomach begin to growl up a storm.

"Holy guacamole! Maggie must have been baking overtime! Everything looks so delicious." Since Paige couldn't make a decision and the tiny human had promptly fallen asleep on the job, she'd go for a variety.

"Maggie's put *me* in charge of all the baking," Mariah said. "I'm really enjoying myself. It's been so great to have the freedom to be creative."

"Well, good for you! I think you've really found your calling," Paige said, gesturing at the overflowing dessert case. Caleb's former wife, Ellie's mother, had been working hard to transform her life in the best way possible—with delicious-looking results. "I'm sure Maggie is beyond thrilled, and my tummy is about to be thrilled, too. I'll start with a couple of pieces of the chocolate-swirl cheesecake." Paige also wanted something crunchy. "Hmm…tell me about your brownies," she invited.

"It's James Beard's recipe, with a few tweaks of my own. They have a delicate crust on the outside, and they're chewy and moist inside. But if you really want crunchy, I'll throw in some of the chocolate-chip cookies I just pulled out of the oven, on the house. They're still on the cooling rack. Back in a sec." Mariah returned with three chocolate-chip cookies in a brown paper sack and handed them to Paige. "Anything else?"

"Well, Harper's a big pie fan. What kind do you have today?"

"New Mexico bourbon pecan and Dutch apple."

"Let's go for the pecan. Then, I'd better leave some goodies for your other customers."

"Okay, here you go. Oh, I wanted to tell you, I'm planning to bring an assortment of holiday cookies to the wreath-making workshop on Saturday. Thanks for agreeing to hold it at one of the studios."

"Of course! We're thrilled you suggested it. It's good for us too— it's a great way to bring people to the ranch at one of our slowest times of the year. I'll see you Saturday, then. Thanks for the delicious treats!"

Paige headed back to the ranch, munching on a chocolate chip cookie. Mariah Johansson had become a friendly and familiar face at Maggie's. Over the past few months, Paige had enjoyed watching her transform from a very ill and frightened young woman, to a cheerful loving mother with a secure job, one that now allowed her to creatively stretch her wings in the kitchen.

From what Paige had seen, Mariah had done a great job reconnecting with Ellie, too. The little girl she shared with Caleb was happy and healthy, and she seemed to be adjusting well to all the recent changes in her young life. Now, Ellie was looking forward to being the flower girl at her daddy's wedding to Harper, in the spring. Which reminded Paige that she needed to keep looking at maternity gowns for super pregnant women, whenever she could manage to summon the enthusiasm. *Good times.*

Bright and early the next morning, Paige got a call from a 505-area code number she didn't recognize.

Hello, this is Tom Price, an attorney representing Edward Barrett. Are you free to talk, Ms. Crawley?

"Um, yes, I have a few minutes," Paige said, feeling a shiver run up her spine.

In the state of New Mexico, establishing paternity is an important first step in determining child custody and support, and there is a specific procedure that needs to be followed.

"What process, exactly?" Paige asked.

As Mr. Barrett's attorney, I'm not permitted to discuss the details with you, directly. But if you and your attorney are agreeable to a meeting, I'll have my secretary call you and Ed to work out a time for you all to be here.

"I…guess that's a reasonable thing to do, Paige asked, hearing the unsteadiness in her own voice. She should have pulled her head out of the sand, months ago. *Now, she had to face the music…and call Cherie Gonzalez.*

Paige had plenty of work to keep her mind occupied while she waited for her appointment with Ed and his attorney. For starters, she and Mariah were holding a holiday wreath-making workshop in the Coop Studios.

Harper and Caleb had taken Ellie to buy Christmas gifts for her mom, and for Kate and Bill Henderson, her grandparents who lived in Santa Fe. This morning, Mariah was bringing some of her holiday baking to share with their class, along with newly-printed business cards for her custom-baking venture. She planned to start small, but Mariah eventually hoped to branch out to birthday cakes and custom wedding cakes.

Mariah had asked Paige if it was all right to promote her baking business at the wreath-making workshop, and Paige had enthusiastically agreed. Verde Springs needed more successful small businesses, and Paige expected big things from her friend, down the road. Like her sister, Mariah simply had a gift.

A dozen people had signed up for the workshop, and some of them would bring a friend or family member. They'd likely get a few latecomers, as well. The workshop was another opportunity to bring people to the ranch, give them a look inside the newly renovated Coop Studios, and hand out brochures for The Inn at Verde Springs. Summer weather, which brought summer weddings, was only six months away.

Paige and Mariah had worked together to come up with a list of materials, and Harper had ordered them through her landscaping supply vendors. The workshop was coming together nicely, and if people seemed to enjoy it, wreath-making would join the late-summer Renaissance Faire as another annual event on the calendar for The Inn at Verde Springs. She and her sister, with Caleb's help, needed to do whatever they could to build something real, sustainable, and meaningful for all of them.

Bright and early Saturday morning, on a gorgeous blue-sky day, cars began pulling up outside the rustic Coop Studios. The former chicken coops' weathered exteriors and barn-red trim, set amidst the snow-covered high desert landscape, made a perfect setting for all things Christmas. Soon, they had a full house of women, along with a couple of men, happily chatting and applying their creative skills to making holiday wreaths, swags, and centerpieces. The scents of balsam fir, western red cedar, and juniper perfumed the air. Paige had placed a stockpot of spiced cider to mull on the compact woodstove, lit with fragrant piñon firewood, making the studio smell even more like Christmas in northern New Mexico.

Mariah proved to be a good teacher, warm with encouragement and praise for each of the workshop's participants. *Maybe she should ask Mariah if she'd like to use the Inn's kitchen to teach a holiday baking class. She could already picture it…*

After the fresh greenery had dwindled to slim pickings and people were proudly showing their handiwork to each other, Mariah set out a dessert table covered with her holiday baking, along with a discreet stack of business cards.

Paige praised everyone's creations as well, and ladled out mugs of hot cider. All in all, the wreath-making workshop had been a very successful event.

As they cleaned up together, Mariah asked, "How are you feeling, Paige? You look so much better—the morning sickness must be easing up."

"Yes, thank goodness! It's pretty much gone, now, except for an occasional twinge," Paige said. "I'm just trying to make up for all those weeks by eating as well as I can. I'm finally starting to get a little bit excited about having a baby! At this stage in my life, I feel like I'm really ready."

"It's nice that you have your sister for back-up. It's tough to get through the last few months of pregnancy, and the first few months of being a new mom, without family close by to help out," Mariah said.

Paige nodded. "I can believe it. I *am* grateful to have Harper, and I owe her for taking such good care of me when I was down and out. But, as it turns out, I might *not* be doing this totally alone," she said. It was the first time she'd considered making that shift in her mind.

"Oh? Well, that's good!" Mariah said. "Does that mean that the baby's father wants to be involved? Sorry—just tell me to butt out if I'm being too nosy."

"No, you're not," Paige said, waving a hand. Over the past few months, she'd gotten to know Mariah well. Although they came from different parts of the country and were nearly a decade apart in age, they'd spent a lot of time chatting over coffee and pastries at Maggie's. Paige sometimes found herself in the role of a mentor, which came naturally to her after years of teaching college students. The younger woman had been through a couple of rough years, so Paige had found herself doling out encouragement and entrepreneurial advice in equal measure. In turn, as Mariah gained greater stability in her life, Paige had found her to be a warm and empathetic person and a wonderful listener. "It's still early days. But I have a meeting with the baby's father and his attorney later this week to go over the process of establishing paternity. I guess New Mexico does things a certain way."

"It's a good sign that he wants to be involved, though. Do you think everything will go smoothly?" Mariah asked.

"I hope so. Ed's a good guy, and I like him a lot. I'm just not 'in love' with him, and I think two people need that 'spark' to make it over the long haul. But, unless I see some behavior from Ed that's a concern to me, I'm really happy to have him involved in our baby's life."

"Ed? Isn't that the guy who helped you set up the Renaissance Faire, last summer?" Mariah asked. "Does he kind of look like a friendly lumberjack?"

"That's the guy. He's not quite my usual type—and an over-consumption of mead might have played a role the night we made this baby." She placed a hand over her growing baby-bump. "But that really doesn't matter to me, now, and I'm *happy* to be pregnant," she said. "I'm getting pretty close to forty, and this might be my only chance to be a mother."

"I guess it's not surprising that Ed would want to be involved. He's a pretty standup guy. And at least he's got the resources to take care of his child—you too, if it came down to it." At Paige's raised eyebrows,

Mariah paused. "It's not my place to say, but there's a lot more to Ed Barrett than meets the eye. I mean, you obviously already know that. You two have so much in common—you're both go-getters with sharp business minds. You could definitely do worse, Paige. Unfortunately, I speak from experience."

Paige was struck momentarily silent. Yes, she supposed there was probably *a lot* more to Ed than met the eye. He'd certainly stepped up quickly to assert his rights as the baby's father, and apparently, he had the resources to hire a sharp attorney.

"I'm not exactly sure what you mean. If there's something about Ed that's important for me to know, I'm listening."

"I'm sorry, Paige. Anyway, I'm not the one you should speak to. Maggie knows Ed really well, though—they've been good friends for years, ever since he first showed up in New Mexico. I think she's kind of like...his big sister? But you could also look online. I promise he won't be hard to find, and that's *all* I'm saying on the subject. I have to head home now and get dinner started for Ellie. Caleb should be bringing her home soon," Mariah said, glancing at the antique farm-house clock on the studio's wall.

"Okay, well, thanks, Mariah. This was a lot of fun! Let's do this again next year, if you have time. I was thinking...you could teach a holiday baking class, too," she said, throwing caution to the wind. "You can use the Inn's kitchen—it'll easily hold a class of ten. I'll ask Harper, but I'm sure she'll agree."

"Wow, really? You have a gorgeous kitchen! I'll give it some serious thought tonight after I put Ellie to bed. Maybe we could meet for coffee on Monday and talk about it?" Mariah said.

"Sure, that'll work. I'll help you carry this stuff out to your car," Paige said, picking up a box of florist supplies. "So, I guess I've got my homework cut out for me, tonight," Paige said, reaching up to help Mariah close the hatchback.

Mariah looked up. "Oh?" she asked. "I thought you'd be done for the day."

Paige shrugged, "I need to find out who my baby's father really is. I have a feeling I've got a lot of catching up to do."

There was obviously more to Ed than a penchant for playing medieval stringed instruments and dressing in fifteenth-century clothes. His business experience and sharp mind had been essential in setting up the Renaissance Faire last summer. And she'd genuinely enjoyed dancing with him at the Faire's featured ball. *Apparently, she'd enjoyed it so much that it had led to more than dancing.* But she hadn't expected to form a long-lasting connection with him—certainly not a connection that would last for the next eighteen years.

CHAPTER FIVE

*T*yping "Edward Barrett, Santa Fe" into Google's search bar, Paige scanned through half a dozen images she didn't recognize before one jumped out at her: Ed's warm brown eyes in a clean-shaven face. He had a small cleft in a strong chin, but with the big lumberjack beard he perpetually wore, now, who knew? The name under his picture was "Reggie Barrett."

Following the thread, Paige typed in "Reggie Barrett" and found another photo of Ed, clean shaven and standing at a speaker's podium. This variation of the photo wasn't so tightly cropped, and the background included a banner that read, "Harp, Inc. *Make Your Home a Safe Home, with Harp Smart-Home Technology.*"

And there he was, with a neatly-trimmed beard, standing next to a well-known Colorado environmentalist and philanthropist. He appeared to be speaking on behalf of a joint conservation program to protect threatened and endangered species in the Southwest. Another photo showed a younger Ed with a less-robust figure at a green building conference in Palo Alto, wearing a t-shirt with the "Harp Home" logo in white lettering on a forest green background.

Paige recalled her own words as she'd chatted with Ed at last summer's Renaissance Faire, just prior to taking him on a rambling tour of Harper's beautiful high-desert gardens: *"So, you can play a dozen medieval instruments, you can dance and sing, and you drive a Porsche,"* she'd teased. *"What aren't you telling me? Are you the secret love child of Frank Sinatra? Do you own an international tech startup?"*

Ed had smiled mysteriously, and said, "I thought you were going to show me some trees..."

What had she gotten herself into?

Early the next morning, Paige decided to take Mariah's advice. Maybe Maggie would have the answers to her questions, if she had a few minutes to sit down and talk. Paige picked up her purse and keys and headed out to Ethel. The recent dusting of snow had melted off in yesterday's low winter sunshine, and the roads were clear. All around her, the landscape was surprisingly colorful: red earth, olive-green junipers, and the bright, nearly royal blue of the New Mexico sky.

She pulled into a spot on the opposite side of the town square and walked diagonally across the winter-brown grass toward the diner. Inside the warmth of Maggie's Diner, it smelled enticingly like breakfast in Verde Springs: pinto beans, roasted green chiles, and carne adovada—New Mexico style pork stewed with red chiles. The scents of good coffee and freshly pressed tortillas rounded out today's menu.

"Hey, would you have a minute to chat? I think I need someone to fill me in on a few things," Paige said, when Maggie looked up with a smile of greeting.

"A few things regarding what?" Maggie asked, as she finished packing up a to-go order for a waiting customer.

Paige didn't want to shout specifics across a countertop in the busy diner, so, she discreetly pointed at her expanding belly and Maggie caught her drift.

"I'll take my break as soon as I get this next order out. What can I bring you?" she asked.

"A glass of orange juice and a blueberry-raspberry muffin?"

"I'll see if we have any left—they've been flying out the door today. Mariah is such a terrific baker! We'll be lucky to have her for as long as we can keep her."

Fifteen minutes later, Maggie joined Paige in the booth, handing over the OJ and muffin. "You got the last one, but Mariah will bake more tomorrow. By the way, our mutual friend gave me a heads up this morning: I'm guessing you have some questions, regarding Ed Barrett? Who, by the way, is pretty well known around here," Maggie said, taking a sip of her coffee.

"You got it in one," Paige said, taking a bite of her muffin, as she felt a blush take over her whole face.

"But, of course, you're not from around here, so you might have been a little out of the loop," Maggie said, nodding her head in understanding.

"Something like that—and I feel like a total idiot! Ed knows about the baby now, and he's stepping up and getting involved—as in, *legally* involved." Paige took a deep breath, "Maggie, should I be worried?"

"Okay, you want the primer on Ed Barrett? I've known him for almost a decade—we met not long after he moved to Santa Fe. First off, his name isn't really Ed. He just uses that with close friends and when he's hanging out with the Renaissance folks, which he does to blow off steam after wheeling and dealing in the cut-throat corporate world. He's mostly into high-tech home security. But Ed has a real knack for organization, so he's also dedicated to keeping the Renaissance Faire movement afloat in New Mexico. And that makes a lot of people around here pretty happy, including me. Those fairs are solid money-makers. I've even been known to have a booth at the annual Santa Fe Renaissance Faire—it's good business."

Maggie continued, "Ed's *real* name is Reginald Edward Barrett III, although I've never heard him use it. His folks were loaded, and he went to all the right schools, mostly on the West Coast. His MBA is from Stanford. His folks were pretty well connected in Palo Alto and Silicon Valley, but Ed's always been a free spirit. He didn't want to be locked into the family business, working under his father's thumb—so he rejected everything about that life, bought an old VW bus, and high-tailed it to Santa Fe. At first, I think all he was really looking for was freedom."

Maggie paused to take a sip of coffee, and snatch a bite of Paige's muffin.

"Well, thanks for filling me in. I'm pretty familiar with the Renaissance vibe, but when did the tech stuff come in?" Paige asked.

"The apple didn't fall all that far from the family tree--but I'll start at the beginning. *Before* the tech stuff, Ed fell in with a group of Renaissance performers, mostly musicians, and he took a liking to stringed instruments, especially lutes and harps. The guy is naturally talented, and he has an amazing ear. Then, one day, when he was browsing an estate sale in Santa Fe, he saw a collection of door harps. You know, those small, stringed harps that play a tune when you knock on the door? They were popular for a while when Scandinavian and modern design were all the rage.

"That was Ed's lightbulb moment. He decided to combine home security technology with door harps so that the surveillance devices would be naturally inconspicuous, and Harp Home Security was born. He became a millionaire almost overnight, but that was only the beginning. Ed has a flair for entrepreneurship and business start-ups—including jumping on high-tech security, the kind you can operate from your smart phone—which has led him to be *wildly* successful. These days, Harp Inc. offers user-friendly home security throughout the world. Which is why you two would actually be *great* together—you're both smart cookies. Now, I'm going to say this as *your* friend *and* his: don't make the mistake of under-estimating Ed—too many people have."

"Too late," Paige sighed. "Guilty as charged. I owe Ed an apology, a huge one. But my main concern, now, is what will happen with our baby."

"I guess that's up to you," Maggie said, shrugging a shoulder. "But you should know that Ed loves kids, and he's wanted to be a dad for a long time. This is his chance—and I don't think he'll let you, or anyone, take that chance away from him."

"Thanks, Maggie. I appreciate it. You've given me a lot to think about."

On the way home, Paige made a mental note to call Cherie Gonzalez. She'd make sure she had equally competent representation when she met with Ed and his attorney. *If she wanted to finish strong, she'd need to start strong.*

On Monday, Paige met Mariah at the Inn, and they ironed out the details of Mariah's cooking class to be held there the following Friday evening.

Then, in the afternoon, she spent half an hour speaking on the phone with Cherie Gonzalez, in preparation for Tuesday's meeting with Ed and his attorney.

So, when you establish paternity, that sets up a legal foundation, Cherie explained. *And that legal foundation, in the eyes of the State of New Mexico, means that the baby's father can legally file for custody and establish a right for equal time with his child, as well as make decisions regarding what's best for the child. Of course, establishing paternity, or voluntarily claiming it in this case, means that you'll qualify for child support from the father to help in the care of your child.*

"But I don't intend to ask Ed for anything—I can take care of myself *and* my child." Paige protested. "I've worked hard for two decades to build a good career. I can do this on my own."

I wasn't implying you weren't capable, Paige. Now, Tom Price is a straight shooter, and from what I've heard, Reggie Barrett is, too. But it makes sense to establish a minimum amount for child support that you'd like to ask for, in case the question comes up. You'd want to make sure to cover add-ons for things like school and activity expenses, things that you might not think of right now. There's also the matter of your medical expenses, and the baby's. For instance, how good is your current health insurance?

"I'm still on COBRA from the insurance I carried when I was teaching in Virginia. Do I need to look for a new policy that will cover my maternity medical expenses? And do you know how that works *after* I give birth? When does medical insurance kick in for the baby?"

A COBRA policy would ordinarily cover maternity expenses. But since leaving Virginia, you've likely moved out of network. I think your best bet is to obtain a family policy. Your insurance company can advise you on further details. Meanwhile, establishing paternity will put your baby in a position to benefit from the father's medical insurance policy, even if you're not married. We can talk about at the meeting tomorrow, Cherie said. *"I'm happy to bring the topic up."*

"Thanks, I'm glad you're on board. This whole custody, co-parenting thing is definitely out of my comfort zone," Paige admitted. "Frankly, I'm not used to a man stepping up the way that Ed seems to be—Harper and I were raised by a single mother. I haven't heard a word from my father since I was eight-years-old."

Well, thank goodness that's not the case here. I know it probably feels overwhelming, and I'll try to give you as much support as I can, Paige, but you should be prepared. Many states, including New Mexico, consider joint custody the best way to keep both parents engaged in the child's life. So, you might want to consider changing your thinking: this will not only be your child. Your baby will also have a father, one who's making a substantial effort, even this early, to be involved in his or her life. My advice is to try to establish a cordial relationship with the baby's father now, Cherie said. *Believe me, it'll make things much easier for the next eighteen years of co-parenting.*

"I hear you," Paige said, "And I only have one more question. Ed has asked to be present at my next ultrasound appointment, and presumably, at any other ultrasound appointments, from here on out. Is that something I have to agree to?" At the moment, with things still so awkward between them, Paige would rather not even think about the possibility. And knowing that Ed's discomfort and his lack of trust in her was one-hundred percent her own fault, didn't make her feel any better.

On that question, the law is clear, and the answer is 'no.' At this point, Ed has no custodial rights.

And that, at least, gave Paige some comfort: she had time to figure things out, with or without Ed.

CHAPTER SIX

*P*aige faced her antique bathroom mirror and frowned at the puffy racoon eyes staring back at her. She just couldn't seem to get enough sleep, even though she was a few weeks into her second trimester. At least her shoulder-length brown hair was growing like crazy, one of the benefits of pregnancy hormones. It was thick and shiny, almost like she'd paid to have an expensive blow-out. She'd dressed carefully in a crisp white blouse and her favorite Ann Taylor suit in dark navy, which she'd had to dig out of a box that she hadn't opened since she'd packed it in Virginia. She'd frowned when the skirt turned out to be irritatingly snug around the waist. Her business armor usually made her feel invincible, but today, she'd settle for a little respect. *Her body, her child, her choices— surely, that trifecta had to count for something.*

She met Cherie Gonzalez outside the office building where Tom Price's office was located and they headed inside. His receptionist greeted them warmly and invited them to take a seat. After a few minutes, Tom Price came out, shook both of their hands, and asked them to come in. Ed was already inside, waiting; a *total power move.*

Financially, they weren't on an even playing field, but she felt confident with Cherie representing her.

"Thank you for agreeing to meet with my client so promptly. This is just a preliminary get-together. It's important to establish a working relationship so we can proceed smoothly going forward," Tom Price said, by way of introduction.

"We're happy to be here," Cherie Gonzalez said, agreeably. "I'm Cherie Gonzalez, Ms. Crawley's legal counsel today, and for the foreseeable future."

"Yes, thank you for making that clear, Ms. Gonzalez. Now, we're here so that my client can begin the process of voluntarily claiming paternity of the child you are carrying, Ms. Crawley. For the record, Mr. Barrett would like to know the baby's due date. It's very important to have some sense of the timeline we're working with."

Cherie glanced at Paige, and Paige nodded. "Ms. Crawley is approximately sixteen weeks pregnant, and her due date is April twenty-sixth"

"And how are *you* doing? Have there been any complications, health concerns? " Ed's attorney asked, in a friendly tone.

Cherie glanced at Paige. "You're not required to answer that, or provide that level of information."

Paige decided to disregard Cherie's comment and speak for herself. "At this stage, everything with the baby appears perfectly normal. And Ed already knows that I was quite ill for much of my first trimester."

"My client would like to be certain that Ms. Crawley is getting the best prenatal care possible—"

Before Paige could speak up, Cherie answered for her, "Ms. Crawley's prenatal care is protected health information, and she is not obligated to disclose."

"May I say something?" Paige asked.

Cherie nodded, but gave her a glance of caution.

"I'm more than satisfied with the care I've received, and I've not been made aware of any problems"

Ed exchanged a mild glance with Tom, but Paige noticed that he wasn't making eye contact with *her*, the mother of his child.

The stuffy formality of the meeting began to make Paige's skin crawl. She and Ed were two functional adults who'd hooked up and unknowingly created a baby, following a night of extreme merry-making at last summer's Renaissance Faire. *Everyone in the room was aware.* "Guys, it's just Paige—there's no need for formality. We all know what we're discussing and why," Paige said, politely but firmly. The entire meeting struck Paige was rather ridiculous—and a total waste of time. She'd had had more than enough, and she badly needed to pee, again. "If these are the kinds of things that Ed wants to know, then *Ed* can ask me himself," Paige said, establishing her own voice in the strange third-person discussion. It was especially awkward with Ed sitting right across the table from her.

Tom Price cleared his throat. "The goal, here, is just to get us all on the same page—to start the two of you talking. It's not a formal meeting at all."

"Well, if *Ed* wants to be part of the process, then *Ed* can ask me himself. Maybe the two of us should go somewhere private and start a conversation *without* our lawyers, because *this* isn't getting us anywhere."

Addressing only Ed, this time, she said, "You have my number—if you want to talk, give me a call." Then she stood up and walked out the door.

Cherie followed her straight into the first-floor lady's restroom and waited near the wash basin.

When Paige had finished washing her hands, she said, "I'm sorry if you think that wasn't cool, but it's the *only* move that felt right to me. Ed and I hung out as friends, for weeks! We danced and kissed and made love. And apparently, despite using a condom, we made a baby. I think we know each other well enough to have an adult conversation."

Although, as it turned out, Ed had failed to clue *her* in on some things, too. *Like his professional and financial status.* Not that she was mercenary—she wasn't. She'd been capable and self-supporting from the age of eighteen, and parentless since she'd been old enough to legally purchase alcohol. But she'd lived through some tough times growing up in a frugal single-parent household, after being abandoned by her deadbeat father. So, in fact, raising her child with *two* parents capable of providing financial security *meant* something to her. *And why wouldn't it?*

"Ed and I are responsible adults, and we can work this out if we both want to. Thanks so much for being here, today, Cherie. If I think I need the firepower of an attorney, I'll give you a call."

When the elevator reached the ground floor, they stepped out into the brisk winter air.

"I agree, Paige, things weren't going well in there. But I think, as Tom pointed out, it *was* just a preliminary meeting to get the two of you talking. I have to be in court in a few minutes—so I don't have time for a debrief, today," Cherie said, glancing at her cell phone. "But if you need anything or you just want to talk, go ahead and reach out." She smiled and moved quickly toward her car, calling over her shoulder, "Say hi to your sister! Oh, and tell her thanks for the 'save the date' card." Don't you just love weddings?"

Paige gave Cherie a half-hearted smile. She loved weddings, too—she really did. And now she could look forward to a lifetime of helping other happy couples plan their celebrations.

Ed Barrett paced his lawyer's office and considered his next steps. "Well, that didn't go exactly like I'd hoped it would. What did you think, Tom?"

Tom waggled his head side to side. "I'm not overly disturbed by Paige's attitude. Not all families look like they used to, with two-parent households, two good-lookin' kids, and a golden retriever. Maybe it's best if the two of you work out whatever custody plan fits your situation best. And let's not get too stressed about today, Ed. We still have time, and there's nothing we can do, legally, until the baby is born, anyway. So, you can decide if you want to take Paige up on her offer to meet and talk, and let me know how it goes."

Ed sighed. "Bottom line: I want my name on my baby's birth certificate. As far as meeting with Paige goes, I'll have to think about it." He glanced at the time. "But not today—I have to meet with an investor in a little over an hour."

Tom nodded. "Take your time. There's no hurry. I'll put you in touch with a good attorney whenever you're ready."

"Thanks for your help today. I just…wanted my voice to be heard, and for Paige to know I'm serious about being involved. I'm sorry things didn't go quite as I'd hoped."

Tom shrugged. "In law, as in life, they rarely do. As I said, family law isn't my expertise. I set this meeting up as a favor to a friend, hoping the two of you could get on the same page—but moving forward, you'll have some decisions to make."

"How did it go with Ed?" Harper asked.

"The whole process rubbed me the wrong way from the get-go," Paige huffed. "And Ed's acting as if I'm enemy number one. I *know* I should have told him about the baby right away—but it's not as if I lied about it, or pretended someone else was the father, or used a generic sperm donor and then pinned it on Ed because he's richer than Bill Gates," Paige said.

"First off, Ed may be rich, but I sincerely doubt he's quite in that level of the economic stratosphere. Second, no one is saying that you lied, *overtly*. Not even Ed."

Paige's ears perked up. "Overtly? What do you mean?"

"Well, just that…*not* telling Ed in a timely manner, when you had plenty of opportunity, *could* be seen as a lie by omission. That's just a fact. Gauging by Ed's reaction and his rush to seek legal counsel, that's probably the way *he* sees it," Harper said.

"But, remember, I was back in Virginia when I suspected I might be pregnant, and then, for weeks and weeks, I was throwing my guts up! And, there's the fact that telling a man you're carrying a child is something that really needs to be done in person, and Ed was out of the country! I'll admit I dragged my feet after I knew for sure, especially after Ed got back from Europe. But I would have told him eventually—I *did* tell him eventually. It's just that…I knew hardly anything about Ed. I didn't even know what he looked like in twenty-first Century clothing!"

That was only a slight exaggeration—she'd mostly thought of Ed as 'Renaissance Guy'—a lumberjack of a man who wore britches and stockings, played the lute, and spoke in an Old English accent. As far as dating material, Ed Barrett was completely unfamiliar territory, unless she happened to be into time travel. *You liked him enough to sleep with him.* She told her conscience, firmly, to shut up.

"Calm down before you upset the baby. I know it was incredibly hard to tell the man you spontaneously hooked up with that he fathered a child—and to subject yourself to the possibility of denial, blame, or rejection. But, Paige, you spent a lot of time with Ed while you two were organizing the Renaissance Faire last summer. Did you really think he was going to react badly? Or were you afraid of something else? Maybe you were *really* afraid that Ed would want the whole package—the baby *and* you?"

"What? Do not put words in my mouth! I wasn't *afraid* of anything. I just needed *time*, and no one wanted to allow me that, not even you. Pregnancy can be overwhelming—especially a surprise pregnancy with severe morning sickness when you're single and nearing forty. The baby could have problems, you know. I could have problems, too."

"I would think that's all the *more* reason you'd want the baby's father on board, especially a man like Ed. He seems to have his act together."

Everything Harper had just laid out didn't immediately resonate with Paige—but it *did* immediately irritate her. The flood of hormones surging through her body might also have something to do with the emotions swirling around her foggy brain.

"I don't know anything, Harper. I'm floundering in the dark, and I don't appreciate everyone piling up on me. I *know* I screwed up, big time! *Mea culpa*, and I am well aware. Maybe I *couldn't* get it together to do everything with exactly the right timing, the way I know I should have, and the way I normally would have. But *I'm* the one who is carrying this baby, and I'm the one who will decide what's best for both of us. All I want right now is some peace—and a giant chocolate chip cookie. I'm going to run into town and have a late lunch at Maggie's. You're welcome to come with me, *if* we can talk about anything other than the obvious," she said.

"I'm sorry, Paige. I really can't right now. I have potted Christmas trees being delivered this afternoon, and I need to be here to organize that. I'm trying to generate some cash flow for us in the off-season. Anyway…I think maybe you could use some time to yourself," Harper said.

"Why does everyone think they know what's best for me?" Paige demanded, before marching out the door, car keys in hand. She needed a rapid infusion of her three favorite pregnancy food groups: *carbs, fat, and chocolate.*

As usual, Maggie's Diner was filled with the enticing scents of two things that were off-limits for the foreseeable future—real coffee and long-haired, easy-going New Mexico cowboys who smelled like leather and campfires. *Who was she kidding?* She'd never been promiscuous in her life, at least in the "before times." It was just the magic of that warm summer evening, dancing with Ed under the twinkling lights at the Renaissance Ball, and undeniably, a little too much mead.

But she'd *wanted* to make love with him, that night—at least that much she could remember clearly. *Just not all of the details that followed.*

Mariah was working the counter at Maggie's, and as she turned toward Paige, a friendly smile lit her pretty heart-shaped face. "Hey, good to see you, Paige. You're still looking great. Any new developments?" she asked.

Nothing good—but actually, nothing terrible either, Paige reminded herself, focusing on the positive developments in her life. "The baby is growing by leaps and bounds, and everything looks normal, so far. My eighteen-week ultrasound is coming up in a few weeks, so I have that to look forward to."

"That's a big one. Ultrasounds can show so much more these days—the internal organs, the brain, even the baby's gender, usually."

"I know, and I can't wait! But I'm still debating on whether to find out if I'm having a girl, or a boy. I mean, it would be really wonderful to have that surprise at the birth, but it's much more practical to know now, isn't it? And I guess I have a lot of planning to do," Paige said.

"That's true, and more than you think," Mariah said, with a laugh.

Paige was momentarily distracted, as she began to mull over an idea: *she had a branch filled with olives to offer to her big, burly, baby daddy. Ugh! She needed to come up with another term.*

"Hey, can you bag me up a bunch of chocolate-chip cookies, and a piece of chocolate-swirl cheesecake for Harper? I have some making nice to do. I bit my sister's head off this afternoon, and this time, she didn't deserve it."

"You can blame the pregnancy hormones," Mariah said. "Take my word for it—they're *real*."

Paige nodded, knowing the more serious story behind her friend's words: Mariah's life had been completely derailed by severe, long-lasting post-partum depression following her daughter Ellie's birth, five years ago. "Thanks, Mariah. You're a really great listener! Have you ever considered studying to be a counselor or therapist?"

"Oh, my gosh. Definitely not!" she said, shaking her head. "I'd take everything people told me too much to heart, and I'd probably have a really hard time letting go of the trauma. Boundaries have never been my strong point—that's something I'm always working on. Besides, I'm pretty sure I've found my calling." Leaning forward, her hazel eyes sparkling, she said, "I'm hoping to open my own bakery, right here in Verde Springs, and I'm almost there. Speaking of—do you know any potential investors with a giant sweet tooth?"

Just one—but she didn't even know him well enough to know if he had a sweet tooth. "I'll keep an ear out," said Paige. "Do you have a name picked out yet?"

"I do! The name came to me almost in a dream, right before I fell asleep: The Rise & Shine Bakery and Cafe."

"I like it! Are you going to offer full-service meals?" Paige asked, wondering if Maggie would mind the friendly competition. Verde Springs was a *very* small town.

"No, I wouldn't do that to Maggie—she gave me a fresh start. I'll probably focus on baked goods, tea, and coffee. But I might offer some take-away things like rustic tarts, both savory and sweet. Bread will be a mainstay—do you know how far you have to drive to find freshly baked bread around here? And as the business grows, I'd like to start making bread deliveries as far as Santa Fe. Maybe even Taos, if I can afford to hire a reliable delivery person."

Paige shook her head in admiration. "Wow, Mariah! It all sounds wonderful. Let me know if there's anything I can do to help." The next few months would be the ranch's slow season, and she'd have plenty of time on her hands.

"Well...I *could* use some help setting up a website. I'll only be doing wholesale baking now, by word-of-mouth—but I'll need a way for customers find me and place orders. Then, when I find the right brick-and-mortar storefront, maybe I can just upgrade the website," Mariah explained. "I've got my eye on the old general store across the square, or the smaller building just adjacent to it. They've both been vacant for a while."

Paige nodded in agreement. "Those are both great locations! Meanwhile, my advice would be to take the best digital photos you can of all the baked goods you're producing here and keep them in a computer file. People will gravitate to clear, vibrant images of your baked goods. If you needed someone to take photos, I could try to look up some of the wedding photographers that covered the weddings we hosted last fall."

"Thanks, Paige, but I'm pretty good with a camera. I'll play around a little and see if I can come up with some good shots. Could I email you a couple to see if I'm on the right track?"

"Sure! I can't wait to see them. And, if you come up with whatever wording you want for the website, I can look it over and give you feedback."

"Thanks, Paige. You and Maggie have been like my fairy godmothers," Mariah said, smiling with gratitude. "I'm so lucky."

"Are you kidding? *We're* the lucky ones! Everyone in Verde Springs is glad you're back, especially Ellie. Anyone can see that she's happy and thriving. Oh, gosh, time flies. I'd better run. Catch you next time," Paige said, giving her friend a quick hug, before heading back to Ethel.

After walking to the car in the icy wind, the SUV was a haven of warmth. Paige sat and nibbled on a chocolate chip cookie while she went over her upcoming conversation with Ed. She wanted to convey three things: that she was extending an olive branch, that she'd meet him halfway, and that she sincerely regretted the way she'd handled things. *Or, mishandled things.* But since she wasn't quite halfway through her pregnancy, she hoped it wasn't too late to change the tense dynamic between the two of them. She'd hold onto that hope and do her best to be transparent and inclusive from this point forward. It was her responsibility to do whatever she could to make things right between them—it was the right thing to do, and it was what *she* wanted, too.

CHAPTER SEVEN

*E*d wore a soft, navy, V-necked sweater over a plain white t-shirt, pressed khakis, and classic leather loafers. He'd neatly trimmed his full, reddish-brown beard and wandering eyebrows, and applied just a hint of the woodsy men's cologne he favored. He wasn't trying to make anyone fall in love with him—he just wanted to look like an approachable, responsible, dad-to-be. Coming up on forty, he had a broad chest and shoulders, perfect for accommodating a sleeping baby. *His* sleeping baby. *That was what mattered.*

Although he'd been discouraged by how their meeting at Tom Price's office had ended, he'd immediately accepted Paige's olive branch in the form of last week's short phone call. Paige had made the first move to include him in the process—and he was more than willing to meet her halfway. *After all, he'd never been in her shoes. How would he have handled a surprise pregnancy?* His initial anger had cooled enough to admit that he was happy and excited to be a father, something that he'd thought was out of reach, for a very long time. His feelings toward Paige weren't what was important, right now. *For all he knew, they were irrelevant.*

As he drove to the address Paige had given him, he committed himself to keeping an open mind. Although he wanted the safest possible birth for his child, he recognized it was *Paige* who would be carrying his baby for nine months, and *Paige* who would be giving birth. In Tom's office, she'd denied having a written birth plan. But from the work they'd done together last summer, he thought he had an insider's view into the way her sharp mind worked. He suspected she had a pretty clear idea of what she wanted—and as the baby's father, he'd like to be involved, too. He hoped this first appointment would go smoothly, because if he did anything to rock the boat, now, she'd probably just shut him out of any future decisions until after the baby was born. *He couldn't even let himself think about that possibility.*

When he walked into the reception area and spotted Paige standing at the desk, checking in, he gave her some space and found a seat out of earshot.

"How are you, Ed?" she asked, after taking the adjoining chair. "Thanks for coming."

"I'm good. You're looking well. How are you feeling?" he asked, politely.

"Pretty good, actually. Now that my hormones have settled down, it's just an occasional twinge of nausea, especially when I'm riding in a car driven by my sister," she said, giving him a tentative smile.

"I'm glad you're doing better. So, are you excited about finding out the gender today?" he asked, attempting to keep their conversation going. "At eighteen weeks, it should be possible. At least that's what I've been reading."

"I haven't decided if I *want* to find out. I've had plenty of time to think about it—but it must be one of those 'you know the answer in the moment' things," she replied.

"But the doctor will know, right? Won't it be strange to have someone else know when *you* don't?" Ed asked. He very much wanted to know—discovering his surprise baby's gender would help make the whole thing more *real* to him. And since he'd been late to find out he was going to be a father, he needed that.

"I guess so—and I realize it's important for *someone* to know. Okay, just to get the ball rolling, Ed, I'm not going to be seeing a doctor. I'm perfectly happy with my nurse practitioner, Janice Romero, who is also a very experienced certified-nurse-midwife."

"So, you've not seen an obstetrician at all?" Ed asked.

Paige shook her head. "I haven't had any reason to—everything is perfectly normal. I'm very healthy, and except for my age, I'm not in the high-risk category. Janice assured me, if any concerns come up, she'll refer me to a specialist. But for now, I'm more than satisfied with the care and monitoring she's providing."

Although he didn't agree, Ed nodded. *Don't rock the boat.* He'd definitely prefer to have an obstetrician on board—preferably, a world-class obstetrician. Still, one concern came to mind, immediately. "So, a midwife? Surely, you're not considering a home birth—not with the ranch being so far out of town."

"Actually, I agree with you," Paige said. "The ranch is a little too far out from a Level-3 NICU for my comfort level. So, I'm planning to give birth in the independent midwifery center that's located adjacent to the hospital, here in Santa Fe. If, for some reason, my midwife determines my pregnancy to be seriously high risk, I'd probably relocate to Colorado Springs or another major city for the last trimester, and maybe give birth in a specialty women's hospital there. That's the plan that makes the most sense to me."

"I agree. Thank you for clarifying. But I'm glad you don't want a home birth. It's *way* too risky," Ed said, again.

Paige knew a lot of people, mostly women, who would disagree, but she didn't have the energy to argue. *What was taking so damn long?* She'd been drinking water like a camel at an oasis all morning, and her bladder was about to rupture. Surely, that was enough to try anyone's patience.

"Ms. Crawley? We're ready for you," said the cheerful young nursing assistant, holding the door open to the clinical area. Paige had never heard more welcoming words.

"Should I follow you in?" Ed asked. "Or, would you like privacy?"

Paige shrugged. "You're already here, and I'm wearing loose clothing. You probably won't see too much—just the part of my belly Janice needs to access for the ultrasound," she said.

The nursing assistant nodded her agreement, then she motioned for them both to follow her down the short hallway. She settled them in a clean patient room and gestured for Paige to make herself comfortable on the exam table. She turned some knobs and dials on the ultrasound machine, then dialed a number to let the nurse practitioner know they were all set up.

Ed sat quietly in the small, claustrophobic space, avoiding eye contact with the four surrounding walls of graphic life-size vaginas filled with babies' gigantic heads. He took deep cleansing breaths and tried to think of a calming song to sing silently in his head. Suddenly, "Three Little Birds," the reggae tune made famous by Bob Marley & The Wailers, filled his brain with a joyful beat. He couldn't help but smile. Maybe, every little thing *would* be alright. Glancing at Paige, she *seemed* relaxed. *Was she?*

"You doing okay?" he asked, tentatively.

"Yeah. I'm just a little nervous. It's not *just* the gender, you know. They'll be able to get a pretty good look at the organs and the brain, too. I'm almost forty. What if there's a problem?" she asked.

"Then we'd deal with it," Ed said. "We'd get the best people on the job, and we'd make the best decision for our child, together."

"That sounds good to me," she said, closing her eyes and taking slow deep breaths.

He hoped she meant it. He hoped Paige understood that she didn't *have* to do this on her own. As the involved father he vowed to be, his job started *now*, before his child was even born.

A few minutes later, Paige's nurse practitioner, Janice Romero, entered the room. She was a tall woman with short dark hair, bright blue eyes, and a cheerful smile. "Hello, Paige, it's good to see you. And you must be the father. Hello, I'm Janice Romero," she said, greeting Ed, but not shaking his hand. "Excuse me, but I'm all washed up and ready to go. So, shall we get right to it?"

Paige nodded and pulled up her loose knit sweater, exposing her gently rounded belly, which made the baby situation instantly real. Ed rose awkwardly to a standing position, trying not to hover—trying not to do *anything* that would annoy Paige.

"You can come closer," Janice said with a smile, waving him over. "I promise there's nothing invasive about a fetal ultrasound, and I'll point out what I can to both of you," she said, gesturing to the screen with her free hand, while she moved the probe over Paige's gel-covered belly.

She twisted a knob to the right as she spoke, "You'll hear your baby's heartbeat in a second."

After a few false starts, the dramatic sound of a rapid heartbeat filled the room, and Ed grinned. "It's so fast!" he said, in a whisper of excitement.

Janice nodded. "Almost twice as fast as Paige's. And that's good. *Normal. Healthy. Strong.* I don't hear any abnormalities. Now, let's see if your baby is ready to make its screen debut." Again, she fiddled with several different knobs, using her knowledge and experience to produce the best possible image. She focused on the head first, and the brain in particular. She stayed silent long enough for Ed's insides to begin to tighten. "Well, so far, everything looks good. There's no hydrocephalus, and, I'm seeing really good development for the age of gestation," she said.

He and Paige both sighed in relief. This state-of-the-art ultrasound really *was* a picture worth a thousand words. They could both see the image fairly clearly. This was the child that they had created together—and at a basic level, nothing else mattered.

"Now, before I go any further, based on the brain development we're seeing here, we *should* be able to determine the sex of the baby.

Is that something you're both wanting? If not, I can screen it off from your view. But *I'll* need to check to determine if there are any issues, of the urinary tract, in particular."

It was showtime or go time. Paige looked at Ed, and he nodded. "It's up to you, Paige. I'll go along with whatever you decide."

Paige closed her eyes and listened to her baby's heartbeat, muffled now that Janice had turned the volume down. *Did she want to know? She knew Ed did—and she, too, was practical by nature. What was the harm in knowing?* Besides, she'd already grown tired of calling her baby an "it." If she found out, now, she'd have another twenty-two weeks to come up with the perfect name for the tiny human developing inside her.

Then, Paige did something she hadn't expected to do at all: she reached for Ed's big hand and gave it a gentle squeeze. It was pleasantly warm and comforting, and the layer of ice that had grown between them began to thaw, just a little. *And every little bit would help.* "Let's go for it. Let's see what the ultrasound shows, pink or blue."

CHAPTER EIGHT

*S*till holding Ed's hand, Paige's eyes were glued to the screen as a swirl of space-dust shifted and consolidated into her baby's body. Two tiny arms waved at her, and two tiny feet were tucked up under its bottom like a cross-legged frog. She saw its little face, the outline of its nose and lips—a person in miniature. The nickname "tiny human" fit perfectly. Janice moved the probe at a slightly different angle, exposing the fetal genitals, and Paige saw a rounded sac rather than two delicate folds. Above it, in the warm waters of her womb, waved a teeny, tiny penis.

"Well, I'd say it looks like you're having a boy!" Janice said, unnecessarily, smiling at both of them, in turn.

"We're having a little boy!" Paige said, smiling at Ed for the first time. *A genuine smile.* She was so happy to be having a baby boy, and equally happy that Ed was here with her. He was a good, solid guy who would show up for her and the baby—he'd already begun to show her that. *Could she learn to put her trust in him? Possibly a first, for her.*

Looking at this magnificent tiny human they'd created together, she needed to share her good news with her sister, who'd been with her through every step since the home pregnancy test had been positive. *Long before she'd let Ed into their lives.*

"May I make a phone call?" Paige asked the nurse practitioner.

"We don't usually allow cell phones to be used in the exam rooms, but since you're my last appointment of the day, I'll make an exception."

"Thank you," Paige said. "I'll be quick." She pressed Harper's number and waited for it to ring.

What's up? Harper asked. *Is everything okay with the baby?*

"Everything is *perfect*—Ed and I are having a boy! Can't you just see him, wearing Oshkosh overalls, and tiny swimming trunks, and those adorable little sneakers with the rubber toes? Okay, I have to go. But I'm coming home soon, and there will be *pictures!*"

Congratulations, Paige! Congratulations to Ed, too! Is he there with you? Harper asked.

"Yeah, he's right here, and I think he's pretty happy about this," she said, glancing at the wide grin on his ruddy bearded face.

This is fantastic news, Paige! I'll ask Mariah to bake some blue cupcakes, Harper said.

"No, no artificial dyes," Paige said.

Then, vanilla cupcakes with cream cheese frosting and real blueberries, Harper suggested.

"Nix the cream cheese, too—at least while I'm pregnant. But plain buttercream frosting and berries will do," Paige said. "See you soon!" She disconnected the call and tried to relax, but she couldn't stop smiling ear to ear.

"You know, it's perfectly fine to eat cream cheese, as long as it's pasteurized," Janice said, wiping the sticky gel off Paige's abdomen. "Go ahead and clean yourself up, and then you can get out of here.

I've printed up some pictures for you to take home. This guy's a little cutie—but not that *little*, as it turns out," she said, smiling. Glancing at Ed, the midwife said, "Size *is* something we'll want to keep an eye on—especially since you're on the petite side, Paige."

"Okay…well, I *feel* fine. I trust you to keep an eye on us, Janice," Paige said. "And I'll be back in a few weeks for the next ultrasound."

"All good news! So, what now?" Ed asked. "Should we go to lunch, my treat? After all, you're carrying the next Reginald Edward Barrett IV."

"That name is bigger than the baby currently is! And I'm still getting used to the idea of a *him* rather than an *it*," Paige said, laughing. "I'd like to head home to Verde Springs, because the tiny human wants lunch, but *he* wants a very *specific* lunch. Why don't you follow me to Maggie's?" she invited. "We can have an early dinner together and share the good news with everyone. Besides, Harper's already planning a surprise celebration for us."

"Are you sure? Aren't I persona non grata in Verde Springs for accidentally, you know, getting you with child?" Ed asked.

Paige smiled at his antiquated expression. *It was possible that he spent a little too much time in The Renaissance period.* "You're still one of Maggie's favorite people. If anyone gives you the side-eye, just tell Maggie, and she'll put too many jalapeños in their food, or something."

"Okay, then. To Maggie's it is," he said. "I'll follow you, and make sure you get there safely."

"Maggie's Diner, how can I help you," Mariah Johansson answered the phone.

Mariah, it's Harper. How busy are you guys, right now?

"It's a little past the lunch rush, so not too busy. Why?" Mariah asked.

Paige and Ed are on their way to have a late lunch at Maggie's. How fast could you come up with some cupcakes topped with blueberries, or some kind of naturally-blue frosting? Harper asked. *My treat.*

"Oh, right, Paige's ultrasound! So, she's having a boy?" Mariah asked.

Yes, and she sounds thrilled, Harper said. *Ed is too.*

"I just took some vanilla cupcakes out of the oven. I could do vanilla-blueberry frosting, maybe with a hint of lemon," Mariah said.

That sounds perfect! They're on their way from Santa Fe right now, and Caleb and I will be over as soon as we pick Ellie up from school. You should join us, Harper invited.

"It'll depend on the timing and how busy we get, but I'll try. Thanks for the heads up. I'm really happy for Paige! And I'll see you soon," Mariah said, disconnecting the call.

By the time Paige and Ed walked through the door, Mariah had arranged the blue-frosted, blueberry-topped cupcakes on a tray. Maggie got in on the action, too, whipping up a non-alcoholic, lemon-blueberry "shrub." The happy expectant parents placed their dinner orders, claimed Maggie's largest booth, and waited for Harper, Caleb, and Ellie to join them.

Mariah kept an eye on the table, too, waiting for Harper to arrive with her ex-husband and their daughter. She still cringed a little inside when she was around the annoyingly happy couple—but she was *very* glad that Harper was loving and kind to Ellie. *Her daughter's wellbeing was the most important thing.* She'd made the terrible mistake of walking away from her daughter once, and she was determined to try to make up for that terrible mistake by being the best mother she possibly could. By necessity, that meant she *also* had to be the most cooperative ex-wife and co-parent she could be.

She'd learned to face the hard facts. Even after they'd divorced, Caleb had waited for her for nearly two years; and when she hadn't come back, he'd moved on with someone else. At least Harper genuinely loved Ellie, which was a wonderful thing, since she'd soon be Ellie's step-mother. *Everyone was making an effort, because that's what healthy adults do.*

The three of them came in the door, all smiles and exuberance. When Ellie spotted her and came running, Mariah stepped out from behind the counter and caught her daughter in her arms. "I'm so happy to see you, pumpkin! How was school today? Did you have a good time?"

"Yep. I like all my friends. And we learned a new shape today. A hexa-hexa…hexagon. Guess how many sides it has?"

"Um, five?" Mariah asked, giving Ellie the chance to correct her.

"No, six! Like how old I'm going to be on my next birthday," Ellie said. "Can you make me a hexagon cake, Mama?"

"I can do that. Do you want to see what I baked today? Something special?" Mariah asked, in a whisper.

"Yes. Show me," said Ellie.

"They're a surprise. Today, Auntie Paige learned that she's having a little boy, so I made blue-frosted cupcakes," she said, pointing at the tray hidden discreetly behind the counter.

"I want to try one," Ellie said.

"And you'll get one. But first, I want you to eat something that's not sweet—an afternoon snack, like a grilled cheese, or maybe half an egg salad sandwich, okay?"

"Okay. Maybe the egg salad. Then a cupcake, and can I have a glass of milk? I'm *so* thirsty."

"Sure thing, jelly bean. Now, why don't you go join the little party they're having over there, and I'll bring you your sandwich," she said, resting her hand in Ellie's light-brown curls for a moment, a privilege once beyond her reach.

"Okay, Mommy. I love you, love you," Ellie said, wrapping her arms around Mariah.

"I love you more," said Mariah. Ellie made it incredibly easy to practice an attitude of gratitude, which had a big influence on keeping her grounded. Since finding the courage to return to Verde Springs last spring, she'd been rewarded with all the help she needed to rebuild her life. *How many people got the gift of a second chance?*

Maggie and Mariah took a break and joined the two couples.

"To Paige and Ed, and their baby boy!" Harper toasted, and six blue glasses were raised in the air.

Words of "Congratulations!" echoed throughout the diner.

"To Reginald Edward Barrett IV," said Ed, in a booming voice full of pride.

We'll see about that, Paige thought, smiling. But nothing could dull her happiness today—not even the possibility of a name more suitable for a medieval lord than the scrappy son of a single mother who would more than likely be raised on a humble, former, chicken ranch.

CHAPTER NINE

$\mathcal{P}$aige had been friends with Ed, first, before the 'Mead Incident.' They'd always enjoyed each other's company—including lively conversations and a shared sense of humor. She admired his intelligence and business savvy, and more importantly, she knew he was a good person. Now, as the weeks of her second trimester ticked by, communication between Paige and Ed began to smooth out, almost naturally.

In order to keep the communication lines open, they'd agreed to meet once a month, as friends, in addition to meeting for lunch or coffee after her appointments. So far, so good, and neither of them had any motivation to change that.

Ed was present for Paige's twenty-two-week ultrasound, and this afternoon, they'd had the twenty-six-week scan. Fetal development had appeared normal in both, but Janice Romero expressed concern about the baby's growing size. Paige was petite, with slim hips and a narrow pelvis. Ed was worried, too. Going forward, he wanted both her and the baby to have the safest birth possible.

While they were eating lunch, Ed spoke up. "Paige, I wanted to ask you, again if you'd be willing to have a second opinion from an obstetrician. I know she's highly regarded, one of the best in the area, and she's not too far away—just in Colorado Springs. We could drive up for the night, find a nice place to stay, and you could have your appointment in the morning when you're rested," Ed proposed. "She's willing to squeeze you in as a special favor to me. Nina Johnson is an old friend—we graduated from Standford the same year."

"I know you're worried, Ed, but Janice said she'd refer me to a specialist if there were any reason to. She hasn't recommended that yet, and I trust her," Paige said.

"I know. But if I had to guess, I'd say she's leaning that way. In fact, if you asked Janice directly if she thought you might need a C-section in the end, I'd bet her answer would be yes. I know how much you were hoping to have a natural birth, Paige. But have you considered the alternative possibility at all?"

She put down her fork, swallowed, and took a good look at the enormity of him. *Maybe she should have slept with the court jester, instead.* In contrast, Ed had powerfully broad shoulders, and he towered over her in height. "Ed, do you know how much you weighed when you were born?"

"Yes."

"Well, how much. Tell me the truth—I can take it," Paige said.

"Just shy of eleven pounds," he said, wincing.

She threw up in her mouth a little. Eleven pounds of kid coming out of *her* vagina?

"Oh my God! What have I gotten myself into?" Paige said. Reaching for hope, she asked, "How about your siblings? Do you have any sisters, or, better yet, brothers? How big were *they?*"

Ed looked sheepish. "Just one sister. Both of us were well over ten pounds, and my mom is a lot taller than you," he said. "Paige, I'm only looking out for your best interests, and the baby's. *Please* promise you'll consider seeing my friend Nina for a second opinion," he said.

"Okay. I'll talk to Janice and see what she says. I'm not promising anything, yet, Ed, but…you've definitely given me a lot to think about." *Understatement of the millennium—her son's head was probably going to be the size of a volleyball.*

First, Paige prepared a list of terrifying questions, and then she scheduled a phone consult with Janice Romero. Apparently, her hormones had recently shifted, her brain fog had lifted, and her sharp, efficient brain had kicked into high gear, just in the nick of time.

"Hi Janice. Thanks for taking the time to talk with me. So, um, Ed and I are a bit concerned about the baby's size. Ed and his sister were both over ten pounds at birth, and neither of them were overdue," Paige said.

How big was Ed himself?" Janice asked. *These things have a tendency to correlate.*

"Nearly eleven pounds. Ten pounds, fifteen ounces, to be precise," Paige said. Taking the bull by the horns, she continued: "Ed wants to set up an exam with an obstetrician he knows in Colorado Springs. He says she's the best there is."

Janice was silent for a moment. *We'll have a much better idea of size at your thirty-week ultrasound. But there's no reason you couldn't have that scan done with the OB in Colorado Springs. Please ask them to provide me with the records and scans from that appointment. Do you happen to know which doctor he's thinking of?* she asked.

"Dr. Nina Johnson—a college friend of Ed's. She attended Stanford Medical School, and he said she really knows her stuff. Of course, after I'd spoken with you, I was going to do some background research. There's no point in driving all the way up to Colorado Springs if we don't have to, especially in the middle of the winter."

There's no need, Paige. You're in good hands—Nina Johnson is highly regarded, and she specializes in high-risk and geriatric pregnancies. She does a neat C-section, too. Being in the general, geographic area, I've seen some of her work. You know, Paige, after your last ultrasound, I was beginning to lean in this direction anyway. This is going to be a really big baby. If you can get an appointment with Nina Johnson, you should definitely take it. It'll save me trying to get you in somewhere here in Santa Fe, when you're already well into this pregnancy. Let me know what you decide to do, and I'll be happy to facilitate on my end. I'll email you a release of information. If you can sign the form and get it back to me, we'll have it in your file when Dr. Johnson's office requests your records.

"Okay, then. I'll get working on it. Thanks for being so honest with me, Janice, even if the probability of a C-section wasn't exactly what I wanted to hear."

Of course! I understand. But we all want the same thing—a healthy baby and a healthy mom. I'll wait to hear from you, Paige. Take care, and stay well.

CHAPTER TEN

*E*d picked her up at the ranch and they made the long drive to Colorado Springs—north on I-25, through the snow-covered Sangre de Cristo Mountains and over the pass into Colorado. The roads weren't icy, but the edges piled high with dirty snow made Paige anxious. Now ending her twenty-ninth week of pregnancy, she felt vulnerable and exposed. *Anything could go wrong.* Meanwhile, "little Reggie," who she'd long since ceased calling "tiny human," was still growing, and growing, and growing.

With his bottom pressed against her bladder and his feet tickling her diaphragm, she was constantly uncomfortable. Ed patiently stopped to allow her to use the restroom in nearly every gas station and convenience store they passed along the way, but in the stretches in between, she had to squat on the side of the road in Snow Parks, using the SUV for a privacy screen. Squatting in dirty snow while heavily pregnant, in the middle of a northern New Mexico winter, was not something she'd ever imagined herself doing. The man was rich, *dammit! Couldn't he have flown her up to Colorado in his private helicopter, or something?* Even though that crossed the line into diva behavior, Paige now deeply regretted not asking.

In total, the trip took them nearly five hours, since Ed had to be extra-careful driving on roads that weren't totally dry and might possibly be coated with black ice. Thank God, he'd reserved rooms at one of The Springs' finest hotels. She planned to pamper herself for as many hours as she could before the appointment that determined whether, and when, she went under the knife.

Despite his considerable size, little Reggie still wasn't quite thirty weeks of gestation, which meant that he *might* survive a premature birth—but with lungs that weren't quite ready to breathe on their own, he'd require a lot of assistance. Thinking like the mother she already was, she vowed to do everything in her power to keep him inside her until he was fully cooked, lungs and all. *She refused to allow herself to accept that, sometimes, bad things happened no matter how hard you tried to do everything right.* She could fully admit that she was something of a control freak—and now, everything was *not* within her control.

Having recently moved from Virginia, Paige hadn't yet been to Colorado Springs, and she marveled at sight of the Garden of the Gods' standing red rock fins. With fresh snow dusting the surrounding pines and firs, the view was a scenic postcard come to life. If only she were hiking-fit like her sturdy sister, she could hit the trails. Maybe someday in the distant future, she could bring Reggie here, and he could climb all over the rocks to his hearts content. *Boys liked to climb rocks, didn't they? And where would Reggie's father be? In the boardroom*

of Harp, Inc? On a plane to Silicon Valley? Could she begin to see Ed in the movie of her son's life, or her own?

"Okay, we're here. I think you'll like this place, Paige. I always stay here when I'm in town for just a night. For longer trips, sometimes a buddy of mine puts me up at his house for a few days—it's up in the foothills. But the facilities here are very nice. I know it's not safe for you to sit in the hot tub, right now, but maybe you can dangle your feet in the pool. If we had time, I'd schedule a massage for you—the spa here offers them."

"I think I just need to get horizontal before I give birth right here in the parking lot," Paige said, only partially joking. The trip had pushed her limits, considerably, and she felt a heavy ache in her nether regions.

"*Somebody's* a bit grouchy," Ed said, but in a patient voice. "Let's get you settled. Then I'll order whatever you want brought up to your room. I hope it's okay that I got us adjoining rooms."

It was more than okay—it was thoughtful and generous. Ed had also done a world-class job of driving questionable roads, and he'd brought them safely to their destination. He deserved some sort of medal, not to be burdened by an enormously pregnant cranky-pants. *But she'd have to think about that, later.*

Paige lay on her left side, as Janice had recommended, the safest position for optimal blood flow in the third trimester. She envisioned her body's circulation carrying nutrient-packed blood through the miraculous placenta that nourished her giant baby. Little Reggie seemed to be taking advantage of the quiet, lack of motion, and extra space to stretch out, and he seemed to be sleeping, too.

A few minutes earlier, Ed had placed a room service order for chicken soup, a grilled cheese sandwich, and a side of cottage cheese with fruit. And he'd requested hot water for her to make her pregnancy tea, which she'd grown to find warm and soothing.

Now, Ed knocked on the connecting door and she called "come in." But she wasn't expecting to find him wearing silk pajama-bottoms with little musical instruments on them. She identified horns, and something that looked like an oboe, and what were those stringed instruments? Oh, *harps*, of course. *Duh.* His muscular shoulders were covered with an Eddie Bauer fleece jacket in a rich olive green. His reddish-brown hair stuck up in all directions, as if he, too, had slept, but only on half of it. *He was, frankly, an adorably large teddy bear. His deep voice reminded her of country singer Chris Stapleton's—his full beard, too.* She swallowed her confusing emotions, allowing only the joyful hope that Reggie would grow up to be exactly like his father.

"How's Reggie?" Ed asked.

"Reggie's…just waking up." Paige looked up at the father of her child. When her heart made a leap entirely of its own accord, she was far too tired to resist. "Come on over here," she whispered, beckoning him forward.

Ed cautiously approached the bed and sat down on its edge.

"Give me your hand," she whispered. That large catcher's mitt of a hand was incredibly gentle and always warm, and dry, and comforting.

Paige put his hand on her belly over her knit maternity top. "If you're lucky, you'll feel something." Then she closed her eyes and let her drowsiness win, just for a moment…

※

Ed felt the warmth of Paige's belly and inhaled the particular, sweet scent that had captivated him from the beginning. Paige had only grown more beautiful and feminine in her pregnancy, her light-brown hair thick and lush and tumbling around her shoulders, her skin aglow with a mysterious light of wellbeing. Being around her was a constant and painful reminder of what he wanted more than anything, and could never have. Now, he felt a dome begin to rise under his hand, filling his palm and expanding, then contracting, like a slow-motion volcano. *It was wild!*

"What the heck is *that?*" Ed asked, in a stage whisper.

"*That* is your baby's butt," Paige answered, drowsily. "It's big, I know, like *scary* big. I think he's curling and uncurling as he wakes up. Keep your hand there for a minute," she said, covering his big hand with her small one. "If you're lucky, you'll feel him turn over. Sometimes he even does a series of cool, gymnastic moves, like some sort of double pike named for an Olympic athlete. Are there any hidden talents in the Barrett family?"

Ed shook his head, "No, I'm afraid we're all duds in the athletic department. Good brains, though," he said, smiling.

"And kind hearts," Paige added, opening her eyes and returning his smile. "Thank you for forgiving me for being such an idiot."

Ed considered her words. "Who says I have?" he asked her, curiously.

Paige met his eyes for a long moment. "Actions speak louder than words, Ed. Didn't anyone ever teach you that?" She patted the bed beside her. "Here, lay down for a minute. You can keep your hand there—let little Reggie know someone's watching over him. I'm going to fall asleep in about two seconds," she said, giving a tremendous yawn.

They lay there for a long while until he heard Paige's long, slow breaths. He ignored the server's knock on the door—they could leave the tray in the hallway. He wanted to soak in this peaceful moment and remember every detail for the rest of his natural life.

CHAPTER ELEVEN

*F*irst thing in the morning, Paige had her ultrasound, and this time, Ed held her hand the entire time. Dr. Nina Johnson was a woman of few words and an intent gaze, and minutes after meeting, she was totally focused on her work. She measured the dimensions of Paige's belly and compared it to the precise number of weeks, of which Paige was very sure.

Dr. Johnson sat back and nodded. "It's really good that you came to see me when you did. I'm not going to sugarcoat it, folks. Even without seeing the ultrasound, I can tell this is a *very* big baby. I'd say *if* you were to go to full-term, you'll *certainly* need a C-section. It would be safest for both of you."

"What do you mean, *if?*" asked Paige.

"I haven't been following your entire pregnancy, Paige, but if you were *my* patient, I'd try to get this big boy out a little sooner, rather than later."

"Isn't that dangerous?" Ed asked. "I mean, wouldn't he be premature?"

"Yes, a little. But there's also a danger with overly large babies—they don't always do well. They often have blood sugar problems, but there can be other problems, too. A very large baby's shoulders can become trapped under the mother's pelvic bones, which can damage nerves in the baby's neck, or even break his collarbones."

Paige and Ed exchanged horrified looks.

"There are risks to the mother, too, with really large babies. As I've said, it's likely you'll need a scheduled C-section, but if the baby were to come early, and unexpectedly, you could be at risk for multiple birth-related injuries, Paige, including tearing of the vagina and rectum," Dr. Johnson said.

Paige could only stare at Dr. Johnson, open-mouthed in horror, and she couldn't meet Ed's eyes at all. She felt all the blood leave her face, replaced by a decidedly queasy feeling in her stomach that she hoped would be temporary. After all, she had another five-hour car ride to look forward to.

"For the rest of your pregnancy, I'd advise you to stay close to a good hospital with a Level-3 NICU and have help available at all times. Until you give birth, you shouldn't drive *anywhere* alone, in case you were to suddenly go into labor. Given the baby's size, we should aim for a scheduled C-section around thirty-five or thirty-six weeks. Some babies get cooked sooner than others, and *this* is a baby that likely doesn't need to get to forty weeks, which is really just an average. I'll go make some notes and give you two a few minutes to take this in. Try to think of any questions you'd like to ask me," she said, "and we'll meet up in my office whenever you're ready."

Feeling a little queasy, himself, Ed attempted to sit down—but Paige wouldn't let go of his hand. He looked into her soft green eyes and saw the fear in them, even before she said, "This is scary," in a voice he'd never heard before.

"What can I do?" Ed asked.

"Just, don't let go. I need a minute to absorb all this—what it all means for me, for *us*. I live way out on a ranch an hour from Santa Fe, and even Santa Fe's NICU doesn't provide the level of care this baby might need—I've already checked." With a catch in her voice, she continued, "I don't think it's going to work, Ed. I thought that after I got through that terrible period of morning sickness, the rest of the pregnancy would be a breeze. And the last few months *have* been pretty easy, until now. This is all coming as a shock, but we have to do what's best for Reggie."

"What's best for Reggie is for *you* to be within a few blocks of a Level 3 NICU and under the care of a high-risk obstetrician," Ed said, Paige nodded her head slowly in agreement. *You could only make decisions on the information you had at any given time—and now they had it.*

When Paige let go of his hand, Ed sat down and typed a few key words into his phone's search bar. "There are two Level-3 NICUs in Albuquerque—and the University of Colorado Health System has Level-3 NICUs in Denver, Colorado Springs, and Fort Collins. Let's talk to Nina and see what she recommends."

"I don't want to be so far away from Harper. I need my sister with me," Paige said. "We've been through everything together, our whole lives. It'll be hard enough, as it is, and I don't know if I can do this without her."

Ed nodded slowly. "Well, then, that means either Presbyterian or Lovelace, in Albuquerque. Or…we could stay right *here*. Dr. Johnson already knows our situation, and she's the best there is. Harper could get here in less than five hours, and Caleb could make the drive with her. It's doable, and I think we need to consider it."

"We don't have to decide right now, do we? Dr. Johnson says I'm not showing any signs of dilation, just yet."

"No, I don't think we need to make a decision right now, or even today. But let's wait to hear what Dr. Johnson has to say."

Paige simply nodded. She'd had a lot to take in today, and she needed more than a minute to accept that life would be changing for her in a big way. *And soon, everything would change for both of them.*

They assured Dr. Johnson that they'd keep in close touch and let her know what they decided. In turn, she agreed to send duplicates of Paige's records to Janice Romero, who would continue to monitor her very closely until they'd made a decision. Then they headed out to Ed's SUV, feeling as if their lives had been taken over by forces beyond their control. *Although that wasn't very much of a stretch, it wasn't a comfortable headspace for either of them to be in.*

"You know, Paige, we could stay another night and head home in the morning. Today has been a lot to take in. What do you want to do?"

"You're right, this has been a weird day, but I'd rather head home. I need to talk to my sister—and I want the comfort of my own bed, with my pregnancy pillow, and Harper sleeping just across the hall."

Ed nodded. "Okay. But we should think about what this news means for you *after* today. I know you want to head straight back to the ranch and spend some time with your sister—I get that. But after what Dr. Johnson told us, it's not safe for you to *stay* there for very long. If you go into labor, you're at risk, and the baby is at risk. So, we're going to have to make some decisions pretty quickly, Paige. We can't wait."

"Ed, I'm sorry, but I can't take in any more right now. My head is spinning, and I think my blood sugar is circling the drain. Let's pick up some lunch to go, and then head back to the ranch as quickly as we can."

"Got it. Gas, food, a quick look at the weather, and then we're on our way. Just hang tight. Hopefully, you'll be sleeping in your own bed tonight," he said, reassuringly.

When Ed stopped to fill up the gas tank, Paige made her way into the mini-mart, first using the restroom *again*, and then loading up on road snacks. For once, she threw nutritional caution to the wind: potato chips, chocolate, sports drinks, and plenty of bottled water.

They headed south on I-25, following the snow-covered Sangre de Cristos, straight toward the New Mexico border. When Ed checked the weather report, it showed scattered flurries in the higher elevations, but nothing much happening in the foothills. The twilight landscape rolled by, high desert mixed with patches of pine forest on the north-facing slopes, and in the draws, the ghostly stems of aspens reached for the wintry sky.

Driving through Pueblo and Walsenburg, they hit a couple of snow squalls—with extreme winds coming off the eastern flank of the Sangre de Cristos. Powerful gusts sent snow skittering across the pavement. Twice, Ed had to pull over due to lack of visibility. The fierce winds made driving farther dangerous, as they caused the snow to drift over the road, unpredictably.

"I know you wanted to make it over Raton Pass and keep going, but we don't have any choice. With these high winds drifting the snow like this, they'll likely close the pass until tomorrow morning—and they'll have to send the snowplows out before they reopen it. We could be stuck here for a while," he said, with a glance in her direction.

"Well, let's try and make it as far as Trinidad, which is about the dumbest name I can think of for a town in this freezing pit of hell. I just hope they have a hotel, a decent restaurant, and cell service," Paige grumbled, wishing she could find a way to comfortably elevate her swollen feet and ankles. As much as she needed a bathroom break, she drew the line at baring her bum in the middle of a snow squall, in the pitch dark. *Guys had it so much easier...*

"Trinidad is named for the daughter of an early resident named 'Trinidad Baca'—not a Caribbean Island nation, so don't take it personally. We'll be passing Ludlow, soon, and then, it's only a little way to go. Hang in there, Paige," he said. Reaching for her hand, he gave it a gentle squeeze. "Maybe a quiet night is just what we need after today's news. And I promise to try to have you home tomorrow, by mid-afternoon at the latest."

Ed was right—flashing signs soon let them know that the Colorado highway department had closed I-25 at the border, stranding travelers headed south into New Mexico. By the time they pulled up to the Western Family Inn, which was conveniently adjacent to a diner, the sprawling motel was down to one room with two queen beds.

"We'll take it," said Ed, handing over his platinum credit card. "And we're lucky to get it," he said, simply. "Now let's get you settled in. You can change into something comfortable, and we can have dinner at the diner, or I can get you something and bring it back to the room."

Paige nodded. "Thanks for taking care of the room, Ed. I appreciate it. I need to lay down for a while. If I rally, I'll come to the diner with you. If not, maybe you can bring something back for me."

Paige was beyond exhausted. After changing into pale blue velour maternity pants and a matching hoodie, she curled up on her left side and let sleep take her under.

Ed covered Paige with a thick, fleece blanket and left the room, leaving her a note on the nightstand: *Gone for dinner. Text me if there's something you want. Otherwise, I'll bring you back what sounds good.*

When eating in a roadside diner like this one, he tended to stick with the basics: An open-faced turkey sandwich with gravy and mashed potatoes hit the spot. He ate all of the coleslaw that came on the side to meet his daily requirement of veggies, and he asked for a piece of pecan pie to go. He scaled it down a bit for Paige—a club sandwich and chicken noodle soup. She'd had a really rough day, so he brought her a piece of pecan pie, too. If pie didn't make her feel better, nothing would.

When he returned to the room, she sat up, shaking off sleep. "You're back. I must have really conked out. Is that food I smell, and do I deserve it? I've been more than a bit cranky today. I don't know how you can stand to be in the same car with me!"

"Yes, to food—and yes, you deserve it. Who wants to hear they might explode from inside, because they're carrying a ticking time bomb the size of a watermelon?"

"Thanks. I wasn't thinking in quite such visceral terms," Paige said, dryly, "but the news we got wasn't the best, I'll give you that." She held out her hand for the takeout bag. "This looks great! A turkey club, and hot soup, and my sugar quota for the day? Keep this up and I might ask you to marry me."

Obviously, just a slip of the tongue, but he couldn't help wincing.

She began devouring the food, which was a cut above typical diner quality—oven-roasted turkey, thick-cut bacon, dense whole-grain bread, and real mayo. "Pecan pie, too? *That's* really going above and beyond."

"I'm glad I could make you so happy. Maybe I should take you to roadside diners more often," Ed said, smiling. He flicked through the news channels to check the weather, confirming what he'd hoped: the storm was expected to blow through that night, making it safe to drive mountain passes in the daylight. They'd just need to wait a few hours until the roads were plowed.

"Looks like we'll have no problem getting you home tomorrow. But we need to talk about what's next, and make a decision. I'm hoping Harper can help you pack enough stuff to get you through the next two or three weeks, a month tops, and it's Albuquerque or Colorado Springs, take your pick. I'm fine either way, although my gut says you should be under the care of the best obstetrician we know. Nina has a stellar reputation. She tells it like it is, and I, personally, have a lot of faith in her. But I want to hear what *you're* thinking."

Paige sighed and waggled her head side-to-side. "I see your point, and I almost can't imagine meeting yet a *third* health practitioner, somewhere closer, like Albuquerque—and then going through all of the poking and prodding, again, and answering all the same questions. It's just that…I don't like being so far from Harper. She's busy running the ranch, and it's not like I'll be gone for a couple of days—it'll be more like a couple of weeks." She hesitated a moment. "If I agree to stick with Dr. Johnson, can you promise me one thing?"

"What's that?" he asked, hoping it would be within his reach.

"I know I'm going to sound like a total diva…but is there any way we can arrange to fly me up here? I dread making this drive again in the middle of the winter—you know, with the ticking time bomb inside me, and all. I think the chances of getting in an accident, or being stuck by weather or road conditions, makes it too risky. Don't you?"

"On that, we agree. I think medical transport could be arranged," he said, easily, "as long as you don't get too used to the extravagant lifestyle. I'm more of a sturdy, used-SUV kind of guy, and I have kind of a love affair with old VW hippie vans." *His GT Silver Porsche was an exception—but then, you really had to make an exception for a Porsche, top down, beautiful woman in the passenger seat, glossy brown hair blowing in the wind, sassy green eyes full of delight…*

"You'd get along well with my sister," Paige said, smiling. "And actually, I love that about you. I *love* that you haven't let money or success go to your head. And thank you for dinner, which was really delicious. I think, after a good night's sleep, I'll be able to waddle down to the dining room for breakfast in the morning, so, you won't have to bring me room service again. But I *do* appreciate it."

"Whatever the pregnant lady wants, the pregnant lady gets," said Ed. *Even a helicopter on stand-by.* He unzipped his overnight bag and pulled out some sweats and a long-sleeve t-shirt.

"My hero! Now, care to come over here and experience an amazing rhythmic gymnastics event?"

"Maybe," Ed said, smiling, "our boy is just a pie man." He sat on the edge of the bed and placed his hand over her rounded belly. Being snowbound with the mother of his child after a satisfying meal was warm and comforting. And, somehow, it didn't feel awkward at all. They were both totally focused on their baby, and the rest would figure itself out, in time. *Wouldn't it?*

CHAPTER TWELVE

"So, you're leaving? Just like that?" Harper asked.

"Yep, just like that," Paige replied. "If Reggie gets any bigger, he could get trapped in my pelvis, like those kids in that horrible cave in Thailand a couple of years ago. I don't want anybody to have to go spelunking—or, for my poor baby boy to end up with a broken collarbone or blood sugar problems." At her sister's dramatically raised eyebrows, she continued. "Think of it like this: Little Reggie is lightly toasted and just beginning to brown, and Nina says he only needs three or four more weeks in the oven."

"Okay, then. If that's the way it has to be, that's the way it has to be," Harper said, firmly. "I'll help you pack. Just tell me what you need and I'll be your personal valet. Really, you just need lots and lots of sweat pants and warm socks—I read that sometimes when you're in labor, your feet can get cold. And Tums. I read that women in labor can chew on Tums to relieve nausea, or heartburn, or leg cramps. And you should pack some huge, comfortable, stretchy tops—no one expects you to be a fashionista when you're about to pop."

""We're actually hoping to *avoid* having me go into labor. And can you please not use words 'huge' or 'pop' around me—they hitting a little too close to home at the moment. But I appreciate you helping me pack. Let's change the subject. How's Caleb?"

"He's good. Yummy. Squeezable. It's been so great to find the love of my life in my thirties. I didn't think I would. I mean, Kevin's regular harem of interns made it obvious that he wasn't 'the one' for me, at least not the one who would last a lifetime."

Paige nodded her head in firm agreement. "It's time to let that go and just be happy. Update me on your wedding plans. Is everything on track?"

"Yes, everything is on track. But you can ask me that again, after you're safely settled in Colorado Springs. I've got some time. Caleb's booked the band, we've updated Maggie on the catering, and my dress is perfect. Those were the only essentials on the to-do list this month." Harper opened Paige's closet and rummaged around under the hanging items. "Which suitcase do you want to take?"

"Suitcases, plural. Who do you take me for?" Paige said. "Bring out the whole Louis Vuitton set. If I'm going to be sitting around proofing like a loaf of Mariah's sourdough bread, I might as well do it in style."

"That's your second food analogy in the last five minutes—do you need a snack?"

"No, Dr. Johnson said not to eat before the flight, in case of air sickness. It's only a few hours, and I'll eat when I get there."

"Okay, then, let's finish getting you packed. Are you bringing all of your undies, or will the servants be doing your laundry?" Harper teased.

"Please. I'm not *that* much of a diva. Pack all of my pregnancy undies—I don't, for a single minute, want anyone but me doing my laundry. And all of my comfy pants, my stretchy pregnancy bras, and the long tunic sweater to keep me warm. Hey, I wonder if Ed would lend me one of his old t-shirts? I bet it would be great to sleep in, and since we've been spending so much time together, I find his scent kind of comforting. *Is that weird?* Don't answer that. Oh, and don't forget my boots. It snows a lot more in Colorado Springs, and I think I can still fit into them."

"Paige, I've got this. So, when is the whirly-bird limo arriving?"

"Ed said that if his pilot has a good weather window, he'll be here by eleven o'clock. I've never flown in a helicopter before. Have you?"

"No, but then I've never been knocked up by a multi-millionaire before. This is a real interesting situation you've gotten yourself into," Harper said, wryly.

Paige sighed. "I guess 'interesting' is one of the kinder words you could use. But...I'd rather not think about what's going to happen with Ed and me—everyone says I should avoid stress."

"I agree, but we haven't had a chance to talk about this, yet. Do you think Ed's forgiven you yet?" Harper asked. "You know, for being an idiot."

"Gee, thanks—I know I can always count on you for support," Paige said. "I'm not exactly sure, but I think he's *working* on forgiving me. The fact that he injected me with a ticking time bomb that might, as Ed puts it, 'blow me up from the inside,' has done a lot to earn me sympathy points. And so far, I haven't argued about naming the baby after him. But, if our kid comes out looking like a Daniel or a Rowan, I reserve the right to change my mind. *Rowan Barrett* has a nice ring to it."

"Let's just hope Rowan doesn't make an unexpected appearance. I like my sister's tummy just the way it is," said Harper, giving Paige's enormous baby bump a friendly little pat.

"I like my private parts just the way they are, too," Paige said, snapping the stuffed suitcase firmly shut. "And I'll do pretty much anything to keep them intact."

Paige packed the accordion folder of Pinterest pages she'd printed, her laptop, and her hard-copy files of the various projects she was working on, including one that was close to her heart: Mariah's bakery project. She'd also packed the fancy three-ring-binder she'd picked up on her last trip to Costco, a package of brightly colored markers, and her planning calendar. She was putting together a wedding binder for her sister, so the event would run like clockwork on the big day, when the matron of honor/ wedding planner would be newly delivered of a gigantic newborn by C-section. The timing could hardly be worse. But Harper and Caleb deserved their big day, and she'd do her part to make sure everything went off without a hitch. *She might be four hundred miles away, but she wasn't helpless.*

Finally, Paige heard the whirring of the helicopter blades overhead, and a moment later, Harper poked her head in looking suitably impressed.

"That bird is *slick!* I'll carry everything downstairs for you, and I want to be there when you take off. Is Ed already on board, or will he be meeting you there?"

"You know, we didn't even talk about that," Paige said, "or if we did, I can't seem to remember. I guess I'll end up where I'm supposed to end up. I just really wish *you* were going to be with me, or at least a couple of hours closer. This is going to be hard enough, without you there with me."

"I'll be with you when the time comes, no matter what, Paige— even if Ed has to send a private helicopter for me, too. And I'll call you every day. Just try to give me a heads-up as soon as Dr. Johnson says it's time to pull the plug."

"God! That is a totally inappropriate thing to say! Just promise me you'll come." Paige and Harper hugged for a long minute, then Harper led the way, spotting for her sister as she made her cumbersome way down the long staircase and out onto the widest part of the gravel drive, since the Inn didn't have a fancy green lawn or a helipad. Just past the entrance garden, a large, shiny helicopter waited like an out of season winged insect, waiting to carry her up into the sky.

Ed *wasn't* on-board, but a flight nurse with a specialty in high-risk obstetrics was. As fit and sun-tanned as an entertainment director at Club-Med—she wore a stethoscope around her neck and projected an air of cheerful confidence. Paige felt her body begin to relax almost immediately.

"Hi, I'm Laura, your flight nurse! I've already been briefed on the situation by Dr. Johnson, and I'm fully prepared to get you and the little guy safely to C. Springs. Hop on-board," she said, holding out a strong helping hand, which Paige gratefully accepted.

But there would be no "hopping" of any kind...

"Have a seat and make yourself comfortable. You'll need to put on these headphones to block the noise and so we can communicate.

Then I'll make sure you're secured with a flight harness for the duration. Barring any unusual conditions, the flight should take about two hours. Then, someone will meet us at the airfield and take you to your destination."

"Which is?" Paige asked.

"Sorry, but no one has clued me in about that," Laura said. "I'm sure someone will be meeting you." She placed a blood pressure cuff on Paige's left upper arm, and a pulse oximeter on the opposite index finger. Then she turned and gave a thumbs up to the pilot—and up, up, and away they went.

Paige felt a brief rush of vertigo, but after the helicopter leveled off, the flight smoothed down and it was largely like any other, with a lot more decibels. She'd reclined her seat to make room for her belly, so she wasn't able to see much through the helicopter's windows. Her only goal was to get to Colorado Springs in one piece, maintain herself like a pampered houseplant for a minimum of three weeks, and pop this baby out at the optimum time. *Oh, and, keep my private parts intact,* she added.

After an uneventful flight, Paige felt the peculiar slide into vertigo as the helicopter began to quickly descend. And then they were on the ground and the rotating blades slowed to a stop. She heard the sound of a car approaching, which she took as a good sign. Laura the nurse unfastened their flight harnesses and turned her attention to a clipboard containing paperwork.

Now that they were safely on the ground, Paige sat up and looked out the window. A dark SUV pulled up alongside the chopper, and she watched Ed's tall form unfold and step out. Then he ducked his head and approached the helicopter.

"Hey, in there. Anybody home?"

Ed's warm reassuring voice was exactly the welcome she needed. *He had come—and he'd be by her side as she moved on to the next stop on this journey.* She closed her eyes to hold back tears, and when she opened them, Ed was holding her hand and smiling down at her.

"Have a nice ride?" he asked. "Has the ground stopped moving yet?"

Paige smiled and nodded. "You're here!"

"Where else would I be? Sorry I couldn't come along—there's a weight limit, and they couldn't have both baby Reggie and me on board at the same time," he said. "Just a little dad joke. Actually, I was back at the house, getting everything ready for us."

"I'm just glad you're here now," she said, squeezing his hand. "So, where to next? Do you own a mountain chalet you haven't told me about?"

"Ah, no, but my friend Steve does, and he's happy to let us stay here for the duration. He spends his winters in Belize. Sometimes Panama, or Columbia."

"Oh, wow! That's incredibly generous of him. He doesn't even know me."

"No worries at all, Paige. Steve was one of Harp's first investors, and we've made him very, very rich, so he's happy to do me a favor. You'll love his place—he's got an amazing view, and it's very private. Plus, we'll have plenty of space, so when the time comes, Harper and Caleb are welcome to come up and stay as long as they like, and we won't all be on top of each other."

"Thank you so much for arranging all of this, Ed. I don't know what I'd have done without you. I'd probably have parked myself in a motel in Northeast Albuquerque." Then, laughing in response to the abnormally loud gurgle from her tummy, she asked, "Will you be feeding me soon? Reggie says he's starving—and Nina had said not to eat much before the flight, just in case I had some motion-sickness."

"First, let's get you out of here and on terra firma. Second, let's go get you some and Reggie some breakfast."

"That sounds really good to me."

The house Ed brought her to was constructed of big timber and native stone, with high, beamed ceilings. The view looked out at the mountains and caught the spectacular silhouette of majestic, red-sandstone fins, courtesy of Garden of the Gods. In addition to providing a comforting presence, Ed had hired a private nurse to handle anything Paige needed. Best of all, he'd left Paige completely in charge. *She* could decide if and when she needed help. A bright obstetric-specialist nurse named Nadine was happy to be with them for the duration, catching up on her reading and working on some freelance health writing. Apparently, Nurse Nadine was a master at multitasking. More importantly, she was careful to provide a friendly but not overly intrusive presence.

Paige called Harper to check in, which they'd agreed to do on a daily basis, if only for a few minutes.

"How are things at the ranch?" Paige asked.

We're all pretty darned happy here at the ranch. In fact, I was happy three times last night!

"Shut it! I've been living the life of a nun for longer than you can shake a stick, other than the *one time* I slipped up—and *now* look at me."

You can't fool me, Paige. You're thrilled to be pregnant, and everyone knows you're going to be a fantastic mom. All you have to do now is lay in your comfortable bed, watch romantic comedies, and gestate baby Keiko.

"There's no need to refer to my baby as a giant marine mammal," Paige said, mildly offended.

That's a compliment! I love Keiko. I watched Free Willy *with Ellie, like three times. You know, it was filmed in the Pacific Northwest, in the San Juan Islands, I think. Watching that gorgeous scenery always makes me a little homesick for the ocean, and for mountains covered with trees. But I guess you can love a place and still not want to live there anymore.*

"Well. Thanks for the movie trivia, Harper. For your information, I won't just be laying around during my 'laying in.' I'll be doing leg exercises to help prevent blood clots, and some gentle prenatal yoga with Nurse Nadine. And I'm not on strict bedrest—I just mostly need to be close to a hospital. On top of gestating, I'll be helping Ed with meal prep, even though he'll be doing most of the actual cooking. It's kind of hard to stand on my feet over a hot stove these days—my arms can barely *reach* the stove."

Ed sounds like a man of many talents. Is he a good cook? Harper wanted to know.

"I'm sure he is. Ed is good at *everything* he takes on—the man's a genius. I hope Reggie inherits a big helping of Ed's formidable talents. They'll help balance out any slightly-geeky parts."

Speaking from past experience, geeky can be surprisingly good. And, FYI, when you two were getting it on the night of the Renaissance Ball, neither of you sounded geeky to me, Harper said.

"Yeah...," Paige said, her voice trailing off. "Thanks for the reminder. I don't actually remember much about the rest of that night—just the taking him upstairs and tucking the big guy into my bed part—and I'm not touching medieval beverages, ever again. But no matter *how* it happened, I'm looking forward to becoming a mom. And, for now, I'm trying not to worry too much about anything else. It's not healthy for Reggie."

You're right—chilling should be your top priority. But, still, failing to remember the juiciest details of how your love child came to be must be kind of difficult—like you're missing out on something. Anyway...changing the subject, when is your next appointment with Dr. Johnson?

"Friday afternoon. I have a whole week to chill until then. Do you think it's too late to take up knitting?"

It's never too late to do anything, as long as you're willing to go for it. Goodnight, Paige.

Was it too late to realize you'd fallen in love with the father of your baby, just as you neared the end of your ginormous pregnancy? Paige really hadn't expected to go down that road with Ed Barrett. It's just that he was so kind, and decent, and he took such good care of her. His hands were always warm when they massaged her aching back and comforting when they rested lightly on her swollen belly. So often, Ed surprised her with his sensitivity, intuitively doing the right thing— like reaching for her hand when she'd landed in the helicopter, and more importantly, arranging for her to see Nina Johnson at *exactly* the right time: too soon, and she'd likely have resisted; too late, and things could have gone horribly wrong, for her and for Reggie.

But love and other urgent questions would have to wait until her baby was safely born. *Equally important, she had absolutely no idea how Ed was feeling.*

CHAPTER THIRTEEN

"*Y*ou're *very big* for thirty-three weeks, Paige, but the baby's heartbeat is nice and strong. Ideally, I'd like to wait another couple of weeks before we schedule your C-section. But we'll start some prep work—get your baseline labs and a blood type and cross. Then we'll work on your birth plan. I know a high-tech birth isn't at all what you envisioned, but we'll tailor everything to your needs as much as possible. For example, do you want to have Ed in the room with you? Given your situation, maybe you'd like to have a different support person—or you could have two support people. More than that and we don't have enough room to do our jobs."

"You're right, my brain is still trying to adjust to the idea of a C-section, rather than the natural birth I wanted. And yes, *of course*, I want Ed to be there. And my other support person will be my sister, Harper," Paige said.

Dr. Johnson finished checking an assortment of boxes on the lab form and handed to Paige. "I'll make a note on your birth plan. Just give this to the assistant down the hall, and she'll draw all of the blood samples we need. We'll go over everything in your birth plan at your next visit, but I don't want to wait a whole week. Now that you'll be here in town, I'd like to see you twice weekly on Tuesdays and Fridays, if that works for you."

"Thank you, Nina. I appreciate you watching everything so closely, so you'll know exactly when it's the right time," Paige said, feeling grateful. *Once she'd gotten past her intimidation, she'd begun to see Ed's fellow Stanford alumnus not only as the talented physician she was, but as a friend.*

"I'm feeling confident, Paige, and you should, too. In just a few weeks, you and Ed will have a healthy baby—just a nice big one."

Paige called Harper that night and gave her the scoop. "Why don't you and Caleb plan to come up here next weekend? I'll have one of my last appointments on Friday, and I'm sure Nina will want to schedule the birth early the following week, as long as the baby seems healthy. She said a *few* weeks, but my intuition tells me it won't be that long. I think I can already feel things changing inside. Maybe gravity and Reggie's weight have already combined to get the baby moving? Anyway, Nina won't want to risk having me go into natural labor."

Oh, wow, you must be so excited! I know I am. I'll talk to Caleb tonight, we'll keep an eye on the weather, and shoot for arriving on Friday afternoon or Saturday morning. I'd rather not drive over Raton Pass in the dark, if we can help it. Call me after Tuesday's appointment, okay? And ask Ed to let me know, immediately, if something changes and you're admitted to the hospital.

"I will. Thanks, Harper. I'm getting kind of anxious, and I'll feel a lot better knowing you're here."

※

At Tuesday's appointment, Paige mentioned the changes she'd felt, and Nina asked Ed to step out of the room. The obstetrician did an internal exam and came up frowning—not the expression Paige was hoping to see.

"Paige, your cervix is already beginning to dilate slightly, and it feels like the baby's head is already partly engaged in the pelvis. Have you had any active contractions?" she asked.

"I don't think so—just a few twinges, and a general discomfort on the outer edges of my abdomen. Internally, more like a heavy ache, I guess. Why? Am I in labor?"

"Well, your body is definitely getting ready to be. And the baby's size and weight, plus gravity, have a powerful effect. At this stage, every day from here on out helps the baby's lungs to develop. And baby boys *need* that extra time—even a few days can make a difference in a good outcome for him. From here on out, Paige, beginning with the wheelchair ride from this exam room to your car, you are on *strict bedrest*, and I mean it! No getting up except to use the restroom, and then straight back to bed. I'll also give you a thin foam wedge to put under your hips. It's not uncomfortable, I promise—but it'll help take some of the weight of this big baby off of your cervix. I'm hoping that will help slow things down a little.

"I'll do another internal on Friday, and if you've progressed at all, I'll want to prep you for surgery straight away. Until then, *talk* to your baby and ask him to stay right where he is. Even four or five days can make a difference. According to your dates, which match up with your ultrasounds, Friday will be just past the thirty-four-week mark.

If there's no progression, and you can keep the baby in until you reach thirty-five weeks or even thirty-six, that's all the better. Let's keep all our fingers and toes crossed, okay?

"Now, I hate to be alarmist, but if your water breaks or you go into active labor, Ed will need to call an ambulance and have the EMTs page me, STAT. Don't even *think* about having him drive you to the hospital—it could be dangerous for you *and* the baby. This is a high-risk situation, Paige. I know you're healthy and feeling good, and right now, the baby is healthy too. But, because of the risk factors we discussed at your previous appointment, we can't afford to take any chances. I'd admit you right now and keep you here for the duration, but the hospital is jam-packed and we're really short-staffed. With an OB nurse like Nadine on board, and the short distance to the hospital, you and the baby should be fine. She knows what to do, and I trust her."

"Alright, I'll be a model patient. But can we call Ed in so you can explain all of this to him, too?" Paige asked, absorbing every little detail Nina had outlined. "He's the one watching out for me."

"I'll be happy to—he should be prepared, too. And *you* can prepare by having Ed or a Nadine help you pack a bag for the hospital. Remember, no spicy food, no exercise, and no sex—let's just keep this fella in a little while longer."

"Got it," said Paige, although Nina's cautions weren't exactly relevant: she wasn't a fan of spicy food, exercise was definitely out, and it was no one's business that she wasn't having sex with Ed or anyone else. There wasn't a whole lot of room in there right now, anyway.

Ed sensed that Paige needed some comfort, so he held her hand on the way home, glancing at her profile from time to time. "How're you doing?"

"As well as I can be, I guess. I'm not a fan of this whole ticking time bomb scenario," Paige said, letting out a shaky breath. "I'll just be glad when Reggie's out of my belly and in my arms. Then we can stop worrying about me being torn to shreds, or Reggie falling into a blood sugar coma."

Ed shook his head. "Good times," he said, which he knew was completely and totally inappropriate—but it brought on a laugh from Paige. He'd do anything these days to see her smile. *Meanwhile, he held the vision of his healthy baby boy in Paige's arms, and her pretty face smiling up at him with delight.*

*

"Hey, do you want to learn how to knit with me?" Paige asked. "The yarn store in C. Springs delivers—I already called and asked. I can have them bring an extra pair of needles for you."

"Whatever you need, darlin'. I'm pretty good with my hands," Ed said, smiling, which brought out the crow's feet at the edges of his warm brown eyes.

Suddenly, the last bit of lingering fog cleared, and after all this time, Paige could remember: Oh, yeah, he *was* good with his hands. *How could she have forgotten that? What other hidden talents had she forgotten in her post-mead haze?* Right now, with her pregnancy hormones surging, she wanted to kiss someone more than she'd ever wanted to kiss anyone before. She looked at Ed's full beard, which—given the size of him and the Pendleton wool shirt he was wearing—made him look decidedly like a lumberjack, or a taller Chris Stapleton with an expensive haircut. They had the same soulful brown eyes. On top of Ed's kind heart and clever mind, sometimes...he was just dead sexy. And, the icing on the cake, Ed gave her the best, most authentic bear hugs.

But when it came to the opposite sex, Paige had developed her specific tastes in college—which happened to be the Ivy League. The preppy East Coast men she'd dated had almost never had facial hair. She just wasn't used to it. *Hmm.*

"Would you ever consider shaving your beard?" Paige asked, thoughtfully, having exactly zero idea how Ed would react. She'd only seen him clean-shaven in the photos she'd found snooping online. But he had a nice strong jawline, and without the beard, he looked so different.

He smiled in her direction, which seemed like a promising start. "Well, I know it's March, already, but can I wait until the weather feels a little more like spring?"

Paige smiled in return. *He didn't hate her.* In fact, if she had to guess, she'd say he was well on his way to forgiving her. Which was a good thing, because, after all the time that had passed, she *knew* she wanted a second chance with the father of her child. *And the man she'd fallen in love with.* She wanted to be physically close to him again, after their baby was born. He was the kindest man she'd ever met, and she couldn't imagine raising their baby without him. But she wanted much more from him—and this time, she wanted to savor every moment and remember every detail. More than anything, she wanted to offer Ed everything she had to give, in return.

The universe works in mysterious ways: these weeks together in Colorado Springs, waiting for their baby to be born, had been exactly what they needed. They were becoming a team. Who knew what beautiful surprises the future had waiting for them? *She couldn't wait to find out...*

Back at the ranch, Caleb and Harper were preparing to leave for their trip north to Colorado Springs. "Hey, I have some good news," Caleb said Friday morning after breakfast. "Ellie's grandparents are coming down for the weekend, and they offered to pick her up after school. And, since Mariah has Sunday and Monday off from Maggie's, we can be gone for a long weekend. So, when do you want to hit the road?"

"Soon, if it works for you. I have a feeling that this baby won't wait until the weekend, and so does Paige. I really want to be there, and I know my sister wants me there for the birth," Harper said. "If we leave right after lunch, we could be cruising into Colorado Springs by about five-thirty, and if necessary, we can head straight to the hospital. Ed said he'll keep us in the loop."

"Okay, it won't take me long to throw a change of clothes in my pack. The truck already has a full tank of gas."

"Thanks, that's great. I have a few things to wrap up with the grounds crew. Then, let's head into town, pick up a thermos of coffee and some sandwiches to go at Maggie's, and hit the road. But first, give me a kiss that'll make me forget the ants in my pants."

"I can think of *another* cure for the ants," Caleb said in his deep voice.

"Another time, babe—I'll give you a rain check. But I appreciate the offer."

Ed called just as they were just descending from Raton Pass into Trinidad. *Hey, I have some news. Are you guys close?*

"Yes, the roads have been clear all the way, and we're just coming down the pass. What's up?" Harper asked.

Paige just finished her appointment. Even without active contractions, she's progressed to four-and-a-half centimeters. Nina doesn't want to wait any longer. There could be a risk of infection or precipitous labor. She's scheduled Paige's C-section for this evening. We're getting some preliminary prep work and last-minute labs done, now, which will take about an hour. We're waiting for the anesthesiologist to get here anyway, Ed said.

"What's the ETA? Will we get there in time?" Harper asked.

Well, Paige's water hasn't broken, and they're monitoring her closely, so we've got a little time. But I'll call you in an hour with an update. If I know Paige, she'll make everybody wait until you get here. So, I'm giving you guys a heads up—you might want to step on it.

"Got it. Thanks, Ed. You've been so great—my sister is lucky to have you." *Dumb, Harper. That could be interpreted so many ways.* She had no idea *how* her sister currently felt about Ed, or visa versa—their relationship seemed to be constantly evolving, with no public declarations from either party. *God help them when they actually became parents, and time was no longer on their side…*

"Hey, babe, in this last stretch between here and C. Springs, you might want to step on the gas," Harper said.

"So, this is happening tonight?" Caleb asked.

"This is happening," she confirmed, nodding her head. "I guess I should find out who the patron saints of childbirth are…"

"Well, you've got a couple to choose from," answered Caleb, who'd grown up a good Catholic boy in northern New Mexico. "Saint Gerard and Saint Gianna are probably the most important. Saint Anne comes later, after the baby is born. She helps ensure a good milk supply for breastfeeding moms."

"Wow! You really are The-Man-Who-Knows-All-Things. Thanks, babe. I'm going to start praying now. I know I have a lot of years to make up for, but maybe the next hour or so will count for something."

With the lavender-blue twilight descending, they drove through the Spanish Peaks Country between Trinidad and Walsenburg, then past Colorado City and down into Pueblo. The traffic wasn't too bad for a Friday night as they made their way through C. Springs and toward the University of Colorado Medical Center. Caleb dropped Harper off at the door and went to park the truck.

Following the overhead signs, she headed toward the elevators, but there seemed to be people coming down and stopping at every floor. Its progress was excruciatingly slow. When Caleb joined her, the doors finally opened and they made their way up to the Family Birth Center.

Harper had called Ed for an update just as they'd reached the hospital, and he'd given her directions for how to find him. When they found the correct surgical waiting room, Caleb kissed her on the cheek and waved her away. "Go find your sister. I'll be here, resting my eyes and waiting for the good news."

Harper knocked on the door of the surgical suite and poked her head into the prep area. Ed had just finished scrubbing, and the OR nurses were donning him in green cotton scrubs, baby blue footies, and a hair net. Two hair nets—one for his full beard. Another friendly OR nurse showed Harper what to do and quickly talked her through everything. Appropriately garbed, she joined Ed in the big, airy, surprisingly cool room where her sister lay, scrubbed and prepped, with her enormous belly coated with orange-tinted betadine solution. Ed stood at her sister's shoulder, holding her hand tightly.

"You made it! You're actually here!" Paige said, tearing up a little. "I'm so glad, Harper. Look at this big guy! Doesn't Ed look adorable in scrubs?" Her green eyes shone with nervous anticipation.

"We're ready when you are, Paige," Doctor Nina Johnson said, smiling down at her. "The whole procedure should take about forty minutes, give or take, but that includes suturing you back up. It won't take that long for us to get your baby out. We have a neonatal nurse, Andrea, ready to receive him, and a neonatal pediatrician, Dr. Collins, standing-by to do his APGAR. You wanted to be awake for the procedure, right? Any second thoughts on that?"

Paige shook her head. "No, I *definitely* want to be awake. I want to see his little face right away, and I want to hold him, as soon as I can."

Nina nodded, smiling behind her mask. "We'll try to keep you awake the whole time, but it'll depend on how the baby's doing, and how fast we need to get him out. Okay, Dad, are you ready to meet your son?" she asked Ed.

"Ready. Paige, I'm here for you. I'm not going to let go of your hand for a second. If you need to squeeze mine, squeeze away. I can take it."

"Thanks for being here. Thanks…for everything, Ed," Paige said, her eyes glittering with emotion. "Okay, I'm ready. I can't feel a thing, Nina," she said. "Is that normal?"

"That's just the way we like it," the doctor said, her eyes smiling above her blue surgical mask.

CHAPTER FOURTEEN

$\mathcal{R}$eginald Edward Barrett IV came into the world at 6:58 pm on the fourteenth of March. Their big baby boy was a tad over thirty-four weeks, and healthy.

"He's beautiful and perfect—and huge!" Harper cried, tears streaming down her cheeks.

Paige smiled and closed her eyes for a moment to take it all in. *Everybody was safe and healthy and whole. She was grateful to Aunt Sabina, for setting everything in motion nearly a year ago, when she'd left them the ranch; to her enterprising sister, for having faith in what it could become; to the Stanford School of Medicine and Dr. Nina Johnso; and to the Virgin of Guadalupe, who watched over them all with love and compassion. But most of all, she gave thanks for the kind and generous Lord of the Renaissance Ball who had made her a mother—and to her beautiful baby, Reggie, for hanging in there for over thirty-four precious weeks. If she could just magically sleep for thirty seconds, and then be wide awake...*

"I can't wait to get the official weight on this guy," Ed asked, his broad chest puffed out with pride.

"Nurse Andrea needs to get him over to the exam table, first. We want to make sure his lungs are good, and she'll get a tiny drop of blood for a metabolic test we do on all newborns. Then we'll see. How're *you* doing, Paige? Everybody's focused on the baby, and *you're* the one who went under the knife," Dr. Johnson said.

She startled to full alertness. "Oh…I'm okay, just tired. Reggie is beautiful and perfect. But I can't believe a baby *that big* came out of me—and he wasn't even full term! Is he alright?" Paige asked. "I haven't heard him cry."

"We'll monitor his blood sugar round the clock, and for the next week at least, he'll need to be looked after in the NICU. After that, if his breathing passes the test and he's nursing well, we can start to talk about getting the two of you home. But you're right—I'd love to hear a good squawk out of him. A vigorous cry is important."

Dr. Johnson continued her careful, neat sutures while her expert team looked over the baby, head-to-toe. She applied a neat dressing over Paige's incision, followed by a loose abdominal binder to help hold it in place.

Paige closed her eyes for a moment, taking it all in, and frankly, exhausted. *But she wanted something more than she'd ever thought possible.* "When can I hold him?"

"It shouldn't be long. They're just cleaning him up and weighing him. They'll bring him over when they're done. We're pretty big on mama and newborn bonding around here. Daddy-baby bonding, too," the doctor said, glancing at Ed. "Big Congratulations, Papa Bear."

"Thanks so much, Nina. For everything. *My* kid is going to call *me* Dad—at least until he's a teenager. That's gonna take some getting used to." Ed turned his attention to Paige, just as the nurses placed a not-so-little bundle in her arms. "How does it feel to be a mom?" he asked, his warm, reassuring hand resting lightly on her shoulder.

"It feels amazing, like I'm the luckiest girl in the world," she said, looking down at her son His perfectly formed head was covered with a thatch of dark hair. His eyes were shut against the light, so startlingly different from the darkness of her womb. She thought his features resembled his father's, even in infancy. *Ten fingers, ten toes, two tiny shell-like ears.* He was perfect. And he was hers. *Theirs,* she amended, looking up at Ed's smiling face.

"So, you wanted to know his birthweight? This baby boy weighs a whopping eleven pounds, four ounces," said neonatal nurse Andrea— and for some reason, everyone laughed. Well, *almost* everyone. Paige didn't think it was all that funny.

Ten days later, on a Monday afternoon, Paige, Ed, and the baby, along with Harper and Caleb, were "home" in the beautiful log and stone home that would always be special to her. This was the comfortable haven that had nurtured her and kept her safe during a precarious time, and now it held all of their joy, too.

Caleb poured drinks for everyone, and they chilled in the comfortable family room. Paige reclined on the sofa, propped up on pillows, practicing her football hold and nursing baby Reggie. Ed moved easily around the kitchen, finishing up dinner, and Harper sat in a rocker near Paige, cooing over her precious giant nephew.

"So, when do you think you'll be ready to bring him back to the ranch?" Harper asked.

Paige glanced at Ed, seeking his input. *She'd been doing a lot more of that lately—it just seemed to happen, naturally.* "Well, I don't think we're in any hurry. Ed's friend Steve, who owns this beautiful place, isn't due back until mid-April. Besides, it's really nice having this time for Ed and me to bond with Reggie. I have a two-week follow-up scheduled with Nina in a few days—so, I'd like to stay at least until then. And I might need a few more days after that before I'm up to the five-hour drive back to Verde Springs."

"I agree," Ed said, easily. "I can work from home a while longer, and, for now, this place *is* home. Since Paige and I don't live together, this might be our only time to bond as a family, or at least, as Reggie's parents," he said, before he stopped abruptly and turned back to the stove.

"I get that," said Harper, quietly. "Well, more power to you guys. Reggie's a wonderful addition to the family." Changing the subject, she looked at Caleb and grinned. "I can't wait until Ellie sees this little guy—she's not going to be able to keep her hands off of him!"

"Hey, who are you calling little?" Paige protested, with a grin. "So, are you guys still planning to head back in the morning?"

"Yeah…weather permitting. Work at the ranch is piling up, and the wedding is only a few weeks away. There's always something that needs to be done last minute. And you're absolutely right—the three of you need to bond as a family. Or, as Reggie's parents," Harper amended, lightly.

Ed jumped into the slightly awkward breach. "Well, dinner's ready. Harper, would you mind bringing the salad to the table? Paige, I'll make you up a plate and bring it to you. What would you like to drink?"

"Thanks, that would be nice. Just water to drink. Reggie isn't big on bubbles, and too much dairy makes him gassy." *Ugh*, she cringed a little. *Is this what conversations were going to be like for the next few months of life with a newborn?*

And then there were three. Paige lay in bed with Reggie sleeping by her side, and Ed sat in a chair by the window, glancing at his laptop and typing something with great deliberation.

"What are you working on?" Paige asked. "Unless it's a new, top secret, home security device that you're not ready to talk about, yet."

"Uh, no, it isn't. When I'm done, I'll go over everything with you. It's pretty important," Ed said, in a serious tone.

Paige waited patiently, something that seemed to be coming more easily to her now that she wasn't hugely pregnant and filled with the stress of carrying a ticking time bomb. Also, something strangely pleasant seemed to happen when she nursed: her milk letdown felt like a soft sigh wrapped in a gentle hug. *Prolactin and oxytocin were wonderful things. Seriously, they should bottle this stuff.*

The sensation she experienced when nursing was the exact opposite of the "fight or flight" stress response that had taken over her life during the chaotic years following her mother's sudden death—and which had hung around for the better part of her twenties. *Oh, how her mother would have loved Reggie.* Then she realized something too terrible for words—her baby didn't have a grandmother. *Or, did he?* Her earlier online snooping hadn't extended to the Barrett family tree.

She was about to ask him when Ed finished what he was doing and came over to the bedside. "Do you mind if I sit on the bed? I don't want to disturb you or the baby, but I'd like you to take a look at this before I email it to Tom."

"Sure, go ahead. Are you working on something legal?" she asked.

"Well, once we go over it and Tom makes a few changes, it'll be legal—it's my will."

"Your *will?*" Paige asked, astonished. "Isn't that sort of premature? You're not even forty. I happened to see your birthdate when we filled out the forms for Reggie's birth certificate."

Ed gave her a serious look. "Age doesn't always matter. Accidents can happen, anytime, and even young people can die from a serious illness. If something like that were to happen, I would want you and Reggie to be taken care of. Reggie's my son, and you'll always be his mother. You're *both* important to me."

Paige nodded, unsure what to say. Ed seemed to know exactly what to he wanted to do. Obviously, *she* should make a will, too. If something were to happen to her, she would want Ed and Harper to find a way to raise Reggie, together—even though, as Reggie's biological parent, Ed would want, and likely get, full legal custody. *Time to focus.* "Okay, I'm following. Can you explain the particulars?"

"I've set up a trust fund for Reggie that he can access in two phases: when he turns eighteen, he can access a flexible trust fund for college; and when he's twenty-five he can access a more sizeable trust fund."

"That's very generous, she said. "You've really thought about this, but isn't twenty-one more typical?" Paige asked.

"Maybe. But when I was twenty-one, I was still rebelling against my parents and hanging out with a crowd of people who weren't going anywhere in life. They aren't bad people—*none* of us were serious about what we wanted to do with our lives then. I think Reggie will need those extra few years of maturity to put his inheritance to good use, especially if I'm not here to guide him."

"Okay, what's next?" she prompted Ed, not wanting to consider that terrible possibility. She wanted him to be a part of his son's life, always.

"It's another document I'm working on, for basic support. I grew up in a wealthy family, which I *don't* necessarily want for my son. Excuse me—*our* son. But I would never want Reggie, or you, as his mother, to have to struggle. So, I'm setting up a modest monthly support fund which you have full access to. Please use it however you see fit. Or, if you like, you don't even have to touch it—you can just let it accumulate."

"That's...very thoughtful of you, Ed. But once the Inn is up and running this summer, we'll be in our second full season, and we already have lots of weddings and special events booked. I don't think I'll have any trouble supporting myself, or Reggie."

"Please, let me do this for you, Paige. It'll save a lot of hassle in the long run. No matter what happens between *us*, the money will always be there, for both of you."

"This is...really unexpected, Ed. Can I have some time to think about it?" she asked.

"Whatever makes you feel comfortable," he said, shrugging. "I have something else I'd like to talk to you about. I know it's early days, and Reggie is still so young, but I don't like the idea of being so far from my son. Santa Fe can be an hour from the ranch in light traffic, and on weekends, when people are heading back from Taos, it can be double that. It's important for me to be a *real* part of Reggie's life, not just an occasional weekend dad. I know it's too early to talk about sharing custody, because you're nursing him and I'd *never* do anything to interfere with that. But, you know, eventually, we'll have to talk about it, Paige."

"Well, I guess you've thought of everything," she said, lightly. *Except the possibility that they could be a real family one day. They could have a real relationship, and maybe, even a real marriage. All she needed was a second chance—but timing was everything.* Paige let out the breath she'd been holding. "Here, take your son and burp him, properly. I'm going to take a shower."

She needed to rinse the sour-milk smell off under a generous rain-fall shower. Her body hadn't felt like her own for nearly eight months, and it didn't feel like her own, now. She had giant, veiny, nursing-mama boobs; she still peed a little when she coughed; sneezing was completely out of the question; and her legacy of stretch marks was the pregnancy gift that kept on giving. As the warm water rained down on her head, she took a moment to be thankful for her strong, adaptable body that had grown a child to more than eleven pounds and safely delivered him into the world, with the help of an excellent doctor. *Everybody was fine.* But this certainly wasn't an ideal time to be thinking about relationships of any kind.

Give yourself a break, the logical part of her brain shouted. *Yes, she should probably do that. And getting twelve hours of uninterrupted sleep would be awfully nice. Wouldn't it be wonderful if she could just put every-thing else in her life on "pause" for a while?* She needed to focus on the joy, and hope that her body was just as resilient as it had proven to be strong.

Ed held his sleeping son tenderly against his broad chest, but at the moment, his thoughts were on somebody else. Paige looked even more beautiful now than she had in the full bloom of her pregnancy. When she nursed Reggie, she looked so happy and peaceful. She was incredibly attentive to his son's needs, always following her mother's intuition.

He sighed. It was crushing to be *so* in love with her and not be free to express it. The two of them had naturally grown closer during her high-risk pregnancy with Reggie. But for him, it had been *more* than that: he knew, without a doubt, that she was the only woman he wanted. *But, what did Paige think of him?* Her mind was a complete mystery, at the moment—and she had so many other things to focus on. Important things. He could wait.

Early spring had arrived in the high desert, and Harper and Caleb's wedding was only a few weeks away. Using his phone, Ed pulled up the ten-day weather forecast and noted the steady uptick in temperatures. He waited until he heard the shower turn off. Then he laid a sleeping Reggie in his cozy bassinette and retreated to his bedroom. He stared in the bathroom mirror at his ridiculous beard which he admitted he sometimes hid behind. After all, "Reggie Barrett III" came with a very public persona, at least in big tech circles. And as an introvert, he'd always hated being in the spotlight, and somehow, the beard helped. His personal body armor. *But maybe it was time to let the lumberjack look go for good.* Letting out a breath, he picked up his razor and got to work. He didn't care if Paige viewed the act as symbolic—maybe it was—but something between them had to change.

※

The rest of the week went by quickly. Paige had her two-week check-up with Dr. Johnson, and received a clean bill of postpartum health. Reggie continued to thrive, and her co-parenting routine with Ed was on an even keel. That meant that she finally had the brain-space to think about other things.

Harper and Caleb's wedding would take place in just ten days. Now that the official countdown had begun, Paige was desperate to get back to the ranch. "You could come too, Ed. The main house has plenty of bedrooms, and you could set up a work space in the Coop Studios. It would be quieter, there, especially with a newborn in the main house. But we could share all of our meals together, and you'd still see Reggie every day. What do you think?"

"I guess that could work for a few weeks, at least until after your sister's wedding. And then, with Caleb and Harper away on their honeymoon, maybe you could use an extra hand around the place until they return. Let me think about it, Paige. When we head back to the ranch, I'll take a look at Caleb's old studio and let you know."

The drive from southern Colorado to northern New Mexico seemed to go by quickly, probably because both she and Reggie slept through most of it. But, poor Ed—Colorado Springs to Verde Springs was a long way to drive without a break.

"Home sweet home," said Paige, gazing out at the big ranch house in the distance, waiting to welcome them home. "Thanks for driving, Ed. Harper said she'd have dinner ready for all of us. But I warn you, cooking isn't my sister's strong point."

Then came the ten-minute scramble of getting a newborn and all of their brand-new baby paraphernalia out of the crowded car and into the house. "Hello? Anybody home?" Paige called out. As if sensing an unfamiliar environment, or because he wanted to nurse, Reggie woke up and began to wail.

"You're here!" Harper emerged from the kitchen and enveloped her big sister in a hug. Ed got one, too—might as well welcome him to the family, properly. "And dinner's almost ready. I just finished tossing the salad. Come on in the breakfast room and join us!"

"Hey, you guys! We're really glad you're back. Ellie's so excited to meet baby, but she's with her mom tonight. Come and sit, Ed. Can I offer you a beer or wine?" Caleb asked.

"Sure, whatever you have," Ed replied. "Thanks."

"Modelo, light or dark?" Caleb asked. "And we're eating Italian, so I have a red blend, as well."

"A glass of wine sounds perfect after that long drive. Thanks, Caleb. Harper, the place looks great! I can't believe how much you've accomplished in only a year. Maybe you can show me around sometime. Paige tells me there's a lot more to see," Ed said. "Although I've heard a lot about them, I've never even been inside the Coop Studios."

"Sure, I'd be happy too. It'll be dark after we're done eating dinner, but we can take a walk in the morning," she said. "And, in case Paige has told you about my less-than-brilliant cooking skills, *Caleb* was the chef tonight. We're having beef-stuffed shells, and let me tell you, my husband makes a mean marinara. But I made the salad—"

"—and Paul Newman made the dressing," Caleb said, moving toward the table with a glass baking dish in his hands. "Okay everybody, let's eat."

"It's wonderful to be home. Even this guy has settled down," Paige said, gently rocking Reggie against her chest.

"Here, let me hold him. You go ahead and eat first, Paige. You're the one burning all the calories," Ed said, reaching confidently for his infant son.

Well, that was very sweet. Harper exchanged a look with her sister. *She could swear that she sensed something going on between the two of them—and she was dying to know the details...*

CHAPTER FIFTEEN

$\mathcal{P}$aige swaddled her giant baby and put him down for the night, or as close to "the night" as a newborn gets. Her sister lay on the bed watching the process with curiosity: swaddling took a little practice, but it worked.

"So, what's up with you and Ed? You two were pretty vibey at dinner. Is something happening there?" Harper asked.

Paige sighed. "I'm still coating my scar with antibiotic ointment every night, and hoping the glaring, purple railroad tracks will fade. I'm hardly thinking about shagging Ed. Or, shagging *anyone*."

"Who said anything about *shagging*? Have you been watching BritBox, again? I saw the way you looked at him when he picked Reggie up at dinner. I just thought…something might *finally* be happening, that's all."

"There *is* something happening, Harper. It's called gratitude. Ed stepped up in such a huge way since accidentally finding out he was going to be a dad—and well, it's really helping me learn to trust him. I mean, it's not like this was all a test—but if it *had* been, he'd pass with flying colors. And…," she hesitated.

"And?" Harper prompted.

Paige sat on the edge of the bed and sighed. "I remembered something about *that* night."

"You mean, the night of the infamous 'mead incident?' That's big news! Was it a *good* something?" Harper asked.

"Yes, it was a very good something, but I'm keeping those details to myself. I'm learning to appreciate *everything* about him. Ed's a great big teddy-bear. He's warm and comforting, he gives a lovely backrub, and he's a fabulous cook. I'd never ask him to, but he's made a will already, so that Reggie and I will always be taken care of. It all means something to me—especially with the childhood you and I had. Can you imagine how different our lives would have been if *we'd* had a decent dad? One who cared enough to stick around? And, one who had the financial means to take care of us?"

"Night and day," Harper agreed. "But, what exactly do they mean, these realizations of yours?" she persisted.

"That's what I have to figure out, because I absolutely can't hurt Ed again. But I also don't want to pretend that my feelings for him haven't changed, because they definitely have," Paige confessed. *She loved him—but she wasn't shouting it from the rooftops until she had a chance to tell Ed himself. But the timing wasn't right.* Reggie fretted, and she gently rubbed his back until he quieted, again.

"Well, then, it seems like you're in quite a pickle. Have you considered doing something crazy, like, I don't know, *talking* to Ed about how you feel?" Harper suggested.

Too close for comfort meant it was time to change the subject. "Let's get you and Caleb married—then we can worry about *my* love life. We only have a little over a week to pull this wedding off. I can help in two- to three-hour increments while Reggie's napping, so I want you to put me to work. I really mean that."

"Okay. Well, Caleb and I have done a lot, but I think I'm starting to regret not hiring a professional wedding planner, even for a wedding as small as ours," Harper said, frowning. "Your gestational timing kind of stinks—but I *do* love the adorable result," she said, tickling Reggie's rounded tummy.

Paige tried not to be stung by her sister's comment. "Oh, ye of little faith! What did you *think* I was doing while I was on bedrest? I wasn't binging Britbox." Paige pulled out the three-ring binder full of calendars and Pinterest photos and the names, addresses, and emails of everyone associated with Harper's big event. She'd even created checklists covering all of the things that needed to happen to make Harper and Caleb officially wife and husband. *And if they'd already checked some, or even most, of the boxes, so much the better.*

"I really missed you, Paige. Now, if it's alright, I'm going to turn everything over to your capable hands. Yell if you need help, or if you need a question answered. Or if you need Caleb to pound something, or me to stick something green in the ground. But, *please* don't overdo it. You're still recovering from surgery, while taking care of a giant newborn. I know you're an over-achiever, but that's, like, a *lot*," Harper said.

"I know I need time to recover—*and* I know I'm a control freak with a tendency to overdo it. But I've decided to focus on developing a new skill: it's called delegating."

Catering adjusted for headcount and confirmed, and deposit placed, so Maggie could place her bulk orders; and delivery details communicated, complete with maps to the ranch. *Check*. Maggie's Diner would be providing all the wedding food. But since asking Mariah to make her ex-husband's wedding cake was over-the-top tacky, Paige had ordered one from a specialty bakery in Santa Fe. Ed had given them a rave review, and the pictures on their website were acceptably gorgeous. *Check*.

Next, music. The bluegrass band that Harper and Paige had hired for the Inn's open house had been available, and Harper and Caleb had nabbed them, immediately. The band members were given dominion over three of the Coop Studios, where they could warm up in privacy and store their instruments safely out of the elements; after the reception was over and everyone had enjoyed themselves a little too much, they could even crash there, along with their spouses and partners. Paige gave them an electronic deposit and confirmed their arrival time. She made a note in her planner, reminding herself to make sure the linens were fresh in the studios, fill the coffee and tea canisters, and stock up the snack baskets. *Check*.

Wedding officiant? Being non-church-goers and relative newcomers to New Mexico, the Crawley sisters had been stumped until Maggie had suggested a friend of hers. Rebecca was a pastel artist and part-time non-denominational minister who lived in the nearby town of Pecos. She'd agreed to help Harper and Caleb craft something short and sweet, so everyone could get to the main event, the after-party. *Check*.

Flower girl? Ellie, of course, looking adorable in a cute spring dress she'd picked out all by herself. Footwear was TBD, and in New Mexico, always weather dependent. Mariah had texted Paige photos, with Ellie grinning ear to ear. *That kid couldn't be cuter. Check*.

Last but not least, matron of honor: her body had gone through some remarkable changes that still boggled her mind. But she could now *almost* fit into an ordinary bridesmaid dress if it had an empire waist and an A-line skirt. Somehow, she'd ended up promising her sister that she'd find one in the next seventy-two hours, so she could tick off that box, too. She and Ed were going into Santa Fe to spend the day, then staying the night at his house, which gave her most of two days to shop. Would she have to settle for a poufy meringue dress, or would she be able find a chic, sophisticated, mother-of-a-newborn dress? Whatever she chose to wear would also need easy access in case Reggie wanted to nurse, which was roughly every three hours round the clock. *I really could have timed things a little better,* she had to admit.

Harper was confident that she had the flowers well in hand. And Caleb's crew had made sure the entry garden's wedding circle, that she'd painstakingly created last summer, was in immaculate condition. If the spring weather tanked, they could quickly move the ceremony inside. But she hoped that wouldn't happen, because the entry garden happened to be the perfect spot for sentimental reasons. It was where Harper had first fallen in love with the old ranch house at first sight. It was where a dandelion-seed of an idea had taken root in the sandy red soil and turned into the *Inn at Verde Springs*. It was where she had first set eyes on the love of her life, when Caleb had stepped out of his contractor's truck wearing his famous toolbelt, full of respect for Aunt Sabina's old ranch house and its one-hundred-year-old history. And it was the heartwarming view she saw every day when she drove up to the house after a quick trip into Verde Springs. For all of these reasons, and more, the entry garden represented "home."

"I made kennel reservations at a nice place in Pecos for Birdy and Sunny. It'll be easier without them underfoot during the wedding and reception. What are we missing?" Harper asked her sister, as they sat at the kitchen counter, finishing up breakfast. Hearing their names, the dogs rose from their dog beds and came sniffing around, smiling their doggy smiles, always ready for a scratch behind the ears or under the chin.

"We need to rent some of those outdoor space heaters," said Paige. "And, we should rearrange the furniture in the entrance hall and open up the sliding doors to both living rooms—so if we do have to move the party indoors, there will be an obvious place for the band to set up."

"Okay, that's a nice idea. Are you on that, or..."

"I'm on it," Paige assured. "But I'll delegate the furniture rearranging."

"Well, then, that about covers it," Harper said. "Text me a picture of your dress when you find one you like, and you *will*. And that's not me being optimistic—that's an order."

"Yeah, yeah, I promise I won't embarrass you," Paige said.

"So...are you looking forward to having some alone time with Ed? You've never even seen his house in Santa Fe, have you?" Harper asked.

"No, actually, I haven't. It's probably so amazing that Reggie and I will never want to leave. Ed even offered to come with me and watch the baby while I try on dresses—which I politely declined. He's been *so* sweet to me."

"You look amazing, Paige! For carrying such a big baby, you're bouncing back pretty quickly. How's the scar feeling, now?" Harper asked.

"Thanks, I'll take the compliment. My incision is pretty much healed, and I'm massaging my belly every night with virgin coconut oil and vitamin E. The abdominal binder is helping a lot, but I won't be swimsuit ready for a while."

"Well, it's only March. You've got time."

At the moment, Paige felt completely out of touch with her body. All she seemed to be doing was producing breastmilk. But since quite a few women eventually had more than one child, she had high hopes that the feeling would be temporary. Because, somehow, she needed to reconnect with the father of her child, who, conveniently, also happened to be the man she had grown to deeply love. *I've never been surer of anything in my life,* she thought. And every day, her certainty grew.

Ed's house was amazing, but not in the same manner as the rustic log and stone house in Colorado Springs. Craftsman homes were a rarity in northern New Mexico, but Ed had somehow found one on the outskirts of Santa Fe a few years ago. The lovingly restored home wore appropriately historic, earthy colors—a cheery yellow ocher on the outside, with a pop of russet on the front door. Mature cottonwoods framed it nicely, but made it look slightly smaller than it actually was.

Inside, the well cared for home reflected Ed's generous personality and his love for music. In addition to his work-from-home office, with all its high-tech bells and whistles, he had a separate room filled with a variety of stringed instruments. Paige didn't doubt he could play all of them.

The living room was warm and inviting, with an original river stone fireplace featuring all the traditional craftsman details. The room's comfortable-looking furniture was a bit large for her taste, but it was perfect for Ed. He showed her the guest room and hung out for a few minutes while she got Reggie settled for the night in his travel bassinette. She liked to keep her baby close, which made it easier to nurse as often as needed throughout the night. Her newborn was a pretty mellow, as babies go, as long as she fed him regularly. He didn't much like getting his diaper changed, but he settled down right after.

Today she'd found an adorable long-sleeved sleeper with a print of a tuxedo on it. The store had one in a three-to-six-month size, which is what her giant newborn was wearing already. At least her son would look adorable at the wedding. She hadn't yet found the perfect dress, but tomorrow was another day...

"So, I talked to Tom Price and he's approved a final version of the will," Ed said. "If you have some time tomorrow, I'd appreciate it if you could look it over."

"I can do that, but I'm glad you said 'tomorrow.' Shopping for dresses with a newborn wore me out more than I'd thought it would."

"Want a night cap? Then to bed?" Ed asked.

"I'd love half a glass of wine, if you have it," Paige said.

"Sure. Red, okay?" he asked.

"Yes, it's perfect. I think Reggie's down for the count, and I brought the baby monitor. Should we take advantage of the moment and sit in your cozy living room?" she asked. "It's so nice to finally see where you live. You have a very nice home, and it suits you, perfectly"

Ed nodded. "Thanks. I'll light a fire." He also put on some soft jazz, which set a nice mood for the evening.

The romantic setting was going to be perfect for the conversation Paige had in mind. "So, Ed, I'm glad we're here, away from the ranch, because I really wanted to talk to you," she began.

"Good. I'm glad you're here, too, Paige. I've been wanting to show you my home—especially the room I've picked out for Reggie. I really want to know what you think. Outfitting a nursery for a baby isn't exactly my forte, and I could hire someone. But it would mean a lot more to have your help."

This wasn't the direction she'd hoped the conversation would go. "About that, Ed. I think we should take a broader view of our family."

"We can structure arrangements in whatever way works best, and when we've come up with a solution that works for all three of us, but mostly for Reggie, I'd like to make it legal," Ed said.

This conversation was swiftly moving from bad to worse—she had to do something. "You know, Ed, I'm really not up for anything serious tonight. I'm still getting my energy back after the birth, and there is something I've been wanting to do with you," she said. *Baby steps.* "Do you have any old photo albums from when you were a baby? Or a toddler? I'd love to see if Reggie looks like you. That would be just my speed tonight, to sit in front of the fire, with you, sipping on excellent wine...and looking at baby pictures. Do you think we could we start there?"

Ed looked at her as though she'd grown a third eye. "Okay...I guess I can try to find them. I think they're in a box in my den. More wine?" he asked.

"No, thanks, I'm good," she said. "Reggie will probably wake up in a few hours, and I'll need to nurse him."

"Okay, back in a few minutes," said Ed, setting his wine glass down.

Paige stared hypnotically into the crackling flames. Contrary to "not thinking about anything serious tonight," her brain conducted a rapid-fire assessment of her life: *She was about to turn thirty-nine, divorced, living with her sister and her sister's soon-to-be husband, and the co-heir of a rehabilitated chicken ranch which she had very little time to turn into a sustainable profit-making venture for all of them—and recovering from a C-section after carrying a giant baby, while trying to repair her fractured relationship with her baby's father.* Obviously, it was tempting to have more than a half a glass of wine, but it probably wouldn't help, and she had a baby to nurse in about three hours.

After a few minutes, Ed returned, carrying an armful of photo albums from the early 1980s. "Here you go. There may be more, but these are most of the early ones." Ed plopped them on the couch beside her.

With the patience of a saint, Paige gently moved the albums to the perfectly empty coffee table and patted the space right next to her. "The albums won't mean much to me without the stories that go *with* the pictures," she said. "Come and sit beside me."

Ed appeared to weigh the pros and cons, but after topping off his glass, he came around to join her. "Okay. So, you really want to learn all about the infant version of Reginald Edward Barrett III?"

"Well, since I just finished nursing Reginald Edward Barrett IV, that would be a *yes*," Paige said, looking up at him. "Go for it."

"Promise me you won't laugh?" he asked, with a hint of vulnerability.

"I absolutely cannot make that promise. They're baby pictures, Ed, and I bet you were really cute," she said, giving him an encouraging smile. *More baby steps, as many as it took.*

Ed shook his head. "That's debatable, but I *was* really chubby. It's been a pretty tough genetic legacy to overcome," he said, more self-consciously than Paige would have thought possible for a creative genius and titan of the home-security industry.

Paige laid a gentle hand on his. Looking up, she said, "So, you were a chubby baby. "I was an *ugly, skinny* baby—completely bald, with a squashed nose that wasn't quite in the middle of my face. I think we both turned out pretty well." She smiled again and gently opened the cover.

Baby Ed lay swaddled in a soft blue blanket, hands clasped like a praying monk, with cheeks like a hoarding chipmunk. Then came some adorably staged black-and-white photos of newborn Ed with his mother. Ed had been born in July, and by the time he was old enough to sit up for a proud photo on the Barrett Family Christmas Card, he'd developed three distinct chins and a baby Buddha belly.

"Ed, you were *adorable!* And that tiny hand-knit sweater is the best! Do you think your mother still has it stashed away somewhere?"

"Maybe. My mother's family sent that sweater all the way from Norway. Most of the Paulsen family still lives near Bergen," he said.

"That's the jumping off point for visiting the Norwegian Fjords, right? I've always wanted to go there," she said, wistfully. "But I didn't get much time off from my job at the university—and for the last few years before I moved to New Mexico, I taught summer classes to pay off the rest of my school loans. So, have you been to visit your mother's family?" she asked. "The pictures of the fjords are breathtaking."

"Oh, yes, plenty of times. We usually visited them at midsummer, when the sun stays above the horizon and you can be outside playing after ten o'clock at night. I had my mom pretty worried, a few times," he said, smiling. "Come on, let's turn the page. This is going to take all night, and you need your rest."

Paige patted his arm lightly. "It's fine with me if it *does* take all night. These are precious memories, Ed. Harper, and now Reggie, are my only family. But I know next to nothing about *your* family—you don't ever talk about them, and when I bring them up, you tend to get dodgy. I don't even know if both of your parents are still alive. Are they? I'd really like to know."

"We're not really in touch," he said, shrugging. "My sister is close to them, and I'm sure she'd let me know if something major happened. For as long as I can remember, my father and I had so much friction between us. He had...very rigid expectations, and they didn't leave any room for me to figure out who I wanted to be. Then, when I chose to leave the family business, he completely disowned me—in fact, he disinherited me. My sister tried to keep the peace for a while, but it just wasn't possible."

"That sounds really rough, Ed. I'm sorry you had to go through any of that. What about your mother?" she asked.

He shrugged. "Eva. She and I used to be close, but my dad ruled the roost and she always went along with him. I get a letter from her now and then, and a Christmas card every year, and that's about it."

"It must be really hard...to have such distance from the people who raised you. Well, you already know *my* family history. It was just my mom, Lilliane, and she's been gone for a long time now. I miss her, especially, now. I...guess I have to ask; do you think our baby will ever have a grandmother in his life? Or a grandfather?"

Ed stared into the fire, saying nothing, and the silence stretched on for an uncomfortably long time.

Suddenly she was struck with a feeling of dread. "You *did* tell them about the baby, didn't you?" she asked.

He hesitated, again, then shook his head. "There would be no good way to tell them about *this*. They wouldn't understand. In *their* eyes, this would be just one more way that I'd screwed up."

Paige's face grew uncomfortably warm. "And in *your* eyes? Are you ashamed of me? Or, of Reggie? Are you embarrassed that you have a baby, when you're not married to his mother?" Taking another breath, she asked the question that she feared lay at the root of everything between them: "Ed, are you ashamed that we made our baby the way we did?"

She was willing to give him a chance to explain. But Ed remained silent for far too long, and Paige had had enough. She stood up and waited for him to do something—to say *something*. She understood family estrangement: her own father had made that choice, and no one had gone running after him.

"Let me try to explain," Ed began. "It isn't exactly…"

But it was too little, too late. "I'm tired, Ed. I'm going to go to bed."

"Alright, I guess we can take a look at the nursery tomorrow, then," Ed said, sounding defeated.

Or never. It wasn't the 1950s! Her son wasn't a mistake or an embarrassment—he deserved to be celebrated! He was her greatest treasure. He'd come into her life at the *perfect* time, and she was beyond delighted to be Reggie's mother.

For the first time, Ed awoke to the sound of a baby crying in his own home. *His* baby. He smiled for a single peaceful moment, until he remembered the abrupt end to his conversation with Paige last night. The outcome had been the complete opposite of what he'd hoped for. Surely, two intelligent adults could figure out how to function as an unconventional family of three, for their child. Unconventional was nothing new for him—he'd been bucking convention his entire adult life.

If Paige didn't want him as a lover, a spouse, or a life-partner—which she'd made perfectly clear through her actions—then they'd be *unconventional* partners who cared about each other, a lot. An unconventional family could work, at least until one or both of them found other partners. *But that was a possibility he couldn't even imagine.* When the three of them were together, he experienced the deep sense of completeness he'd been lacking all of his life—and the mere thought of anyone *else* in that picture was completely devastating.

Sometimes, peopling was hard for him. He had a large group of casual acquaintances in the Renaissance movement, who he hung out with in New Mexico's intense summers, and a smaller group of business associates that he trusted completely. *But romantic relationships? Not so much.* He seemed to have a knack for driving the women he loved away. Now he had much more at stake than just another failed romantic relationship—*Reggie.* His son needed to have the best possible life and the unwavering support of two loving parents—and he'd do *anything* to make that happen, starting with cooking his baby mama breakfast. But first, he needed to take a quick shower...

The hot water revived him and left him feeling more relaxed. After he toweled himself dry and dressed casually in jeans, suede moccasins, and a pullover V-neck sweater that Paige had once said she liked, he tapped on her door. *No response.* He tapped again, listened hard for the sound of the shower or the soft, distinctive sounds that his son made, when he was awake. Then he opened the door: Paige and all of her things were gone, and Reggie was gone, too.

"Are you sure you're not making a mistake?" Harper asked, hands steady on Ethel's wheel. "With you running back to the ranch whenever you two hit a glitch, Ed's going to think we're some kind of codependent weirdos. Besides, don't you think you two need to talk?"

"Well, you and I *are* some kind of codependent weirdos. For most of our lives, we've really only had each other. Besides, what is there to say? Ed's ashamed of us—he's ashamed of the way Reggie came to *be*. But just look at my darling, gorgeous baby! He may have arrived unexpectedly, but our baby is not a *mistake*."

"Paige, I really can't imagine Ed saying that," Harper said, doubtfully. "He's *crazy* about Reggie. What is this about?"

"He hasn't told his family about Reggie," Paige said. "They don't even know that he exists."

"Okay…I hear you. But, from what you've told me, they're not close."

"I didn't even know if they were still living! I have a right to know the basic facts about Ed and his family, don't I? They're Reggie's grandparents! And *they* have a right to know they have a grandchild in the world!"

"I really think that's Ed's call to make," Harper said, at the risk of further upsetting her sister. She suspected that Paige was overreacting. *But she hadn't been there to know what really happened—and, this wasn't the situation she was facing.*

Paige was silent. "Let's not talk about it. I just want to get home. I didn't sleep much at all, last night."

"Was Reggie being fussy?" Harper asked, striving for empathy.

"No, Reggie's a great big angel baby, and I'm the luckiest new mom in the entire world. I was just…too much in my head. I really need to avoid drama late at night. Plus, I think my hormones might be a bit of a mess right now, coming down from the pregnancy. Postpartum stuff. I cried at a dog food commercial. I mean, I *actually* cried!"

"That doesn't sound like very much fun," Harper said. "Well, we're almost home. Do you want to stop at Maggie's and pick up some high-carb comfort food?"

"You read my mind," Paige said.

"I guess that's one of the advantages of being codependent," Harper replied. "But since I drove all the way to Santa Fe and back to come get you, *and* I put gas in your car, *you're* buying."

CHAPTER SIXTEEN

*A*fter days of nursing, pumping, burping the baby, and changing a newborn's gazillion diapers, Paige was pooped. She went to bed soon after putting Reggie down and slept like the dead. Then, a little after 6:00 am, something *very* strange happened. Dozing in and out of sleep, occasionally glimpsing the gray turning to blue outside her window, Paige was startled awake. Eyes wide open, now, she glanced at her son, still sleeping soundlessly. Laying perfectly still, she felt a strange tilting sensation. Then, back to normal—and another strange tilt. On the tail end of a faint rumble, she heard the sound of ceramics breaking on the tile floor below. Paige reached held onto Reggie's co-sleeper and tried to breathe. *What had just happened?* Then her door burst open and Harper and Caleb both entered the room, thankfully, wearing clothing.

"Are you okay?" Harper asked. "And Reggie?"

"I think so—whatever it was seems to have stopped. That was freaky! Do you think the house's foundation is unstable?" Paige asked.

Caleb shook his head. "The house is built on compacted ground, pre-slab-construction. I think this was an earthquake." He opened his cell phone browser. "If it was, it should be showing up here on Google in a few minutes."

"Oh, wow!" said Paige. "That was…weird, like nothing I've ever experienced."

Harper nodded. "They're weird, alright. We had a few in the Seattle area when I lived there, but I didn't know New Mexico had earthquakes."

Caleb nodded. "We've been known to have a few, but nothing very big for over a hundred years. There was a category 6.2 in Socorro, in the early 1900s, and a 5.2 about a decade later, in Cerillos, just off the Turquoise Trail. There were a couple of 4.0 quakes in Los Alamos and Cimarron, just a few years ago. Lots of smaller earthquakes probably occur here, pretty frequently—but it would be really unusual to have a *big* quake here."

"What are they saying? Anything?" Harper asked, leaning over Caleb's phone.

"Um, yeah, a Google alert says it was a 3.9. But that's just a preliminary reading," he said. "It could move up or down."

"And the epicenter?" Harper asked.

"Right now, they're saying it was on the Santa Clara fault, near Española."

"I wonder how far away people could feel it?" Paige asked. At that exact moment, the phone rang, answering her question.

"Hi, Ed," she said. "Yeah, we felt it, here. No, not too strong, but it was the first one I've ever experienced. Reggie's fine. It didn't even wake him up."

Do you want to come back to Santa Fe? We didn't finish talking—and I didn't get a chance to show you the nursery, Ed said.

"It's very nice of you to offer, but Reggie seems really settled here, and so am I. For the time being, we'll just stay here. Of course, you're welcome to come up and see him anytime you want. I would never prevent you from seeing your son," Paige said. She could be a single parent—her mother had done it and everyone had survived. And at least Ed would help out financially, unlike her own deadbeat father.

Alright, if that's what works best for you, for the time being, Ed said. Keep in touch, and call me if you need anything. Oh, and Paige? You might feel a few aftershocks. So, be careful, please, especially coming down the stairs, carrying the baby.

"Hi, Tom," Ed said. "Thanks for the lovely card. I promise to share a cigar with you the next time I see you."

And when might that be? Tom asked.

"Maybe sooner than I'd hoped—I need to talk to you about custody arrangements. I know it's really early, but I need to know what my options are, and maybe get the ball rolling, in case the process takes a while."

Ed, my advice is still to avoid jumping the gun, Tom said. The last time we tried the legal route, it scared Paige off. Maybe it's best if you two work this out together, amicably. But I'll have my secretary shoot you an email with some informational links you can look over Then, if you want the name of the best family lawyer I know, by all means, let me know.

Afraid to leave Reggie alone, Paige brought him downstairs in a front-pack, then joined Caleb and Harper to assess the damage.

"How many aftershocks have we had now?" asked Harper.

"Three. There will likely be a couple more, but they might not all be strong enough to feel," Caleb said.

A few pieces of broken crockery lay on the kitchen floor, and every one of the framed photos had fallen face down on the fireplace mantle. But the urn that held their Aunt Sabina's ashes still sat firmly in its place, as if it had been the single spot of calm in the grand old house. Paige made a mental note to secure the lid of the brass container, in case the quakes continued and the urn took a tumble.

"There doesn't seem to be much damage inside. Should we look outside?" Pagie asked, and Harper got a strange look on her face.

Perhaps it was just pre-wedding jitters—but Harper had a sudden vision of the earth opening up into a huge gaping crevasse into which all of the people she loved were swept—and for a split second, she was horrified. But that was just plain silly. *The earth didn't actually open up like that, did it?* Anyway, New Mexico didn't have major active faults like California's San Andreas. *Or, did it?*

"It'll be okay, Harper. Let's just go take a look," Caleb said, taking her arm, gently.

"I'm staying inside. But I expect a full report, you two," Paige said.

"Wait, don't head off yet, babe" Harper said, pointing a finger upward, as she stepped outside. "Check this out."

"Is there a crack in the adobe?" Caleb asked, turning to look back at the ranch house.

"No, not that I can see. But, look, the *nicho* above the front door is still empty. Remember, we said we were going to look for the patron saint of rain, or of growing things? Maybe we should broaden our search a little—who's the patron saint of earthquakes?" Harper asked.

"Harper, that's a little woo-woo, even for you. Do you really think that some tchotchke made in a factory somewhere has the power to affect plate tectonics?" Caleb asked.

"All I'm saying is, as long as we're committed to being decorative and rustic around here, we might as well multi-task and find the proper saintly figure to protect our home," Harper said. "What's the harm in covering all the bases?"

Caleb shook his head. "While y'all are thinking about 'proper saintly figures,' I'm heading up to the Coop Studios to check for damage. Are you coming?"

"Yep, right behind you." Harper followed Caleb, the calm voice of reason, up to the Coops, lost in thought. They didn't need proper saintly *figures—just one.*

Later than night after Caleb was asleep, Harper did some quick online research. Saint Isadore the Farmer, the patron saint of agricultural workers, peasants, day laborers, and brick layers. Spanish, hometown, Madrid, and not quite right. Then came Saint Medardus, the patron saint of the weather (*that was a little closer to the mark*), vineyards (*should she plant some?*), prisoners, and the mentally ill. Also, peasants, again—and sterility. *She wasn't touching Saint Medardus with a ten-foot pole.*

Next up, Saint Heribert of Cologne, the patron saint of drought. He'd followed a less-than-stellar path to adulthood, after his life's ambition had been thwarted by good old dad. Deprived of his life choice to become a monk by the entrenched rules of the Patriarchy, he'd given all of his money to the poor and chose to roam the streets helping the sick and destitute. Then, during a terrible drought, he led a parade of poor folks to the church to pray. When he rose from his knees, a New Mexico monsoon-style rain came down, saved everybody's crops, and whisked him to sainthood.

Darn it, these old-world dudes didn't feel right at all. A house brought back to life by two women should be watched over by a *woman.* Hmm. *What about new-world saints of the female variety?* Harper could only think of one. She glimpsed her lovely, ethereal face everywhere—especially on the tall white candles sold at mini-marts and dollar stores throughout her newly adopted state: *La Virgen de Guadalupe, traditionally adorned in a deep green cape sprinkled with shining gold stars, and surrounded by a lovely arch of blooming roses.*

Feeling the warm tingle of intuition, Harper typed "Virgin of Guadalupe reported powers," into her search bar and found a suitable definition, courtesy of Pope Francis: "A mother who provides shelter, who takes care of, and is close to her people." Another quote revealed that, "Statues of *La Virgen de Guadalupe* stand in special *nichos* on the facades of countless Mexican homes." And New Mexican homes? She shivered as a tingle ran up her spine. She was fairly sure that the *nicho* on the ranch's one-hundred-year-old home had originally been intended for the brown-skinned Mary of Mexico—and that everybody else in New Mexico knew this except Eastern transplants like the Crawley sisters. Obviously, *La Virgen* had disappeared from her designated *nicho* when the house had fallen into ruin. And she needed to be replaced, *rápidamente,* before the ground opened up and swallowed everyone Harper loved.

*

Ed called Paige again that night. "I *really* think you and Reggie should come back to Santa Fe. We have important things to talk about," he said, as direct as he could be.

The earthquakes have subsided. We haven't had an aftershock since early afternoon, and Reggie's really settled here, Paige said, neutrally.

"So, there's nothing I can do to change your mind? I'm happy to come up and get you both," he offered. He'd do anything to keep both of them safe.

No, we're just fine here, she said, again.

"Alright, then. Good night, Paige. Give Reggie a kiss for me."

He poured himself a glass of merlot, but didn't light a fire. It was time for due diligence, starting with a look at *A Father's Rights to Child Custody and Visitation in New Mexico.* "The best interest of the child is the presumption of joint custody..." he read, and then they got to the part that interested him: "The judge may award primary custody, defined as one parent having primary physical custody for the majority of the time, while the other parent receives visitation with the child." *Not ideal at all.* "When deciding on primary custody, the judge takes into account each parents' ability and commitment to care for the child." He continued on, stopping when he read that, "it is possible for either parent to be awarded primary custody, and for the other to receive visitation. A female parent has no greater right than a male parent." Then, one last sentence caught his eye: "Hiring an experienced family law attorney could potentially affect the outcome of a primary custody battle and could mean the difference between receiving limited visitation and primary physical custody."

Of course, a battle wasn't even close to the outcome Ed desired; he'd *never* want to take Reggie away from Paige. He'd seen the incredible bond between them. But neither did he want to be a part-time dad, seeing his son only on the occasional weekend or summer holidays. And he *really* hated the idea of seeing his son raised by another man, whenever Paige finally found what she was looking for—which apparently wasn't him. He just had to look harder for a better solution.

He tapped in a number on his phone: "Tom, it's Ed. Yeah, I know. But I've read through all of the information you sent me. And now, I really *would* like to speak with the best fathers' rights attorney you know. Local is good, but if I have to drive to Albuquerque, it's not a problem."

CHAPTER SEVENTEEN

*O*n a warm early spring night, Paige opened her bedroom windows and inhaled the incomparable fragrance of the high desert. She'd felt so at peace since bringing her baby back to the ranch, where she was surrounded by her family: *Harper, Caleb, and Ellie—Maggie and Mariah, in town.* With her sister's help, she'd finally caught up on her rest and wasn't feeling tired in the least. And since Reggie would be asleep for hours before his next feeding, she had time to do some discreet online snooping regarding Reggie's West Coast grandparents. If Ed wasn't going to give her much of a peek into that window, she'd have to see for herself.

Reginald Edward Barrett II was a near replica of Ed, or visa versa, but the elder Barrett had the steel blue eyes of a Scotsman. Paige read that Reggie II had inherited his riches from his father and his grandfather. But, unlike the popular adage that says, "the first generation makes the money, the second generation spends it, and the third loses it," Ed's dad had been a ruthlessly successful businessman.

Paige clicked on a different link which brought up a bio for Ed's mother, Eva Paulsen Barrett. She was a lovely, tall and slender woman with Scandinavian features and a familiar gaze. *Ed had inherited his mother's eyes*—warm, brown, and full of emotion.

Eva Paulsen Barrett was an ardent conservationist, along the lines of Lady Bird Johnson, but with old East Coast money. She'd devoted much of her life to helping to preserve endangered flora in Northern and Coastal California, creating a legacy to be proud of. *But would she make a good grandmother? Grandma Eva?* Paige smiled. With a pedigree like Eva Paulsen Barrett's, she'd likely be "Nana," at best. *Any other grandchildren?* Her curiosity soon took her to a whole new level of snooping.

Adding "children of" to the search bar, Paige located the sister that Ed had mentioned as his only sibling: *Elizabeth.* Did Elizabeth have children? She did—two girls, Chloe and Halley, with the surname of DuBois. Tall and slim, they'd inherited the Parker physique, and did not, in any way, resemble their burly grandfather or uncle.

Finally, starting to get sleepy herself, Paige googled "origin and definition of the surname, Barrett." After all, it was now her son's name, too, right there on his birth certificate. Barrett was a common name in parts of Scotland and Ireland, an ancient relic of the Norman invasion, and it came with various interpretations. The one that struck her as most accurate was "Mighty Bear," a moniker derived during the twelfth-century invasion led by Strongbow. *She and Harper knew very little of their own family history, especially on their father's side. When she had time to start a hobby, maybe she'd look into it…*

Paige leaned back in her chair, slowly closing the multiple tabs she'd opened and putting her laptop into sleep mode. She had a feeling that Ed's mother, her baby's only grandmother, would be *thrilled* to know about her new grandson. But as Harper rightly pointed out, that was firmly *Ed's* call to make. As she checked on Reggie before heading to bed, Paige lamented, not for the first time, that her own mother had died so young, only in her forties. Lilliane Anderson Crawley would've been a truly wonderful grandmother, and they would all be so fortunate to have her in their lives. Life wasn't fair. Her mother had left them, too soon, when they were barely getting started in their own lives, and she'd missed out on so much. *They all had.*

Harper and Caleb were finishing breakfast when Paige came down the stairs with Reggie in her arms. At three-and-a-half weeks, he was spending more time alert and focused. Of course, the baby hadn't presented them with any smiles, just yet. It was a little too early for that. As his proud mother, she figured everything would happen when it was supposed to…

"Hey, did you guys feel that aftershock this morning?" Paige asked.

"Yeah, we felt it. It was a pretty big one. Could've been another primary quake, not an aftershock," Caleb said.

"Well, at least we didn't lose any more crockery," Harper said. "And since when did *you* become Geology Man?" she asked her husband.

"Hey, I may have majored in construction engineering, but I minored in geology. I know things," Caleb said, as he carried his plate to the big farmhouse sink.

"Aren't you full of surprises?" Harper said, smiling at him.

"You *love* my surprises," he said, leaning in for a kiss.

"You know, the honeymoon doesn't start for a few more days. Speaking of, is there anything left to do for this wedding of yours?" Paige asked.

"You're the designated wedding planner, and you've been ticking items off your list, right and left. I think if you have a dress, we're all set. So, do you?" Harper asked, a note of challenge in her voice.

"It's...in progress," said Paige. "I'm taking Reggie into Santa Fe with me today for the final fitting. Ed's insisting that we talk, and it's hard to keep putting him off."

"Well, good. *Don't*. You and Ed need to talk to each other more than any two people on the planet," Harper said, carrying her own plate to the sink. "And I want photos of the dress by end of day, or there'll be trouble."

"Well, we wouldn't want *that*, now, would we?" Paige said—apparently with an inappropriate amount of sarcasm.

"Just make sure you have a dress to wear, would you? These grounds aren't gonna get beautiful all by themselves," Harper said, as she headed out the door, gloves and clippers in hand.

"Well now, I think you just irritated my fiancé," Caleb said. "Can't you just agree with everything she says until I put a ring on her finger? That's *my* M.O. for the next few days." He winked at Paige and followed Harper out the door.

Ed took her to lunch at *Matbakh Al Amir*, the place with the fountains, although they hadn't yet been turned on for the season. In Santa Fe, winter sometimes stuck around for at least another month.

"So, big doings this weekend, eh? Are you excited? Nervous? Everything in good shape out at the ranch?" he asked. "I could find some time to help, if you need me to."

"Everything is under control—I don't expect even a ripple on the big day. But Harper's still obsessing about my dress, which is annoying because she doesn't give a hoot about clothes, and everyone is going to be looking at *her* anyway. She's going to look great—I'm the one with the slowly-receding belly. But who cares if I'm a little poochy?" she said, taking a bite of her lamb curry. She was dying for a bite of Ed's baba ganoush, but eggplant made Reggie incredibly gassy.

"I don't think you look poochy—I think you look amazing, even after such a short time. No matter what you wear, you'll look beautiful, Paige," he said, his soulful, brown eyes meeting her green eyes, for a sweet moment.

"Thank you, Ed." *And God and Spanx.* "That's a very kind thing to say. Are you sure you're okay to watch Reggie during the wedding ceremony? I'll be pretty busy," she said, although she was *quite* excited to be her sister's matron of honor on her big day.

"We'll be fine. He's comfortable with me," he said, reaching out to let Reggie tug at his finger. "He already knows I'm his daddy," he said, smiling.

"And a wonderful daddy you are. So, what did you want to talk about, Ed?" she said, taking a sip of her hibiscus tea with a dollop of honey. Nursing moms had to take pleasure in small comforts.

"Well, it's about Reggie. We haven't sorted anything out. I've been going along with whatever was easiest for *you*, with a newborn. But… I've met with a family attorney, and I'd like to at least get preliminary custody arrangements down on paper."

Frankly, she was stunned. "But, Ed. It's so soon! He's just a tiny baby. Well, maybe not tiny, but a really *young* baby. I *know* we need to talk about custody—but can't this discussion wait a little longer?"

she asked. "I mean, have I done or said *anything* that would make you think I'd try to limit your access?"

Ed closed his eyes and sighed. "Paige, I don't want 'access.' I want to be a full-time father to my only son. I'm always going to be in his life, one way or another. We really need to come up with an arrangement that works, for both of us, and of course, for Reggie."

"I never said you *couldn't* be! But I'm nursing him right now, Ed. What do you want me to do? I don't want him to get used to a bottle, just yet. That can be confusing for an infant. And I can't just give you one of my breasts to take home with you."

Ed shook his head. "I want *all* of you," he said, with some emotion.

What? For a moment, Paige's heart skittered wildly, before reality caught up.

"I mean, I want you *both* to move here to Santa Fe—temporarily, for a year or two—until Reggie's done nursing, and he's old enough to be comfortable without you for a few days. I want *equal* custody, as I said, right from the beginning. This is the only way for us to make it work."

But was it? "Or, *you* could move out to the ranch, and the effect would be exactly the same," Paige said, evenly.

"My business is headquartered in Santa Fe—you know that. The ranch is okay for short visits, and I always enjoy my time there. But to effectively manage Harp over the long term, I really need to be here in town," he said.

"And The Inn at Verde Springs is *my* business—how can I run it from Santa Fe?" she asked him. "Hospitality services are hands on, and Harper and Caleb can't always be there. Case in point—they have a two-week honeymoon coming up in a matter of days."

"I realize that, but as I said, it would only be temporary. Maybe you could hire an assistant manager, just for a year or two. Paige, I just want what's in Reggie's best interest. And what's in the best interest of any very young child is to have *both* of his parents under one roof, easily available, and cooperating to provide the best care possible. I don't think what I'm asking for is unreasonable," he said, getting a tinge red in the face.

Paige paused. "This arrangement you're suggesting—I really can't see it working but I promise I'll give it some thought. And I'll want to discuss the idea with Harper. My being away from the ranch would affect her, too. But I don't want to bring it up until *after* the wedding, which is just a few days away. We're all under a lot of pressure right now. Can you give me a little more time?"

Ed nodded. "Of course—but I can't wait *indefinitely*. Thanks for hearing me out, and I hope you'll consider it. I really want you to think about splitting your time. Maybe you could take Reggie to the ranch a couple of two days a week—and the rest of the time you could work from home in Santa Fe. I realize that babies need a lot of care, so I hope you'll *also* agree to help me interview potential nannies. We'll need to find one who'll work well for all three of us."

Nannies? Oh, he was really getting on her nerves, today. "Well, right now, the person Reggie needs most is his *mother*. Since we're done here, I'm going to give him a quick feed in the car, and then head home." She quickly packed up the baby carrier, diaper bag, and her purse. As she proceeded toward the exit, she called over her shoulder, "By the way, have you told your family about the baby, yet?" It was a cranky, post-C-section, nursing mother's version of a mic drop—but she was pleased to see several interested heads turn in her direction.

She wasn't in a hurry to get back to the ranch—but she *was* desperate to get out of a lingering lunch with Ed. *Who did he think he was?* Always getting lawyers involved when they just needed time to work things out amicably, in a way that was best for everybody—but most of all, for Reggie. Of course, she still *loved* the big guy—that hadn't changed. But right now, she didn't *like* him very much...

After nursing Reggie in the car, Paige drove to the bridal shop, parked in front, and hurried inside. She hoped the baby would stay in his blissful, post-feeding nap until she had time to slip into the dress that, in desperation, she'd ended up ordering from the bridal shop over the phone. Since her body shape was constantly changing, she'd arranged to have the fitters make any last-minute adjustments, and today was the day. *She'd nearly run out of time, and she wanted to look presentable for her sister's wedding.*

The young women in the store exclaimed over Reggie. They'd all seen Paige in here, before, in various stages of pregnancy, and now they were excited to see the adorable end-result.

"I'll be happy to watch him for you," a sweet girl named Meghan offered. "And I promise not to wake him up. Go ahead and try it on."

"Bless you. I just need a minute to slip out of my clothes and pull on this gorgeous, gorgeous dress. I *really* hope it fits."

"I can make any last-minute adjustments, if needed, but I think it's going to be perfect," said the owner of the shop, who'd come over to join them and fuss over the quietly sleeping newborn.

Paige pulled the shimmery, dusty-pink dress over her head. *Here goes.* The dress floated on like a dream. It was nicely fitted in all the right places, but generously forgiving in the waist. The length was good too, below the knee, but slightly shorter than Harper's tea-length wedding gown. The simple scooped neckline showed off her breasts, but not in a crass way. She wanted to look elegant and maternal, not like Reggie was overdue for a feeding. She came out of the room to find four pairs of eyes staring at her, the shop girls' and Reggie's, now awake and placid. "Wow, he sure seems to like you!" Paige said to Meghan, who was still holding him. "Sometimes he doesn't take to strangers."

"He's the sweetest baby," she said, smiling down at him.

"And *you* look absolutely beautiful! It's a wonderful fit, and it doesn't look like you'll need any last-minute alterations," the shop owner said. "Shall I wrap it up for you?"

Paige had her Spanx to thank for that. "Yes, but would you mind snapping a photo, first? Here's my cell. Harper is on a tear, and I might need to pacify her with a quick look at the dress."

"Okay, all done. Here you go," the shop owner said, handing her phone back.

"This looks good," Paige said, glancing at the photo. "Well, I think we're done here. Let me take this guy off your hands—unless you want to moonlight as a nanny. My baby's father just threatened to hire one." *She was still steamed about that...*

"Really? Honestly, I wouldn't mind. I love babies, and I only work here part-time," a young woman named Meghan said. "I'm the oldest of a large family, so I have plenty of experience taking care of my younger siblings."

"Wow, thanks, I'll keep that in mind! I'm pretty focused on my sister's wedding, this weekend. But after that, I might be in touch," she said, giving Meghan a warm smile. They exchanged phone numbers, and then Paige carried Reggie to the car, buckled him into his infant car seat, and headed back to the ranch.

CHAPTER EIGHTEEN

"Knock, knock," Paige called out. She held a tray with two plates of breakfast crepes, fruit, coffee, and a pale green vase filled with two dozen, bright-yellow daffodils, since they were now blooming prolifically all over the ranch.

"Come in. Caleb's just in the shower. Caleb, don't come out naked—my sister is here," she called, in a much higher volume.

"Got it," came his muffled reply.

What a guy. "Well, now that your big day has finally arrived, I thought you deserved breakfast in bed. You *both* do, even though tradition says the bride and groom shouldn't see each other the night before the wedding."

"We've already seen every bit of each other—I don't think there are any surprises. But Caleb and I are both big believers in a hearty breakfast. So, thanks, Paige. It was very thoughtful of you."

"Eat up. The wedding festivities start in just a few hours. Are you ready?" she asked her sister.

"As ready as I *can* be, given that the earth moved, again, this morning. Did you feel it? I swear—the last thing we need is another earthquake! At least I'm not nervous about marrying Caleb, and I'm ridiculously thrilled to be Ellie's bonus mom. She told me, yesterday that she's just going to call me Harper, except on Mother's Day, because she thinks it will be fun to have two moms. I think she's more excited for the second Sunday in May than she is about the wedding!"

"That's adorable! And with those dark blue eyes you've both got, you could almost *be* her mom. It'll be *my* first Mother's Day, too, and we can celebrate together! You'll be back from your honeymoon by then, right?"

"Unless we get kidnapped by pirates, or Caleb has something planned for us that he hasn't told me about," Harper said.

At that moment, Caleb cleared his throat, loudly, then came out wearing a low-slung towel around his hips. *The man had abs that went on for days, and...this was Paige's signal to clear out.* "Well, enjoy. But not *too* much. Save something for the honeymoon."

With the wedding set for three o'clock, Ed arrived at one-thirty and immediately took Reggie off her hands, so she'd have plenty of time to prep and help her sister with last minute tasks.

Paige wore a navy and white print shirtdress and sandals, and she'd slip on her dusty-pink matron of honor dress at the last minute. Just as she was fastening the backs on some rose quartz and silver earrings, she heard a loud screech coming from Harper's bedroom. *Her first rescue mission of the day, and she was on it.*

"Hey, what's up?" Paige asked, poking her head in.

"I just took a *shower!*" Harper said, with unusual force.

"Well…it was awfully courteous of you to shower before you stand across from Caleb and pledge your eternal vows," Paige said, carefully.

"And I smell *worse* than I did before!" Harper wailed.

"What? That doesn't make any sense, Harper. Did you use some weird bodywash or shampoo or something? Caleb likes *your* smell—don't go changing anything up last minute."

"Just—get over here and smell me."

"Harper, you're being dramatic," Paige said, as she walked across the room and took a whiff of her only sibling. "Oh, Jesus-Mary-and-Joseph, no you're not. Lordy, you smell like you took a bath in fire and brimstone!"

"What. Is. Happening?" Harper wailed. "And on my wedding day!"

"Well, at least your groom probably smells equally terrible." Paige turned on the faucet and out came a stream of strange, orange-tinted water with a strong mineral odor. *Was it sulfur?* They didn't have time to bring in an environmental CSI team—she had to get her sister married. What she needed was a solution, and fast…

"Harper, stay right where you are. I mean it—don't move. And don't go *near* your dress. I'll be right back." She ran into her room across the hall, picked up the gallon jug of distilled water she'd used to fill the fancy dress steamer, and returned, pronto.

"Okay, remember our Nana Hazel's stories? When she was an army nurse in Korea, she and her friends used to take a 'possible bath,' using only as much water as an army helmet could hold. So, that's what *you're* going to do. I have almost a full gallon, here," she said, handing it to her sister. "Now, get moving and give yourself a 'possible bath,' while I call an emergency plumber."

"Why?" Harper asked, confused. "I don't think fire and brimstone is an actual plumbing problem—it seems like more of an ancient curse-type thing. Maybe we should light some candles, or pray. And what in the hell is a 'possible bath?'"

"Look, it's not rocket science. You just start at the top and wash down as low as possible. Then, you start at your feet and wash up as high as possible. Then, you know, you wash *possible*. And use some soap that smells really good—I have some lovely linden flower soap from France in my shower."

"Hey, wait just a minute! Why don't *you* stink?" Harper asked, hands on her bare hips and elbows out.

"I showered last night, and I was going to shower again right before I put on my fancy dress. But I'm having strong second thoughts about that," Paige said.

"Okay, just bring me your magic soap, and no peeking," Harper grumbled. "I'll just be in here washing 'possible' up, down, and sideways."

"I'll…coach you through it," Paige said, because she didn't know what else to say. Forty minutes later, the two Crawley sisters proudly descended the stairs, arm in arm, and they did not leave a stinky, sulfurous trail behind them. *Thank you, Nana Hazel.*

Dressed in their spring wedding finery, the guests had assembled in the entrance garden. Under their rustic rose arbor, which Harper had spruced up with cheerful spring flowers, Caleb waited patiently with Rebecca, their officiant. Standing next to him was his best person, Maggie Ramirez, who looked regal in a long velvet skirt and silk blouse.

Inside the house, Ellie chomped at the bit, ready to sprint down the path with her wicker basket overflowing with scarlet rose petals. Her pale green dress clashed a little with her favorite hot pink cowgirl boots, but no one cared. She looked absolutely adorable. "Why do I have to go *first?*" she asked.

"Because it's traditional—the flower girl *always* goes first, Ellie. You'll be the one to let the guests know that the wedding is about to begin. I'll go right after you. And after that, Harper will walk up the path to meet your daddy," Paige explained. "Then, your job will be all done and you can just enjoy the wedding. Remember, you're going to sit with Ed and help him with baby Reggie?"

They'd come up with that plan at the last minute, since Ellie's mom wasn't attending her ex-husband's wedding, and Maggie was Caleb's best person.

Ellie nodded. "So, I have, like, an important job?"

"One of the *most* important," said Harper, gravely, giving Ellie a mock-serious look. *She was going to be a fantastic bonus mom, if she said so herself.*

"Okay, I *guess* I can do it," Ellie said, with a dramatic sigh. "When do I go? I don't *like* waiting."

"As soon as the music starts, I'll give you the signal, okay?" Paige said, demonstrating a thumbs up.

The band began playing a clever string-adapted version of John Legend's "All of Me," since it was hard to haul an actual piano out into a rock garden. The song's lyrics were the truest expression of what she and Caleb meant to each other. "*All of me loves all of you*"—*yes, it was like that, exactly.*

Harper gave Ellie the thumbs up. Paige waited a few beats before following her soon-to-be niece down the garden path. Her sister looked stunning in her pale dusty-pink dress. *If Ed didn't notice, the man was thick as a brick.* Then, when the band came around to the chorus again, Harper took the first step toward a future with the man she loved.

Caleb wore the cheesiest grin, as he wiped away a tear with his thumb. *The big goober.* This was the man she could absolutely give everything to. He reached for her hands, and they looked into each other's eyes, and the rest was easy. He was so *easy* to love, and he loved her hard in return. *This time, for both of them, love would last...*

"And so, by the power invested in me by the State of New Mexico, I now pronounce you husband and wife, wife and husband. Now, it's time to kiss the bride—"

But Caleb jumped the gun and pulled her into his arms. It was the kiss to beat all kisses, and just when they were about to come up for air, the earth moved. The crowd looked at each other in shock as the ground rumbled and tilted, and droplets of murky, grayish liquid began to fall ominously from the hazy sky.

"*This* is a huge buzzkill," Harper muttered to the wedding party.

"You were right—we *should* have splurged for the Virgin of Guadalupe statue," Paige whispered, beside her. "Sorry I didn't back you up on that."

"Well, it's only an earthquake," Harper said. "It's not like it was in my nightmares, when the earth split and—"

Her words were cut off by a ripple and crunch that sent chills running up her spine. It sounded an awful lot like the earth being torn asunder—and all around them was a sulfurous stench straight from the depths of hell.

Ed breathed in relief as he saw Paige making her way through the small crowd to reach him. Reggie was tucked into the big, covered stroller, and he held Ellie firmly by the hand.

"Ed, this is horrible! I don't know what's happening. What should we do?" she asked.

"If nothing else, the air quality's going to drive us out," he said, covering his mouth with a hand, as he coughed "I think we need to evacuate, immediately." His eyes met Maggie's across the crowded garden. "One second, Paige," he said, handing off the stroller, and Ellie. "Don't move. I'll be right back." He'd grown up on the West Coast, and was more earthquake-savvy than the frightened guests milling around him. But this wasn't like any earthquakes he'd ever experienced. *Not even close.*

"Maggie. Are you okay?" he asked.

"Yes, just startled, like everybody else. This is awful! I feel terrible for Harper and Caleb—but I think we need to get out of here," she said.

"My thoughts, exactly. Do you have a crew at the diner today or did you shut down?" he asked.

"I have a small crew prepping for tomorrow," she said. "Why?"

"Can you call them? I'm just thinking...the diner's almost ten miles away. If everything's okay in town, maybe we could move the party there?" he suggested.

"Hold on, I'll find out," she said, pulling out her cell and calling her assistant manager. "Hey, it's Maggie. Yeah, that was a big one! We really felt it rock out here at the ranch, too. Is there any damage in town? And is everything still functional? Okay, good. So, here's what we're going to do—we're moving the Crawley-Johansson party to Maggie's."

Half an hour later, the wedding party had been safely moved to the diner, and the rest of the guests followed in a winding caravan. But the matron of honor wasn't in party mode. She was holed up in Maggie's storage room, sitting on a five-gallon bucket, making frantic calls to various emergency-response authorities.

"Hello, this is Paige Crawley, calling from Verde Springs. We've experienced an earthquake on our ranch, about ten miles away—but the most pressing issue is that the earthquake appears to have ruptured something. Why? Well, it smells just awful, like fire and brimstone, and we'd really like to have someone check it out. Well, I don't know. That's why I'm calling. It *could* be a gas line, or, possibly, something natural?" She paused, listening, and frowning. "Well, how am *I* supposed to know whether it's an emergency, or not? Is a ruptured gas line an emergency? You tell me!" She paused to take a breath and count to ten, but only made it to six. "Well, then, who *do* you suggest I call? Ghostbusters? Oh, that's *very* funny, you little shit. I'll be calling first thing Monday morning, and I am going to have a nice, long chat with your supervisor!"

Ed poked his head in, a question in his eyes. She shook her head. "Okay, I'll do that. Thank you very much for the suggestion. I really hope this isn't an *actual* life-threatening emergency that could endanger the lives of thousands of San Miguel County's citizens. No, thank *you*," she said, ending the call. She looked up at Ed. "Well, so far, I've spoken to the local gas company, and three natural disaster people that were no help at all—and the Emergency Disaster Response coordinator is apparently on vacation in Belize. I hope all the disasters were made aware."

"Did you get any suggestions for who to call?" Ed asked.

"Only one that made any sense—someone suggested we call the University of New Mexico's geology department to see if a hydrogeologist could come out to the ranch. I guess there isn't a local spewing-toxic-fumes-from-the-depths-of-hell-specialist on call in the state of New Mexico. But, dammit, there *should* be. How did this happen? And why today, of all days?"

"Paige, take a breath. We're all fine, and everyone is having a good time out there. Come on out and take a break—and you should eat something," he said, holding out a hand to pull her up. "The food is fantastic!"

Paige closed her eyes and took a breath, and with it came a moment of clarity. "Ed, *you* were a lifesaver back there, getting everybody evacuated—and you and Maggie coming up with the plan to move everybody here was pure genius!" She stood up, leaned in, and kissed his cheek. "On behalf of my sister, thank you."

"You're welcome. And one more thing—I never got a chance to tell you how lovely you look today," he said. "In that dress, you're an absolute knockout. I've *never* seen you look more beautiful, Paige. And, I'm feeling extremely lucky tonight."

"Oh?" she asked, not sure what tone to take with him, or if she should take any tone at all. The inner workings of Ed's mind were a complete mystery to her, at the moment. *But she appreciated the compliment.*

"Well, obviously, you *can't* stay at the ranch, now—so it would make the most sense for you and Reggie to stay with me in Santa Fe, at least until this situation is straightened out. Caleb and Harper can even join us. My house has plenty of room. But I *was* wondering… do you know what they're planning to do about their honeymoon? Weddings aren't usually followed by mysterious natural disasters," he said, frowning.

"I don't know—Harper and I haven't really had time to talk. I'd hate for them to cancel their trip because of what happened today—and who knows how long it will take to clean up this mess?"

"It's a little hard to say, since we don't know what we're dealing with. So, what can I do to help?"

"I'll have to think about that, Ed. Thanks for offering. And I guess you're right—I don't want to take the chance of going back to the ranch until I know it's safe, especially with the baby. I might have to borrow one of your t-shirts to sleep in, and tomorrow I'll have to go clothes shopping. God, if this situation didn't suck so much, it would almost be funny: the day my sister marries the love of her life, the earth explodes in noxious gases and sulfurous rain? Does my sister have rotten luck, or what?"

"You can borrow anything you want," Ed said, smiling. "You and Reggie, and Harper and Caleb, are all welcome to stay with me in Santa Fe for as long as you want to, or need to. I have plenty of room, and I'll make it as easy as I can, for everyone."

"You already have," she said, briefly wrapping her arms around his waist. *He gives the best bear hugs—and, as usual, he's a rock in an emergency.* "I'll go talk to Harper."

By eight o'clock, the last guest had departed Maggie's with a heck of a wedding tale, Harper and Caleb were happy but exhausted, and Paige looked ready to drop. But Ed had one last surprise up his sleeve…

"Ready to go?" he asked Paige, gently lifting a sleeping Reggie from her arms. He expertly balanced Reggie against his broad shoulder, and reached out with his other hand to pull Paige to her feet.

"I'm complete *toast*," Paige said.

"Come on. We'll have you home in bed in just over an hour," he said.

"Wait, if Reggie's car seat is in the back, where are Harper and Caleb going to sit?" she asked him.

"I…made other arrangements for them. In fact, I think I hear it, now," Ed said, with a gleam in his brown eyes.

And down from the darkening sky dropped a shiny helicopter. "I thought your sister and Caleb might like riding in style—and that, in a small way, a special ride might make up for the interruption of the wedding night they'd originally planned."

"What? Wow! Harper's going to love it. Are they following us to Santa Fe, then?" she asked.

"I thought they deserved something a little more special, so I booked the honeymoon suite at La Fonda, in Taos. Then, tomorrow, they can either go to Agua Caliente for a spa day, or they can join us in Santa Fe. I'll keep a car on standby."

"Ed, what an *incredibly* thoughtful and generous thing to do! You've really saved my sister's wedding from disaster. I don't know how I can ever thank you," she said, tearing up a little. "So, tonight, it's just the three of us?"

Ed nodded. "Just the three of us."

I'm really starting to like the sound of that, Paige thought.

CHAPTER NINETEEN

*A*fter putting Reggie down for the night, Paige joined Ed in the living room, where he had a fire going and the room was nice and toasty. He handed her a half glass of wine, then retired to a recliner to sip on his own.

"You really know how to treat a lady," she said, with a tired smile.

"You just take it easy, now. It's been quite an emotional day, and your sister is a happily married woman, enjoying her wedding night in one of Taos's finest hotels. Reggie is asleep, and you don't have a thing in the world to worry about," he said, softly.

"Thank you." She closed her eyes and took a deep, cleansing breath, then opened them. "How big was the quake? I forgot to ask," she said.

"5.3. Biggest one in the swarm. That's moderate, as earthquakes go. But it must have released some pressure, along with whatever gasses we were smelling at the ranch, so, hopefully, we won't have another one for a while."

"That would be just fine with me. Mmm, this is good wine, Ed. What am I drinking?" she asked, beginning to relax, at last.

"It's a Tempranillo I picked up in Spain last year. I tasted it in a local bistro, and they mentioned the name of the vineyard. When I had some time to pick up a case, I arranged to have it shipped over here. It pairs really well with gelato."

"I thought gelato was Italian," Paige said, sleepily, her eyes drifting closed.

"Not the kind I buy at the grocery store," said Ed. "I think it's made in Texas, but I promise, you'll love it. Want to try a scoop?"

"Now that you mention it, that *does* sound like a good pairing, and I was too busy to eat much at the reception," she said, with a huge yawn.

"Coming right up. You just hang tight," he said, heading toward the kitchen.

"Okay, gelato, where are you hiding?" Ed asked his deluxe, stain-less- steel freezer. "Don't let me down when things are going so well." But the gelato continued to play hide and seek. By the time he gave up and returned to the living room, Paige was sound asleep on his leather sofa, still wearing her lovely, pink satin dress. He covered her with a warm alpaca throw, turned the fire to low, and left her there to sleep until morning.

Heading upstairs, he opened the door of the nursery to check on Reggie, then took the receiver for the baby monitor with him to his own room. If Reggie was hungry, he'd yell loud enough to let Paige know—the house wasn't *that* big. And, starting with tonight, he hoped it would become "home" for all three of them.

※

Paige woke the next morning, full to bursting. "Oh, my gosh! I have to feed Reggie. I can't believe I didn't hear him wake up," she said, when she entered the kitchen. She filled up a glass with filtered water and turned to Ed, who held the baby against his shoulder, one hand rubbing his sleeper-covered back.

"No worries, the little guy slept all night. I kept the baby monitor with me." But when Reggie heard his mother's voice, he screamed bloody murder, and Ed handed him over. Paige's breasts were already leaking through the bedraggled matron of honor dress. "Um…one second, little guy. Ed." Glancing down at her dress, she frowned. "If I could borrow a spare t-shirt and maybe a spare pair of boxers, I'd sure appreciate it," she said. "I'll be in the guest room."

She fed Reggie, who emptied both breasts in record time, which gave them both a great deal of relief. It was a pretty genius symbiotic system. Baby fed and changed, she waited patiently until Ed knocked on the guest room door.

"Here you go. I have some stretchy bike-short-style boxers that might fit, and my smallest t-shirt. I accidentally washed it in hot water and threw it in the dryer. And here's my smallest pair of sweats. I'm sorry, Paige, but that's the best I can do."

"Thanks, Ed. These will do nicely, for now. But I think I'll need to go shopping after breakfast," she said, really, really hoping there would be breakfast.

"Okay, we can do that. Come on down when you're ready."

After French toast for breakfast, they drove to Santa Fe Place Mall, which had a variety of clothing stores. She'd get the basics in

Dillard's—and for casual everyday clothing, she had the choice of an Old Navy and an Ann Taylor. She only needed to put together an emergency wardrobe that would last for a few days. At least Harper and Caleb had the advantage of having suitcases already packed for their honeymoon, with clean undies that fit and comfy travel clothes. But Paige was pretty sure that didn't make up for the abrupt end to their fire-and-brimstone wedding.

Ed took charge of Reggie, which made everything much easier as Paige quickly shopped for undies, two nursing bras, a couple of stretchy t-shirts. She also bought some black yoga pants, jeans several sizes larger than her pre-pregnancy size, and a light fleece jacket. At Ann Taylor, she bought a comfortable wrap sweater in a neutral color. Over her black yoga pants, it would do for a casual dinner out. She'd pay Ed back for everything she'd spent, when life returned to normal. *When exactly would that be?* Now, properly outfitted out with warm comfortable clothes, she went to find him.

Since Ed had recently dispensed with his former lumberjack look, he cut quite a dashing figure. The man had a sense of style that served him well, and he could afford a really nice men's wardrobe. *Maybe she should rethink the yoga pants and t-shirts?* But she didn't want to spend frivolously—it had been incredibly generous of him to offer her his card for the day. She and Ed had left the ranch in such a hurry that she hadn't had time to take any essentials with her, including her wallet, and she wasn't sure when it would be safe to be back on the property, especially with a young baby.

Spotting Ed, she was amused to see that he and Reggie were surrounded by a cluster of admiring women cooing over her sweet son. "There you are," she said in a sweet, maternal voice—thus establishing her important role in this scenario and scattering the women like brightly colored balls on a pool table. "I think I've got everything I need, Ed. We can head home now, if you like. But if you pass by a CVS, I need to stop and pick up a few things for myself and Reggie."

"Well...I think that can wait. Reggie, here, was just telling me that his mama had a really hard day yesterday, and that she might enjoy going out to lunch. Her choice of cuisine too—that was Reggie's idea."

"What a smart boy!" *A lot like his daddy.* "Hmm, how about Thai? It's not something I can get in Verde Springs, and we can bring some back to the house, so you don't have to cook for me all the time," she said.

"I *like* cooking for you," Ed said, with a smile. "But Thai it is."

Harper and Caleb showed up at Ed's house around dinner time, so it was great that they'd brought extra Thai food home to feed everybody. The glowing newlyweds had loved La Fonda, but they'd skipped the elegant hot springs. They had no idea what was going to happen next, and it was definitely putting a damper on their honeymoon plans.

"What would you *like* to do?" Paige asked her sister, between bites of savory Massaman curry.

"I'd *like* to go on my honeymoon with this handsome dude—but it seems irresponsible to leave when our whole world might be going up in flames. Shouldn't we at least get an opinion from somebody official first?" Harper asked.

"Ed and I are working on that—we're trying to get someone from the UNM up here to check the situation out. But it's unlikely that could happen before Tuesday, at the earliest," Paige said.

"Well, that's good, I guess. Hey, I was thinking...we *could* give Sam a call," Harper suggested. "He's still working in Colorado, isn't he? That's not too far away, if we could convince him to hop on a plane. And Sam's one of the smartest people I know."

"I haven't talked to him for a while," Paige replied, cautiously. Sam McKinney was an old high school friend from back in Virginia. When she'd returned to Richmond after college, they'd dated for a while before life intervened, as it often does when you're both in your twenties and building separate careers. They'd both moved on, long before she'd married Dan, her former husband."

"Or, if Sam still works in Denver, maybe he knows somebody who knows somebody in New Mexico. I think it's worth a shot. Do you want me to call him?" Harper asked.

"No, I want *you* to go on your honeymoon with Caleb. Ed and I can handle this," she assured her sister. "But if you have Sam's contact details handy, you can text them to me. Between Sam and an expert from UNM, we'll know something soon, and I promise to keep you in the loop. As long as you two promise to go on your honeymoon and enjoy yourselves!"

"Only if you promise to buy the biggest, baddest Virgin of Guadalupe as soon as possible, and get my grounds crew to place her in the *nicho*. When they do, have them put on earthquake bracing so she doesn't come crashing down on people's heads."

"I'm on it." Paige said. "I mean, *we're* on it." She smiled at Ed. She really wanted to get better at this, but after being on her own for most of her adult life—other than her brief, failed marriage—it didn't always come naturally.

CHAPTER TWENTY

*P*aige called someone she hadn't spoken to in more than a decade. She and Sam McKinney had been friends throughout high school, and later, had dated briefly after she'd returned to Richmond after college. But they'd broken off their relationship when he'd taken a job with the Geological Survey, in Denver. In her early twenties, she'd found Sam interesting and attractive because *every* female on the planet found him interesting and attractive. But with so many miles between his new job in Denver and her big sister/parental figure responsibilities in Richmond, they'd had to make some hard decisions.

Harper was in her junior year of high school, and until she turned eighteen and moved on to college, Richmond was where Paige needed to be. Since then, she and Sam had only stayed in touch through social media and their Christmas newsletters. But she would always have a soft spot in her heart for the bright, young man he'd been. Paige had always suspected that her sister had had a school-girl crush on Sam, and maybe that was one of the reasons that Harper had kept in better touch with him. While Paige had needed to draw boundaries to protect her heart and learn the hard lesson of moving on.

*

"Hey, Sam, it's Paige. I know…it's been a long time. How are you?"

Well, Paige Crawley, wow! This is a blast from the past. I'm…doing well. How are you? And how's your sister? Sam asked.

"I'm doing really well, and Harper is, too. As it turns out, we're not too far from you. Harper and I are both living in northern New Mexico now, and loving it. We've been here for about a year, now."

What? That's incredible. Small world! It's really good to hear from you. So, how's life treating you?

"Pretty well, but there have been a *lot* of changes in my life. I have so much to catch you up on, but it will have to wait. Believe it or not, Harper and I need your *professional* help. We've run across a problem on our ranch, and we happen to need the services of a hydro-geologist. Harper thought of you right away, so…if you're up for it?"

Wow! Now, that's a surprise. I guess you can tell me why you finally decided to move West, after all, some other time. Tell me what's going on, and I'll see if I can help.

"Okay. Short and sweet, there's been a swarm of earthquake activity nearby, and after a couple of small quakes that didn't appear to cause much damage, something big happened. But we don't know exactly *what*. Our well is contaminated, everything smells like sulfur, and we don't know what to do. And that about sums it up."

Yeah, I've been keeping an eye on that patch of seismic activity on the Santa Clara fault. Near Española, right? So, is that where your property is located?

"We're closer to Pecos. The ranch is fifty-six acres. My sister and I've walked every inch of it, and we've never seen anything out of the ordinary. Then, on the day of Harper's wedding—terrible timing—there was an earthquake, and some sort of event that released a really foul stench. We thought it might be natural gas, but the company said they don't have any lines in this area. Anyway, we haven't felt like it's safe to be on the property until we get things checked out. So, do you think you might be able to help us? Or, do you know of someone closer, maybe even local, who could do figure out what we're dealing with? And, Sam, time is of the essence. Harper and I are also trying to run a business, and we're gearing up for our spring and summer season."

Have you tried contacting someone from UNM? They have a pretty solid geology department.

"Yes, we *have* tried, but they're still on spring break, and it looks like we won't be able to get anybody to come out here until mid-week at the earliest. Is there any way you could possibly come down, tomorrow? I know it's terribly short notice, but we'd pay for your flight," Paige said.

I guess I could. But I'll have to bring equipment, too. There might be some extra baggage fees, he said.

"We'll cover everything," she said. "If you can arrange a commercial flight to Santa Fe, we'll have someone pick you up there." Ed gave her a thumbs up. "If you can come first thing in the morning, we could have you back home later that same evening."

Alright. I can do that, Sam agreed. *Send me the details, and I'll start packing up my equipment. 'Night, Paige. Thanks for thinking of me.*

"Problem solved," Paige said, smiling at Ed. "You'll like Sam. He went to school with me. Harper had a crush on him, too, but he was too old for her, at the time."

"But, not for you?" Ed asked.

Paige could feel her face grow warm. "Why do you say that?"

"I don't know. Something in your voice, maybe?" he said. "It's fine. I have a past too—we all do. It just occurred to me that I don't know very much about yours."

"Well, you'll get to meet Sam tomorrow," she said. "And, he wasn't such a huge part of my past. I liked him a lot, and we even dated for a while. But life just got in the way, like it does when you're in your early twenties and just starting out. If you want to know anything else, you can ask me. I don't have any secrets."

Ed and Paige drove from Santa Fe to Verde Springs, with Reggie sleeping in his car seat. They'd be meeting Sam at Maggie's to further explain the situation, provide him with a map, and get his take on how best to approach the situation. Meeting an old ex, along with Ed, and the baby she'd somehow neglected to mention to Sam, felt surreal. *Oh, and, of course, the earth cracking and venting mysterious noxious gases after an earthquake event had nearly halted her sister's wedding in its tracks was pretty surreal, too.* It was challenging to stay grounded in such strange times, but she was trying.

"Hi, Maggie. It's great to see you," Paige said, giving her friend a hug. "Thanks so much for coming to our rescue after the wedding. Despite the drama, I think everyone had a good time—mostly due to Ed's hustle and your generosity."

"No worries. I was happy to do pull something out of a hat for Harper and Caleb. And everybody seemed to enjoy themselves. I know I did. So, what brings you and Ed out today?" she asked.

"We're meeting an old friend, here. He's a hydrogeologist based out of Denver now, although we went to high school together back in Virginia. We're hoping that Sam might be able to help us solve the mystery and figure out what we need to do next."

"Good luck with that—and let me know what he says. I can tell you, since Maggie's Diner opened its doors, this is the most excitement we've seen in Verde Springs! You and your sister sure know how to bring it."

Paige laughed. "Harper thinks we pissed off a minor goddess or something. I hope she's able to put the wedding day fiasco behind her and is enjoying her honeymoon. But, given recent events, it would be nice if those volcanoes in Hawaii don't decide to put on a big show for them."

"Me, too. If I were Harper and Caleb, I'd skip the big island this time."

"Oh, gotta run. That's probably Sam, now," Paige said, as a dark sedan pulled up. She recognized it as one of the car services Ed frequently used—he'd kindly arranged to pick Sam up at the Santa Fe Regional Airport and shuttle him to Verde Springs.

"Hey, stranger! It's so good to see you," Paige said, embracing Sam in a quick hug. "Come and meet Ed—he's my baby's father. Since the situation at the ranch cropped up, the baby and I have been staying with him in Santa Fe. It's a long story, and I promise to share it another time."

"Geeze, never a dull moment with you, is there, Crawley?" Sam laughed, showing very white teeth. He'd developed a few attractive crow's feet around his blue-gray eyes, and, overall, he looked slim and fit—and like someone who spent a lot of time in the outdoors in the Rocky Mountains.

Paige led him to the table and introduced him to Ed, and the baby, who was now awake and busily taking in the stimulating environment of Maggie's Diner with big slate-blue eyes.

Ed stood to shake Sam's hand. "Ed Barrett. Nice to meet you. Thanks for coming down here on such short notice."

"Sam McKinney. It's nice to meet you, too. I hope I'll be able to help. So, why don't you show me what you've got?" he said, addressing both of them.

"First, we're buying you breakfast. What's your pleasure?" Paige asked, handing Sam a breakfast menu.

Half an hour later, Sam pushed his plate aside. "My god, that was good. If I lived here, I'd be coming to Maggie's for three meals a day. Okay, let's talk hydrogeology. Tell me what's going on."

After stacking the breakfast dishes to one side, Paige spread out the map of the ranch, showing him where the house, the Coops, and gardens lay, and the network of roads they used to access them. She pointed out the tiny circle drawn on the map where Harper and Caleb's wedding had taken place, and the "X" that marked the location of their well. "This is the map of the property. We hadn't had any problems until recently. But in the previous month, we had two smaller quakes, which were presumably located on the Santa Clara fault. On the morning of Harper's wedding, we had another tremor, and then, that 5.3. We felt it strongly at the ranch, and they felt it here in town, too."

"So, the day of the event, what was the first indication that something different was going on, specific to the environment of the ranch?"

"Harper took a shower before she dressed for the wedding, and she came out yelling that the water smelled like sulfur. When I came in to help, I could see that something was definitely wrong: the odor was terrible, and the color was off, too. The water was orangish-yellow, and it had that rotten egg smell that's unmistakable."

Reggie started to fuss, and Ed expertly picked him up and held him against his chest, and he soon quieted.

"He's a cute little guy," Sam noted, with a smile. "So, what happened next?"

"Well, we noticed the problem with the water only about an hour before the wedding. Guests had already begun to arrive. We didn't have time to investigate, so we just went ahead with the ceremony."

"Wow, so Harper's a married woman? I'm glad to hear things worked out for her in New Mexico. I was really sorry to hear about what happened up in Washington. She told me all about it in her last letter." Sam said. "She deserved better."

"Yeah, that was a pretty rough time for her. But I think ending her marriage to Kevin was meant to be—especially since we both ended up relocating to New Mexico. And Harper's new husband, Caleb, is a great guy. He has a five-year-old daughter whom she adores, and the three of them make a wonderful family. Now, back to the situation," Paige said, refocusing.

"You mentioned an event? Can you describe it?" Sam asked.

"We heard a crack, and then a sort of rumbling, whooshing sound that went on for a long time. A light rain began falling, and we could definitely smell that strong sulfur odor in the air. We didn't know whether it was dangerous, or if something even worse might happen, so Ed rounded everybody up and got us out of there. We relocated the wedding party here, to Maggie's, and no one has been out to the ranch, since. We've been in touch with our neighbor, though, and Miguel says things are better. There's just a faint sulfur smell in the air—but it's not nearly as strong as it initially was."

Sam squinted his eyes and thought for a minute. "I can think of a few possibilities, one in particular. New Mexico's hydrothermal features are pretty interesting. Do you know if there are any active vents or hot springs in the immediate area?"

"Well, there's Agua Caliente, near Taos, and there are quite a few hot springs near the town of Jemez Springs," Paige said, looking at Ed for confirmation.

"A little closer, the Pecos River has a few hot springs. And there are more springs down near the Truth or Consequences, but none that I know of within about ten or fifteen miles of the ranch," said Ed, who was more familiar with the area.

"Well, I guess it's time to go out and have a look. I brought a couple of hazmat suits, respirators, a set of walkie-talkies, and a sampling kit. That's about as techie as I could get on short notice, from the gear I keep at home, but I can do a lot of the work remotely from Denver. Ed, if you wouldn't mind following me out to the ranch, we'll do a little exploring. Paige, I think it's best that you and the baby stay here in town. We can reach you by phone, if needed."

Paige nodded, taking the baby from Ed. "That sounds like a good plan. Whatever happened, it wasn't close to the house or gardens, so maybe, you could start by walking the perimeter of the ranch?" Turning to Ed, she said, "Can you please keep in touch with me by phone? And come back straight away, as soon as Sam's finished?"

Ed nodded. "Sure. I can do that."

"And Ed? Be careful," she said, squeezing his hand.

After the two men left on their reconnaissance mission, Mariah stopped by the table to chat. "Can I get you anything else, Paige? We've got plenty of blueberry muffins, fresh out of the oven."

"Oh, I'm fine right now, thanks. Before we leave, I might get some goodies to take back with us to Santa Fe," Paige replied. "By the way, Ed's become a big fan of your baking."

"That's nice to hear. So, was that the geologist you brought in? The guy who left with Ed?" Mariah asked. "He's like…George Clooney level attractive."

"Yeah, that's Sam. Women have been known to drool over him. He seems to have that sexy scientist vibe. He's a hydrogeologist, actually, an old friend from Virginia, but he's lived in Denver for a while, now. I thought we should get an expert opinion as soon as possible, and Sam was someone we already know and trust. Then, when we finally get in touch with someone from UNM, we'll have a second opinion. Hopefully, between the two of them, there will be some consensus on what we should do."

"Yeah, I hope so, too. This whole thing has been pretty scary for Ellie. She's been fussing about the dogs and wondering if they're okay."

"Oh, I'm so sorry, Mariah! I should have mentioned it to her—the day before the wedding, Harper took Birdy and Sunny to a boarding facility in Pecos to keep them out of the way of the guests. They're having an extended stay there, with plenty of doggie friends to play with, and I promise I won't bring them back to the ranch until I know it's absolutely safe," Paige assured her friend.

"That's good to hear—I'll be sure to tell Ellie. She's in Santa Fe visiting her grandparents this weekend. I thought, with Caleb and Harper gone, it would be good to have her occupied. I've been really busy at Maggie's, as we gear up for summer, and I'm spending a lot of time on the plan for my bakery business, too."

"Oh, how's that going?" Paige asked. "Is everything on track?"

"Yes, it's all good, I think. I've heard back from the state, and from one of the private funding organizations, that they're considering my grant proposal. So, at least, I haven't been rejected outright. Meanwhile, I'm using this week to develop new recipes and come up with a preliminary menu. One step at a time. I'm not really in a hurry—I just want to get it right the *first* time."

"You're doing a great job, and you're being very thorough. Now that the pregnancy is behind me, I should have more time to help you with whenever you need. But it'll have to be by phone or Zoom unless we set up a meeting, here. Reggie and I are staying with Ed in Santa Fe for a while, until we know it's safe to go back to the ranch."

"You know, I really *like* Ed, and Maggie's always had good things to say about him." Mariah said. "I think you've got a good guy—someone you can really depend on. Well, I'd better get back to work."

Paige didn't doubt that was true, but she didn't *have* him. He wasn't *her* guy. Still, she didn't know what she and the baby would have done without him, in these past few weeks. He'd been a rock, not just for her and Reggie, but for all of them. Maggie's advice had been spot-on: *don't underestimate Ed Barrett.* The past few months had shown Paige that Ed was much more than a good guy, and a good match for her— he was the man she'd grown to love, hook, line, and sinker. *If only he could see a future together, too.*

CHAPTER TWENTY-ONE

*S*am loaded several large duffels into the trunk, while Ed transferred the two walkie-talkies with him into the front seat.

"It's really nice country, here," Sam said, once they were on the road. "I can see why Paige and Harper like it, but I'd never peg either of them for fans of living in the country. Paige, for sure, was always a city girl. How on earth did they find the ranch in the first place?"

"They inherited it jointly from an aunt on their father's side of the family. She'd operated the ranch as a poultry operation a couple of decades ago. She'd leased it for a while, and then it fell into disrepair. They took on a big project, and Harper spent most of last spring rehabbing the main house and grounds with Caleb, the man she ended up marrying. After the spring semester ended in Virginia, Paige came to New Mexico to help out for the summer—she helped Harper set up the Inn, and they both did a great job. But after Paige's teaching position was eliminated, the Inn at Verde Springs became a whole lot more for both of them. Since then, they've been hosting weddings and garden parties for every occasion you can think of, plus creative retreats and workshops. It's quite the enterprise, and they're justifiably proud of it," Ed said.

"Thanks for the rundown. So, how did the two of you meet?" Sam asked.

"Like I said, they've been hosting all sorts of events at the ranch. Last summer, I helped Paige organize a Renaissance Faire. We seemed to get along well with each other. One thing led to another, and Reggie came along."

"So, do you think two will get married?" Sam asked. "It seems like the next logical step. And you must be close to the same age."

Ed shook his head. "I don't think that's in the cards—but I care about Paige, and of course, I care about Reggie. So, I plan on staying pretty close," he said, giving Sam a cool look.

Sam got the message: *don't poke the bear.* The man was huge, with massively strong shoulders, and he was no doubt protective of Paige and Reggie. Despite Ed's casual dismissal, Sam had a feeling that the idea of marriage wasn't completely off the table. He'd caught a look of frank adoration from Paige, and it was absolutely directed toward the father of her child. *Geez, was the big guy blind?* "Well, thanks for filling me in. I'm anxious to see this place." After that, Sam was quiet until Ed pulled up outside the ranch gates.

"This is the place, as you can see from the sign. I can drive you up all the way to the house—we just didn't know whether it was safe," Ed said.

"Well, let's find out. Can you park on the side of the road and let me get some monitoring gear out of the trunk?" Sam asked.

"No problem."

Sam retrieved a portable monitoring device that could be worn as a backpack.

"What've you got there?" Ed asked.

"This is a basic air quality monitor setup that will detect any noxious gases and analyze the air for particulate. In a few minutes, we should know whether it's safe to breathe the air. I don't detect a strong scent of sulfur, though, maybe just a trace."

They waited in silence while the intake tube drew in a continuous air sample. When the machine beeped, Sam said, "Levels are mildly elevated for a few different gases—ammonia, hydrogen fluoride, and sulfur dioxide—that's the rotten egg smell. Some people think it smells like burnt matches. Nothing's registering in the harmful range, right now. But I think you made a good call, evacuating everybody and bringing Paige and the baby to Santa Fe. It must have been a kinda scary, especially since you had no idea what you were dealing with."

Ed nodded in agreement. "Yeah, it was a little freaky on the day of the wedding. Something definitely happened, and we still don't know *what*—but it seems to have dissipated quite a bit since then."

"Let's drive a little farther. I have an extra setup for you want to wear, but I'll probably want to check things out, first. This equipment is heavy to carry, so it would be good if you could get us a little closer," Sam said.

"Just tell me where you want to go," said Ed.

They drove up until they could see the Coop Studios, then the house. They parked on a little rise that looked over the ranch, while Sam played with the dials on the air quality monitor. Levels for ammonia, hydrogen fluoride, and sulfur dioxide were slightly raised, but still within the high end of normal.

"What do you think?" Ed asked.

"It'll take me a few minutes to unload the rest of the equipment from the trunk and get it set up. I'll get another hazmat suit and respirator for you," Sam said.

"While you do that, I'll grab some things that Paige needs from the house," Ed said. "I'll be back in ten."

Sam nodded. "When you're finished in the house, we'll get you outfitted, and the two of us can walk the perimeter of the property. But I don't think we'll have any trouble locating the source—there's the plume," he said, pointing at the western horizon. In the distance, a thin white plume of steam rose from what looked like a single source. Now that the air had had time to clear, after the initial eruption event, it was easy enough to spot.

"So, *that's* what's been wreaking all this havoc?" Ed asked.

"Most likely. We'll know more when we get over there. Any chance we can drive closer?" Sam asked.

"Not in my car, but we might be able to take Harper's work truck. I'm sure she wouldn't mind. It's got high clearance and four-wheel-drive."

"Perfect. Okay, then," Sam said.

"I'll be as quick as I can," Ed said, opening the car door.

Ed called Paige and she gave him a rundown of the essentials she needed for herself and Reggie.

There's a navy duffle in my closet. Just toss everything in there and I'll sort it out later. It'll be so great to have some of my stuff. Ed, it would be great if you could grab some things from the office, downstairs, especially

my laptop and briefcase. I'll need access to the files for some projects I'm
working on.

"Okay. I think I got everything you needed from your bedroom," he said, after a short scavenger hunt. "Now, where's this office?"

It's really just a corner of the private living room that Harper and I share. Near the windows, there's an old oak desk. Just bring the laptop, the briefcase, and any loose papers you see laying around, and anything that looks like a planner or three-ring binder. That should do it. Thanks for this, Ed, I really appreciate it. How's it going with Sam?

"Good. He's just setting up some equipment, and then we're going to head over to the northwest property boundary to check things out. Sam says there's some sort of plume over that way. Do you think Harper would mind if we borrowed her work truck?"

Go for it. She leaves the keys tucked above the visor. And Ed? Be careful.

"Always. I'm responsible for someone else, now," he said.

With Ed's help, Sam transferred his equipment to Harper's truck. Then he handed Ed a white, hooded hazmat suit. After Ed managed to pull it on, barely covering his tall frame, Sam handed him the respirator and showed him how to adjust the straps for a secure fit.

"Ready?" Sam asked.

Ed nodded. "Let's go see what we're dealing with."

They drove along the gravel road up past the Coops, and angled across a wide stretch of old alfalfa fields. Ed shifted the truck into four-wheel drive when they hit a patch of high desert scrub, weaving carefully between patches of big tooth sage and the occasional cholla cactus, swollen with flower buds. The easiest route followed a draw up to the top of a ridge, then along the ridge to an observation point just above the plume. From there, they could climb down to get closer: Sam wanted to collect water samples, in addition to close-up air samples surrounding the most active plumes.

The truck rumbled along, climbing the ridge without difficulty, and soon, they reached a stopping point. Sam strapped on the air-monitoring backpack and clipped on a walkie talkie. They'd stay in touch as he explored closer to the plumes of steam to obtain his samples.

"Ed, it's best if you stay up on the ridge for now, and keep the respirator in place. When I return, we'll head back to the ranch and I'll give you the technical brief. Okay, I'm off."

It was hard, at first, to tell exactly what Sam was viewing up close. But when the wind shifted, the large plume of steam changed direction. Then, Ed could clearly see the area of disturbed ground that had caught Sam's attention: there was a small pool of orangish liquid with white crusting around the edges, and a few small surrounding vents emitting tendrils of steam. Ed watched as Sam approached carefully, testing the ground ahead with a stick he'd picked up, and stopping frequently to take photos. He walked the perimeter of the active area, then returned to where he'd started. After determining that the ground would fully support his weight, he moved slowly forward, one step at a time, until he reached the edge of the pool. Sam quickly obtained a series of water and air samples. After he'd finished, he turned and waved a hand at Ed, before making his way back up the rocky slope.

When Sam reached the truck, he removed the air-quality-monitoring pack, but kept his respirator in place as he placed his samples carefully into a padded, cooler. Then he sat down in the passenger seat and motioned for Ed to head out. Only then did he remove the respirator so he could talk. Ed removed his as well and looked at Sam, ready for the hydrogeologist's explanation.

"Well? What are we dealing with?" Ed asked.

"I'll know more when I get the samples fully analyzed; but the good news is that the plumes appear to be mostly steam," Sam explained. "I don't doubt that the initial eruption of the main fumarole, or vent, may have emitted an impressive cloud of noxious gas—that would have really been something to see, if anyone had known where to look. But all of the activity seems to have settled down, now."

"Fumarole? I'm not familiar with that term," Ed said.

"Basically, geysers, fumaroles, and hot springs are the three major types of vents that release steam when the water table interacts with the heat from the earth's crust. This is where the study of hydrogeology comes in: you can't *see* it, but there's a network of underground channels that run just below the earth's surface. At certain depths, there can be considerable heat, especially whenever there's been volcanic or seismic activity nearby, and you're pretty close to the Santa Clara fault here. But fortunately, the heated water that's now being released is being diluted by cooler water closer to the surface. So, instead of an explosive geyser or a fumarole, you've got a hot spring. Fumaroles can contain a lot more heat, often up to boiling temperature. They're dangerous—but that doesn't appear to be the case here. Basically, if the subterranean heat source *isn't* hot enough to qualify as a fumarole, then you've got a hot spring."

"So…the ranch has a hot spring?" Ed asked.

Sam nodded. "Whether it's viable to commercialize or not, I won't know until I analyze the samples I collected. Let's head back to the ranch, now. We can stow the gear away and change out of the hazmat suits, then head back to town to tell Paige the good news."

Back at Maggie's, Sam and Ed eased into the booth, grinning like schoolboys who'd discovered a hidden treasure.

"So? What did you find?" Paige asked.

Sam spoke first. "It looks like you've now got a hot spring on the ranch! A fairly sizeable one."

"But...how does something like that just magically appear? It wasn't there before," said Paige. "The ranch is just high desert and old farm fields, surrounded by rock outcroppings."

Sam smiled. "Well, it didn't *magically* appear—it appeared after a series of sequential seismic events. I read an interesting paper about this when I was in graduate school: Occasionally, after an earthquake, there can be hydrologic changes, things like increases or decreases in stream flow; and those changes indicate disruptions in the subterranean hydrologic channels. There's evidence that seismic shaking, like what you'd likely have with a moderately strong earthquake, can clear clogged fractures in the bedrock. Sometimes those fractures happen to be found right over a pressurized thermal reservoir, like the one that apparently exists under part of your ranch. So, the seismic shaking from the earthquake activity must have cleared the fracture of accumulated debris, and that allowed the pocket of pressurized steam that had been building up to finally erupt. I'm sorry it happened on the day of Harper's wedding—but I still wish I'd been here to see it," Sam said.

"So, can we expect more of these eruptions? Or another hot spring to appear, maybe on another part of the property?" Ed asked.

"That's a good question," Sam said. "But we need to think in terms of geologic time—in other words, *slowly*. For now, all of the activity seems to have settled down, and what you have is a steady pool of warm water flowing right from the ground. I've taken water and air samples in the immediate area, and as soon as I've had them analyzed back in Denver, I'll provide you with all the details. For now, I'd wait at least another week, just to be on the safe side. Then I think it would be fine for you to return to the ranch. After that, I'd say you're going to have some decisions to make."

"Decisions?" Paige asked. "With Harper out of town, I hope it's nothing too urgent, Sam. The ranch is a joint venture, and we always make decisions together."

"The most important decision you and Harper need to make is whether or not you want to develop the hot spring," Sam said. "Whatever you decide, the water source is unlikely to go away anytime soon. So, you now have a resource on the ranch that you *didn't* have before— and you might as well take advantage of it. But that's just *my* opinion."

"Well, I think it's amazing news! Ed and I are still waiting to hear from someone at UNM, and we'll want to get your test results back. But wow! Thank you *so* much for coming down on short notice. I really appreciate it, and I know Harper does, too."

"I was glad to help, Paige. Let me know what you decide to do. Ed, I think I'm ready to start heading back now, and I guess you're the man that can make that happen."

Ed nodded. "It'll take a little while for the car to get here, so let's order some lunch. My shout."

Sam was lithe and lean and…objectively *hot*. But Sam wasn't the one she was in love with.

⚹

Later that night, Paige spoke to Harper on the phone. The honeymooners were having a wonderful time in Hawaii. They were both taking surfing lessons, and her sister sounded happy and relaxed.

"I have some news for you guys. But I want you to promise not to spend too much time thinking about it. We won't make any decisions until you get back," Paige assured her.

Okay. Well, don't keep me in suspense. Was Sam able to figure out what happened? And does he know what we're dealing with? Harper asked.

"We think so, although Ed and I decided to go ahead with a second opinion from the university's expert. We should be able to get that sometime later this week, or early next week. But the big news is… drumroll…we now have a hot spring on the ranch!"

Wow, that's amazing! Is it safe to return home, yet? Harper asked.

"Sam still has to analyze the samples he took, so he thinks we should wait another week, just to be safe," Paige replied.

Yes. Being safe is important, and I always know that you and Reggie are safe when you're with Ed. Can't you just stay in Santa Fe until Caleb and I get back? Harper asked.

"Oh, yeah. I imagine Ed would be all over that. I promise I'll think about it," Paige said.

Well, let me know where you and Reggie are going to be, okay? Harper said.

"I will. Ed grabbed a bunch of my things when he was at the ranch today with Sam, so Reggie and I will have everything we need, and I'll be able to work from Santa Fe."

How's it going with Ed? Better, I hope? Harper asked.

"Well, I don't always know what he's thinking—and he probably doesn't have any clue what *I'm* thinking. But on the surface, we're getting along great," Paige said.

Well, there's a cure for that, you know. It's called talking. Maybe it's time to tell Ed how you really feel, Harper suggested.

"I know it is. There's just been so much going on for both of us, that I wanted to let the dust settle for a few days. *She wasn't really procrastinating, again, was she?* I enjoyed seeing Sam again. We should invite him down for a few days—you know, after we've decided what to do about the hot spring."

That's fine with me—I'd love to catch up with him in person. It's been a long time. But, you're right, I'm going to put the ranch out of my mind for the remainder of my honeymoon. Nobody is keeling over, and, according to our neighbor, Miguel, birds aren't falling from the sky in the vicinity of the ranch, so I guess this can wait. Anyway, I'd prefer to focus on my hot husband.

"Yeah, you do that. He's a keeper. Have a wonderful time, both of you," Paige said. "And don't worry about a thing."

CHAPTER TWENTY-TWO

The next week in Santa Fe turned out to be an unexpectedly pleasant surprise, and the three of them strengthened their bond as a family unit. When Reggie cried or needed attention, whoever was free would take care of his immediate needs. While Ed made breakfast, Paige fed Reggie, and then she bathed and dressed him. In the late morning, after Paige had a chance to shower, run a load of baby laundry, and change into clean clothes, she felt fresh and energetic enough to make lunch. In the late afternoon when Reggie went down for his long nap, she and Ed both tried to focus on their work. Dinner, they usually ordered in, and she insisted on cleaning up the kitchen afterwards, leaving everything fresh and clean for the morning. Long after she'd gone to bed, Ed stayed up late putting in a few more hours of work for Harp, but he never complained.

On Friday morning, Sam emailed the air and water sample test results and then arranged to meet with them over Zoom to go over what he'd found.

So, the air quality isn't harmful anywhere—and ammonia, hydrogen fluoride, and sulfur dioxide levels are only elevated to high normal immediately over the main vent and a couple of the smaller steam holes, Sam said. *Even on the ridge where we parked the truck, Ed, the air quality was at safe levels. You might detect a little sulfur dioxide with your nose, but it's not enough to be harmful.*

"That's great, Sam," Paige said. "Does that mean we can return to the ranch?"

Well, hold on. Now, the water coming out at the moment is about 129 degrees. That's good, because you'll be able to dilute the spring water with cooler well water to reach a comfortable bathing temperature if you decide to pipe it into pools. The water itself, while full of minerals, doesn't contain anything caustic. This could be a really valuable resource for you and Harper, if you wanted to develop it.

"This is a *lot* to wrap my head around, Sam. I mean, it's exciting, but I know it'll take a lot of work and money at a time when we're both keeping a pretty close eye on our finances. We'll talk it over after she returns. Meanwhile, should we be concerned about our well? It services the house, the Coops, and all of the landscaping surrounding the Inn. Is the water safe to drink and to water plants? We've invested a lot of money into our gardens, and we wouldn't want to lose them."

Most likely the well was temporarily tainted from the initial release—the pressure may have forced water laterally through hydrologic channels in the rock, including into your well. If it's cleared, now, the water should look and smell the same as it always has. But to be on the safe side, you'll want to get a water quality test done, both of the well itself and from the tap. Especially if there's any unusual color or odor. The New Mexico Environment Department can do the testing for free, and there should be a field office not too far from you.

"Okay, we'll do that. So, is it safe to go back to the ranch now?" Paige asked.

I think it makes sense to wait until you get those water quality tests back. Then you'll be able to use the water in the house without worrying, especially since you have a young baby. That's just my opinion.

"Thank you for explaining the situation so clearly, Sam. I really appreciate your making the trip down here, and I know Harper does, too."

No worries. It was a fun little adventure, and it brought me back to my early days in the field. Good luck Paige, and be sure to let me know if you need anything else. This was quite a find—and I think the new hot spring will increase the value of your property considerably.

"That's good to know, whether *we* decide to develop it, or not. Stay in touch, Sam. Come down this summer when we've got this all sorted, and we have the Inn open again. You're getting a free stay for as long as you want. Bring a guest too, if you like."

Thanks, I'll keep that in mind, he said. *Give Ed my best regards. 'Night, Paige.*

The next morning, Paige and Ed were eating breakfast in the sunny kitchen, while Reggie lay awake but content in his infant recliner.

"When is Harper getting back?" Ed asked.

"In another week. So, Sam thinks I should stay put until I get clear water quality tests on the well and the house's tap water. Would that be alright with you?"

"Paige, you don't even need to ask. I *love* having you and Reggie here with me," Ed said. He finished his coffee and set the mug down on the Mission-style dining table. "As far as I'm concerned, you can both stay with me as long as you want."

"Well, thank you, I appreciate it. We love being here, too." She smiled and took another bite of her granola and yogurt, feeling happy and relaxed. *We're making good progress,* she thought.

"So, any plans? What are you working on now?" he asked.

"Before events start to ramp up with the ranch, I'm helping Mariah finalize her business plan. She's under consideration for a couple of grants. If she gets them, she'll have some seed capital. If not, she might have to keep her wholesale business going for a bit longer. It's not a good idea to start the first year of a new business under-capitalized."

"That's a shame," Ed said. "With the quality of baking she produces, she deserves to have a successful storefront business, if that's what she wants. I might see what I can do to help her."

"What are you thinking, Ed?" Paige asked.

"If Mariah applies for a small business loan, I'd be willing to sign on as her guarantor. I don't know her well, but Maggie thinks highly of her and believes in her potential. That's good enough for me—and her baked goods speak for themselves. I have a feeling Mariah can make a go of a small brick-and-mortar store, especially with you as her business mentor, Paige."

"Oh, that's incredibly generous of you, and thank you for the compliment. But I have to tell you, Mariah says she's *really* committed to making this work on her own. My advice is, before you approach her, let's wait and see if she gets at least *one* of the grants she's applied for on her own. Then she'll know what she has to work with."

She smiled to take any sting out of her words. Ed had already done so much for her, and her sister, and for the people of Verde Springs.

He might be a formidable businessman, but he was really a giant of a man with a heart to match—and she and Reggie were incredibly lucky to have him in their lives. "What are *your* plans for the week?" Paige asked, in turn.

"I have…a meeting with an attorney," he said.

"An attorney? That sounds serious. I hope it's not too stressful," she said. "Everything's been going so well for us, lately."

"I'm just gathering information, getting all of my ducks in a row," he said, neutrally.

"It sounds like you're preparing for battle," she mused, taking a sip of her orange juice.

"I hope not," Ed said, lightly.

Paige's early morning optimism drained out of her all at once, and the juice turned to acid in her stomach. She set her breakfast aside and steeled herself to address the gigantic elephant lurking in the kitchen: "Ed, I really hope this isn't about *us*. But, if it is, don't you think the *first* step should be for the two of us to talk about it?"

He hesitated, but finally faced her head on. "The thing is, Paige… what is there for us to talk about? We *both* want to be full-time parents to Reggie, and we live an hour apart on a good traffic day. I can only think of one solution, but you'd never go for it," he said, shaking his head.

"I'm willing to listen," she said, gently.

After a long pause, he finally continued. "We could get married," he said.

Wow, that was totally not on this morning's bingo card. "Ed, um, if that's a proposal, I think you've missed a few steps," she said, trying to catch her bearings.

He shook his head. "This wouldn't be a *real* marriage—I know you don't want that. But it would keep us under one roof. It would give Reggie the stable life he deserves. It would provide stability for *both* of you. I think we're pretty compatible, don't you? Haven't we both been enjoying our time here together?" he asked.

Ed seemed to be recognizing that point—and throwing it out the window at the exact same time. "Ed, I've *loved* being here with you, with all of us together. But…I think you're talking about something like a marriage of convenience, right?" When he nodded, she took a deep breath and continued. "That's what it used to be called, back in the dark ages—before people figured out how to live authentic lives that have at least a *hope* of meeting everybody's needs," Paige said, evenly, while trying to hold it together and not fall off her chair in astonishment. *What could he possibly be thinking?*

Clearly stumped by her immediate rejection, Ed was silent for a long moment. "Well, do *you* have another solution?" he asked. "The fact that you didn't tell me you were pregnant until we met face-to-face in my favorite restaurant—and I had to find out *months* after the fact—made it clear that you *couldn't* have had any real feelings for me." He shrugged, as if it should be completely obvious.

But it *wasn't* obvious—and what Ed believed was miles from the truth. But he'd made something crystal clear, too: *he hadn't forgiven her at all.*

Paige swallowed hard, then took another deep breath. "I have sincerely apologized for not telling you that I was pregnant the minute I found out. It wasn't right, and I deeply regret that I hurt you. But I can't deny that it happened—and I don't expect you to. *I really messed up.* When I discovered I was pregnant after a spontaneous hookup, at the age of thirty-eight, I needed a minute to wrap my head around it. Maybe because I've been ridiculously responsible for all of my adult life, and I never, in my wildest dreams, imagined I'd have an unintended pregnancy. But, Ed, I *wanted* to make love with you that night—and I guess, in my post-mead haze, I thought a thin piece of latex would be enough to protect us. And I wasn't at all sorry about the outcome. But I didn't have a *clue* about how *you'd* react to the news that you'd fathered a child!"

"Paige, it's all just a bunch of *words*," he said, frustrated, "which your actions haven't exactly matched. And there's something else: every time there's a problem, you go running straight back to the ranch, taking my son with you."

Paige took another deep breath. "I know. I know. It's a *terrible* habit, my running away like that. And I promise I'll work on it, Ed. I'm extremely sorry that I hurt you, and I hope someday you can believe that. And maybe even…forgive me.

"What I want *you* to hear *now* is this: if you want to live an authentic life, if you want to be more of a permanent feature in my life and Reggie's, it's time to think about what we mean to each other. You know, to actually *explore* that, if we're brave enough. And I am willing to take that chance—I *want* to that chance."

"I'm floundering here, Paige. I have no clue what you want," Ed said. Pausing, he ran a hand through his shaggy hair. "When it comes right down to it, what *do* I really mean to you?"

"Everything. You mean *everything*," she said, slowly, hoping he would take in the truth of her words. She swallowed her emotions and continued. "Am I *really* that hard to read?"

"Well, maybe I'm not so great at reading people. Or, maybe, it's hard for me to…" And that was where his words ended.

"Or, maybe, it's just hard for you to *trust* me?" Paige thought she might as well finish his sentence for him. *He didn't trust her. Maybe he never would.*

He didn't disagree. And after another uncomfortably long silence from Ed, Paige got up from the table and went to her room. She heard him head up to his study, which she hoped would give him time to think. But, if the man couldn't learn to use his words before it was too late, it seemed like they were done here. *She'd held off as long as she could, hoping things between them would sort themselves out, naturally.* But today, she'd needed to lay her heart on the table. She'd been as honest and vulnerable as she could be. *You mean everything.* What happened now was entirely up to Ed.

Moving in slow motion—the way you do when you feel all of your hopes and dreams plunging down to earth—she half-heartedly packed up her clothes and personal items, then Reggie's. She gave Ed plenty of time to think. *Plenty of time for the Mighty Bear to come out of his lair and talk to her.*

When it was clear that it wasn't going to happen, she ordered an Uber. It would take a big chunk out of her bank account, but she couldn't stay here a minute longer or she'd lose it. *So much for not running away…*

Being here with Ed was maddening. Every night, she needed to feel his strong arms around her. She craved his warmth and comfort like it was necessary to stay grounded in her new world. She wanted to offer him *her* warmth and comfort, too—to walk up behind him when he was working at the stove and wrap her arms around him. Kiss him on the back of the neck. She wanted him to stop what he was doing, turn around, and pull her into his embrace. She wanted his lips on hers—*and they were so very far away*. She even missed his damn beard!

This was just too hard. She couldn't make up for the first few floundering months of her pregnancy when she hadn't known *how* to tell him they'd conceived a child together. Sure, everybody made mistakes—and she was completely aware that she'd made a really *big* one. But she couldn't take it back. And in the end, she was overjoyed to be a mother, and delighted with the child they'd created together. *Clearly, Ed had some things to work out, and he needed time. Fine.* But she couldn't stand for her greatest joy to be tinged with regret. *Maybe it was truly over between them before it had even begun.*

For as long as she could remember, when life got hard, Paige straightened her spine and prepared to handle everything that came her way, head on. Her personal *modus operandi* included hyper-independence, a coping mechanism she'd depended on since early childhood. First, when her father had left them—and a decade later, when her mother had died, leaving her younger sister in her care. Her hyper-independence had been reinforced, decades later, when Dan had walked out on her, too. Life had taught her that "relying on others isn't safe"—a trauma response that colored every aspect of her life, including her past relationships. Ed Barrett had been the first, and *only* man, to change her perspective. But she could no longer see a way forward.

Having a consistent helping hand and reliable backup was a refreshing and welcome change in her life, which she appreciated more than Ed would ever know. *Being around Ed had allowed her to have faith and trust in a man for the first time in her life.* But there was no way in hell she would ever enter a 'marriage of convenience' with the man she had fallen in love with. It wasn't something she was capable of, and it wasn't going to happen. There had to be a way to fix this. Because the only relationship she wanted with the man she'd grown to adore was a *real* relationship—one founded on love and trust that would last until they were old and gray, or gone. Above all, she wanted their son to grow up with the crucial knowledge that his parents loved each other. And she would never settle for less.

Ed sat in his study, his eyes closed and his head spinning. He'd have welcomed the distraction of hearing his son cry to be picked up and held, but Reggie was still quietly sleeping. Letting out a breath, he picked up his cell phone. With his giant fingers, he carefully typed out a number. "This is Reggie Barret. Yes, that's right, but I'd like to cancel that appointment. No, I don't want to reschedule."

He heard the front door open and shut, and a car pulling away. *Paige leaving, again—taking his son with her.* What a mess he'd made of things. To be fair, what a mess they'd *both* made of things. Reggie seemed to be their single spot of shared joy. And Ed refused to let his son be caught in a tug of war between the two people who loved him most. *No matter what, that just wasn't going to happen.*

Harper and Caleb landed in Santa Fe and caught an Uber to the ranch, since they didn't want Paige or anyone else to make an unnecessary trip. When they pulled up to the main house, she was surprised to see her sister outside, cutting a bunch of late tulips in the entry garden.

Paige was wearing a pair of overalls, with the baby monitor stuffed into the front pocket.

"What in the world are *you* doing here?" Harper asked. "I thought you were staying with Ed in Santa Fe for another week or two."

"Welcome home! You look stunningly beautiful and happy—and that makes *me* happy," Paige said, giving her a one-armed hug and conveniently ignoring her question. "Hi Caleb, it's good to see you, too. Welcome home!"

"Why *aren't* you in Santa Fe?" Harper asked, again, not accepting her sister's avoidance for an answer.

"You really want to do this, now? Okay." Paige let out a breath. "I took your advice and talked to Ed. Things…really didn't go well. Then, as usual, I ran back to the ranch. It's too hard to be with him and not *be* with him—and he hasn't tried to get close to me, even once. There he is, day after day, looking and acting like the perfect man and the perfect father. He's funny, and charming, and ridiculously sexy in that lumberjack way he's got, even without his beard, which honestly, I kind of miss. But he's made it completely clear that we can't be together—at least not in any way that could make either of us happy."

This was quite a spin-out, even for Paige. Could she be overreacting, again?

"Has he, *really?*" Harper asked. Setting her suitcases down, she smiled sweetly at Caleb, and he picked them up and headed inside. *Her husband was a very smart man.* "I mean, *how* has Ed made it clear that he doesn't want you? Don't you think he's just protecting himself because he felt rejected? No one *wants* to get hurt, ever. Maybe it's just as hard for Ed to see you with Reggie, and not show you how much he cares about *you.*"

"Oh, really, you think so? Then why did he suggest a marriage of convenience, when it could be so much more? Something *real*." Paige asked, crossing her arms.

"Ouch! Ed actually said that?" Harper asked. "Oh, Paige, I'm sorry. I didn't know." She rescued the tulips from her sister and herded her toward the ranch house.

"Not in those *exact* words, but that's what he meant. He said we could get married—but 'it wouldn't be a *real* marriage.' Well, dammit, I *want* a real marriage, *with* Ed," Paige said, with tears in her eyes. "Reggie deserves to grow up with two parents who *really* love each other! I want so badly to give him that, and I *know* we can, but the possibility hasn't even entered Ed's mind, despite my telling him that he means everything to me, and that I'm want to take the chance to see if we can *really* be together."

"Yikes! Now, I understand why you're so upset. Come inside. We'll make some tea, and we can talk some more about this," Harper said.

Once she and Paige were sipping on a hibiscus blend and nibbling on a tin of bizcochitos, New Mexico's state cookie, Harper thought of *one* critical question. "Okay, what I want to know is what *you* said to Ed—after his ridiculous marriage-of-convenience comment."

"Well, I talked about authenticity, and I said I thought it was time to think about what we mean to each other. To *explore* that. And that I was willing to take the risk."

"That's *great*, Paige!" she said, encouragingly. "So, what happened?" *Although she couldn't help wondering why Paige just didn't jump Ed's bones when Reggie was down for a good long nap. In her experience, it was usually effective. But in this way, she and her sister were very different creatures.*

"Ed said he was confused, and that he didn't know what I really wanted. Then he asked me straight out, 'What do I mean to you?'"

"Now, we're getting somewhere!" Harper said, encouragingly. "And how did you answer him?"

"I said he meant *everything*," Paige said. "Wasn't that clear enough for him?"

"And, then what?" Harper asked, holding onto a glimmer of hope. Maybe her sister *had* overreacted, which wouldn't be all that much of a shocker. Paige had a tendency to overthink most things.

"Well, he didn't jump up and throw his arms around me. He didn't say anything at all—and I waited around for a good long time. So, I packed up and left again. It's too hard to be around him, when I have such strong feelings for him and the two of us are getting nowhere!"

"Oh. Well. Then I agree with you—the ball's firmly in Ed's court," Harper said. *And it was time to change the subject.* "Now, let me see how much my nephew has grown, and I'll tell you all about Hawaii. Then we'll make a plan to talk about the hot spring. But maybe not tonight. I'm jet-lagged, and I don't want to set a precedent of ignoring my hot husband the minute we get home."

"You're such a good wife. I want to be a good wife, too. I *would* be such a good wife, too, if Ed could only see it."

"I think Ed knows that, Paige—you're a total catch, and you're always taking care of everybody. He just doesn't want to offer you his heart on a platter and have you turn up your nose."

"*That's* not what happened. Okay, maybe I hesitated, at first—but not once I really got to know him," Paige said, defensively.

"But I'm betting that's the way it felt. Obviously, Ed was deeply hurt," Harper said.

"You can be really mean, sometimes, you know that?" Paige said. "It just takes *time* for me to get to know someone, and especially, to *trust* someone. But now I know that Ed never lets me down. *Well, almost never.* And I really like who he is as a person. He's kind, and warm, and genius-level smart. And he can be really funny too. Not only that; I fell in LOVE with him. He…just can't see it."

"I'm not trying to be mean—I just tell it like it is," Harper replied. She sighed, fondly remembering her extremely relaxing two-week honeymoon in the faraway Aloha state. Her sister and the big guy she'd fallen in love with sure needed to work on their communication. Since they'd obviously failed at the spoken word, maybe they could try the telepathic method.

CHAPTER TWENTY-THREE

$\mathcal{P}$aige lay wide awake, restless and unsettled—trying to gather her courage for what came next. Since she'd been the one to leave, again, *she* had to be the one to reach out. That was a no-brainer—even though, technically, *she'd* been the one who'd most recently offered her heart on a platter and had it rejected. *What more did she have to do? Propose to the guy...?* And an idea began to take shape...

"So, do you want to talk about the hot spring?" Harper asked, poking her head into Paige's bedroom.

"Um, yeah, but first, I want to see it with my own eyes. Ed's seen it, but I've only seen the photos that Sam took. If Caleb could keep an eye on Reggie for an hour or so, maybe you and I can go for a little stroll this morning. What do you say? I could use some exercise to clear my head."

"Okay, after I replenish my calories. Caleb wanted to...well, we used up a *lot* of calories," Harper explained.

"Me too. Reggie wanted to nurse half the night. I think we should hire us a professional chef. We can offer employee perks now—like unlimited use of our new hot spring."

A quick thirty minutes later, they hopped into Lucy and drove to the northwest boundary. Then they walked along the ridge until it overlooked the ranch's recent scene of geological chaos: the main vent spewed steam, and thin tendrils drifted skyward from several smaller, active vents. For a moment, a gust of wind blew the steam aside and Harper and Page looked down onto a multicolor pool. A steady stream of warm water spilled out of the lower end of the pool, giving off gentle wafts of steam and turning the once brown high desert into a beautiful ribbon of green.

"Hot damn! What do you think?" asked Harper. "It's almost like finding a pot of gold on your very own back forty! What should we do with it?"

"I think we need to explore the options and get a cost breakdown for each," Paige said.

Harper nodded in agreement. "Where do you think all that water goes?"

"I'd wondered about that, too," said Paige. "According to Sam's report, most of it eventually percolates back down into the ground, which he says helps replenish the water table. "But it probably doesn't *have* to. You could use some of the water to heat a greenhouse in the winter, or we could come up with another idea."

"That's not a terrible idea. Okay, I'll get to work drawing up some plans. Spring is my busiest season in the gardens, and we'll need to gear up for the guests that will be arriving soon—*and* there's the money situation," Harper said. "We both need to be on top of that. We've worked so hard to get the Inn up and running, and we don't want to do anything to risk losing it, including over-extending ourselves."

"I'm with you, there. I know it won't be cheap to develop the hot spring, and we'd need to secure working capital," Paige said. "And we can't ask our guests to go tromping across the high desert just to enjoy a soak. We'd need facilities—and probably more gardens, or, at least some attractive landscaping down there. We have to make sure this hot spring can potentially pay for itself, or there's no point in forking over the money to develop it in the first place."

"Are we ready for this? I'm newly married and building a relationship with Ellie. You're the mom of a brand-new baby, and you're still trying to figure out where your relationship with Ed is going. With the Inn, and our wedding business, and the Coop Studios' workshops and retreats—do we *really* want to add the hot spring to the mix? I'm a little overwhelmed just thinking about it."

"Well, *if* we went for it, we'd need to hire a lot more help," said Paige. "That'll take money we really don't have right now. Maybe we need to think of this as a *long-term* strategy, not a project we're going to jump into immediately. Would it matter if we developed it next year? After we've had another full season of retreats at the Coop Studios and a handful of weddings, we might have enough saved to start laying out the site. But to get a development loan, we'd need to show the bank that we're a good business risk."

"Yeah, maybe we shouldn't jump the gun. Let's just gather some ideas, and try to come up with what we'd like the hot spring to look like if we *did* develop it," Harper said. "There's no rush, right?"

"Yeah. No rush at all," agreed Paige. Even though her entrepreneurial spirit was already bursting to get to work, her focus for the near future was Reggie. *But that didn't mean she didn't have room in her heart, and her life, for someone else. She needed to implement her plan, and soon.*

"So, about the Ed situation," Harper said, as they walked back to the truck. "You *can't* let this silence between you go on much longer, Paige. You two need to talk, soon, before the only possibility that's left is two lawyers gaming it out in court, with Reggie as the football. Is that really the outcome you want?" she asked, bluntly.

"Of course, not! I know it's up to *me* to make the next move. I can't help it if my falling for Ed was a slow burn—not every relationship starts with fireworks. But either way, I got there. I'm in love with him, and I as much as told him so. Which is hard to believe, given his response—or, should I say, *lack* of a response. I've been thinking about our situation non-stop, and...I'm thinking...I might bite the bullet and *propose* to Ed. I don't know how else to prove to him that *he's* the one I want to be with, forever, no matter where life takes us. I want the three of us to be a real family—not for practical reasons, like he suggested. But because I *love* him, so much."

"Now that's more like it! Whatever you want or need, I've got your back," Harper said.

Ed sat in front of the fire in his cozy living room, which felt oddly cold and lonely without Paige and Reggie there with him. He'd totally blown it. *Does Paige really care for me? And what's the point in starting a custody battle with Paige, when it's the very last thing I want?* Without the answers to those two questions, he'd taken the only action that had immediately come to mind—he'd called and canceled the appointment with the fathers' rights attorney.

He'd also given Paige space—she obviously needed time to herself, or she wouldn't have left the way she did. *None of this was easy.* He didn't have to imagine how it felt to spend time with someone you were hopelessly attracted to, someone you wanted with your whole heart, when you knew your feelings weren't reciprocated. He'd been *living* it, for months. How terribly ironic that Paige seemed to be struggling with the same situation.

He hadn't a clue what to do—but he missed Reggie with an ache that wouldn't quit, and as his father, he had every right to see him. To do that, he'd have to head into Verde Springs, which meant he'd be invading Paige's home turf. Considering his options, he could think of only one place that might be considered neutral territory. He picked up his phone and called the mother of his child. She didn't answer. But, given their persistent failure to communicate, that only made his first attempt to reach out a little easier.

"Paige. It's Ed. We don't need to have a serious talk, yet, unless you want to. But maybe you'd like to meet for lunch, or dinner, and the three of us could spend some time together as a family. I think meeting at Maggie's might be the best idea. I'm free Friday night, and I hope you are, too. And Paige…I miss you. I miss *both* of you."

On Friday afternoon, Paige dressed carefully in an outfit that over-lapped nursing-mother and still-sexy at almost-forty. She'd dressed Reggie in an adorable outfit, too. Not that *he* needed any help in the cute department—and Ed already adored his son. *Who wouldn't?* Reggie was growing like a weed, keeping his eyes open more and engaging with both of his parents, and lighting up when he saw them.

Maggie saved them her best booth, a semi-private one in back. Earlier, Harper had dropped off a five-gallon bucket of blooms to make a fabulous table bouquet. Mariah had baked a special dessert, rich and chocolatey, and Maggie had a couple of New York Strips ready to grill. *Was it too much?* Probably. *Unless Ed accepted her proposal.* Then it would be a day to remember, forever, for both of them. *Well, she'd always believed in preparing for the outcome she most wanted.*

If only she could come up with the perfect words that would wash away any lingering hurt and magically bring the two of them together. *She could only speak her heart and her truth.* Whether she came across as sincere and emotionally compelling, or she ended up blubbering like a fool, she was going to ask Ed Barrett to marry her. But *first*, she needed to tell him she was *in love with him*—and he needed to hear it and believe it.

Would those three little words, "I love you," be enough?

Ed thought long and hard about his next step. He'd wanted to give Paige a gift that would show his affection for her—but without putting any pressure on her. He'd only know for sure whether he'd hit the right note when he watched her open the blue velvet box in his hand. Over the past week, when the three of them were miles apart, he'd felt empty inside. It was clear: Paige and Reggie *were* his life, now and forever. *They were his family, and he'd never change the way he felt about either of them.*

After shaving closely this morning, he put on the V-neck sweater Paige liked and his comfortable, stone-washed jeans. If the evening went as he hoped, Paige and Reggie would follow him home to Santa Fe in Paige's SUV, which had plenty of room for the baby's car-seat. But tonight, he needed the confidence boost of driving his Porsche. He hadn't taken it out on the road, or even out of his garage, in months. But tonight, he was perfectly happy to blow the carbon deposits out of the Porche's engine on a gorgeous spring evening.

The sun dipped lower in the sky, and the warm air was scented with sage springing back to life after months of winter. He drove past the string of small villages between Santa Fe and Verde Springs—past Cañoncito, past Glorieta. Coming down the steep hill, he tapped on the brakes, but didn't feel much of a response. He downshifted, which didn't make the Porsche's engine happy, but he was going too fast for the familiar dip at the bottom. The engine strained and he smelled the acrid burn of overheated metal. He pumped his foot again, but the brakes were mush. He knew he was in big trouble, with the deep dip in the road that was coming up next. His last thought was of Paige and Reggie—and then he was airborne and arcing over the guardrail.

Holding her sleeping baby in her arms, Paige waited in the booth at Maggie's, sipping on soda water and waiting for Papa Bear to walk in the door. The appointed time of five-thirty turned into six, and then six-thirty. He hadn't left any messages or texts on her phone, but she wasn't irritated—she was *scared*. If Ed was having second thoughts about the meeting *he'd* proposed, and she'd enthusiastically agreed to, then everything would be over. *And in losing him, she would surely have made the biggest mistake of her life.*

Needing an infusion of support, she picked up her phone. "Harper, Ed's not here. Do you think he changed his mind."

Don't panic. Maybe he got laid up with work. Did you check your voicemail?

"No, no voicemail. No text, either. What do I do now?" Paige asked.

Hang tight—I'll be there as soon as I can. We'll eat, we'll have dessert, and then, Ed will be there. I promise. He would never stand you up, and you know he was anxious to see Reggie.

Fifteen minutes later, Harper arrived and slid into the booth across from Paige. They ordered quesadillas and iced teas and waited together while the clock ticked on. Finally, it was seven-thirty on Maggie's big kitchen clock. *Ed wasn't coming.*

They finished their meals in silence, and then gathered their belongings. After they got Reggie settled in Ethel's backseat, Harper began walking toward Lucy. As she reached her truck's door, Maggie came dashing out of the cafe waving a white bar towel to get their attention. "Wait! Don't leave! Grab Paige and come back inside. I have some news about Ed."

Paige and Harper sat back down in the booth. Maggie took a seat across from them. Taking Paige's hands in hers, she said, "Honey, there's been an accident. Ed wouldn't be a no-show for no reason. I didn't say anything, but…he called earlier today and wanted to make sure I had a certain brand of Champagne on ice. He *wanted* to be here—and he *planned* to be here. When Ed didn't show, I just had a really bad feeling. I called the State Police, and they're reporting an accident between Glorieta and Rowe. A late-model Porsche—silver, just like Ed's. About four-forty-five. I called both of the hospitals in Santa Fe, and the patient, a male in his late thirties, was life-flighted into Christus St. Vincent's about five-fifteen. Then…I told a little white lie. I said that my son was missing, and I gave them Ed's name and description. Paige, I am so sorry to say Ed's been admitted to the trauma center.

"I think you should head down there—Harper can drive you and help out with Reggie. I'll join you after I close up. You two go on, now," she said, gently. "I'm so sorry, honey. I'll be praying for Ed."

Paige's heartbeat fluttered erratically, and she had trouble catching her breath. *This can't be happening.* But, as Maggie had calmly explained, it was—it had. "Harper? Can we get going? Now, please," she said, standing up with trembling legs. She settled Reggie in the car seat once more, and got into the passenger seat. Harper drove towards Santa Fe, quickly and efficiently. She used Bluetooth for directions to Christus St. Vincent's, and then they were pulling into the parking lot. Paige took off, half-running toward the entrance, while Harper unhooked Reggie's car seat from its base and followed her into the hospital.

CHAPTER TWENTY-FOUR

*P*aige explained that she was the mother of Ed's son, and in lieu of other family, his emergency contact in New Mexico. Although she didn't have that in writing, she'd get it on Monday morning from Ed's attorney. Still, the charge nurse could only tell them that Ed had been admitted to the trauma unit.

"The doctor will want to speak to you regarding the patient's next of kin," the nurse continued.

"Was Ed's accident that serious?" Paige asked, her stomach lurching.

"I'm not at liberty to say, but I think you should talk to the doctor. I'll let him know you're here."

Paige took a seat in the waiting room next to her sister, who held Reggie against her chest in a surprisingly maternal way.

"Did they tell you anything?" Harper asked, gently patting Reggie's bottom.

"Not enough. I explained that I was Ed's emergency contact in New Mexico, because we have a child together. And the nurse said the doctor might want to speak to me, which makes me really worried.

Usually, they won't disclose *any* information unless you're a spouse or an immediate family member."

"So, we're waiting?" Harper asked.

Paige nodded. "For as long as it takes."

An hour and a half later, Maggie arrived, bringing a basket filled with muffins, pastries, sandwiches, and juices, but no one was the least bit hungry. "Any news on Ed?" she asked.

"No. We're still waiting. I'm trying to make a decision, though. If his condition is really serious, should I reach out to his family? He said they're estranged. But surely, when something like this happens, they'd want to know," Paige said.

"If Ed were my son, *I'd* want to know," Maggie said. "Ed and I have been friends for a long time, Paige. He doesn't hate his family." She smiled. "Ed doesn't hate *anybody*. He just wanted the freedom to pursue his own life—and anyway, it was Ed's dad who pulled the plug on their relationship, not Ed. I guess Reggie Barret Senior is one of those people who take 'my way or the highway' literally."

"Wouldn't Ed's mother want to know? This is her *son*, and I know how I feel about Reggie. At some point in her life, surely, Ed was her whole world!"

"Ms. Crawley?" a doctor dressed in green scrubs called out.

"Yes, I'm right here," Paige said, standing up.

"I'm Dr. Michael McAllister, the emergency physician who treated Mr. Barrett. Could you follow me, please?" he said.

"Of course. Harper, call me if Reggie wakes up and needs me," Paige said, before disappearing through the swinging double doors.

※

Paige sat anxiously across the desk from the doctor, who had removed his cloth surgical cap. "Please, can you tell me anything about Mr. Barrett's condition?" she asked. "Beyond the child we share together, Ed doesn't have any family here in New Mexico—but I can work on getting in touch with them."

He nodded. "I understand you're Mr. Barrett's emergency contact, and we'll need you to verify that—on Monday, the nurse said. Until then, we will need your help to try to reach out to his family. Mr. Barrett is in critical condition, with head injuries, a possible cervical spine injury, and some nasty chest contusions from blunt chest trauma. We're keeping his body temperature low to decrease the risk of brain damage. And his right leg has been surgically rodded—he sustained a compound fracture of the femur, which led to a great deal of blood loss. We may need to speak to his next of kin. Do you know if Mr. Barrett has a health care directive? And are you in a position to reach out to his family?"

"Ed is estranged from his family, but I'm going to try my best," Paige said. "And I'll be able to reach his personal attorney Monday morning."

"That would be good. Even if Mr. Barrett makes it through the next few critical days, he's facing a *very* long recovery," he said, handing her his Medical Staff contact card. "Please have them get in touch with me as soon as possible. They'll likely need to be involved."

"I certainly will. Is he...stable enough that I could see him?" she asked.

"Yes, but he's limited to ten-minute visits. He's in ICU bed 3. Just ask at the nurse's desk and they'll direct you back."

Paige walked slowly into the ICU pod, which was eerily quiet and so dimly lit that she wondered how the nurses could manage to see their way around. She stopped outside ICU-bed 3 and her breath caught in her throat. The still form of the man she loved lay in the narrow bed, one leg raised on two pillows, his head thickly bandaged. A flexible tube of blue corrugated plastic entered through his mouth and supported his airway, while the machine at the bedside inflated his chest approximately once every five seconds. *It was an eerie sound she would never forget.*

Entering the room, she bent over the bed and kissed his cheek, the only available patch of unmarked skin. He had IV lines in both hands, one administering fluids, the other, blood. The machine on his left kept track of his vital signs. Turning in a circle, Paige noted his dry-erase board, where unfamiliar handwriting informed her that his nurse's name was Stephanie and his respiratory therapist was Luis. Paige sat on the bedside chair and closed her eyes. *Ed had been coming to see her. She'd hoped they were going to open their hearts and speak the truth. She'd hoped they were finally going to work everything out between them and be a real family. Just hours ago, the image was so clear in her mind.*

Paige opened her eyes and glanced around the small room, her gaze lighting upon the plastic ER bag stamped with the Christus St. Vincent's logo. Most likely, it held Ed's personal effects. She'd need his keys to get into his house and track down his family contacts—as well as to be close to the hospital in Santa Fe. She didn't think he'd mind—he'd said he loved having her and Reggie there. Loosening the cotton drawstring, she rummaged around, listening for the jingle of keys, but they'd fallen to the bottom of the bag. Her hand landed on a small, velvet-covered box. *Not a ring box—but she hadn't expected a*

ring. She had been the one planning to propose, with flowers and chocolate.
Her hand drew out a flat box three inches in diameter, from a jeweler
on Santa Fe's central plaza. As she removed it from the bag, her heart
beat a little faster.

Paige returned to sit at Ed's bedside. She talked to him, even
though he couldn't hear her. "I love you, Ed. I really do. I'm so sorry
about your accident. I *know* you were coming to see me. I *know* you
wouldn't let me down. I'm here now, and I'm going to be here every
day until you come home to us."

She took a breath and opened the box to find the most beautiful engraved, oval locket on a fine gold chain. And in the locket was
a photo Ed had taken of her with Reggie in her arms, not long after
their son was born. The other oval framed a photo that she'd taken
of Ed holding Reggie. *It was the perfect gift—all of them together in one
place.* With shaking hands, she removed the locket out and fastened
the chain around her neck. Setting the empty box on the bedside table,
Paige leaned over the bed and gently kissed his cheek. She heard the
steady blip that tracked his heartbeat. She listened to the steady sound
of his breathing, and, for now, it was enough. She whispered the words
like a prayer—*Ed is alive, he'll recover, and he'll come back to us.*

CHAPTER TWENTY-FIVE

*C*aleb had arrived around midnight to pick Harper up, but she'd back in the morning with her own vehicle, and she'd bring everything Paige needed with her. So, for what remained of the night, she was on her own.

Carrying Reggie in his car seat, Paige turned the key in the lock and stepped inside. Without Ed's presence, the house felt huge and empty. It was late, and she really wanted, and needed, to reach out to Ed's family, but she was too exhausted to begin a scavenger hunt in his home office. She still had to nurse Reggie, change his diaper, put him in a fresh sleeper, and get a good night's sleep. Morning would come, and with it, a stressful day ahead. She'd set an alarm and get up early.

As she lay in the comfortable queen bed in the guest room, she remembered Ed sitting on its edge, smiling down at her as Reggie held onto his finger. *Remembering the warm light in his brown eyes, she knew that life would be unacceptable if she were never to see it again.* Reggie fell away from her breast at last, his little puckered lips still continuing to make suckling motions. The midwives called it "dream feeding." She made a nest of pillows for the baby, keeping him close within reach. *Her comfort.* Then she closed her eyes and willed herself to sleep.

She awoke, startled when she heard Reggie's soft cry, remembering that she wasn't in her own familiar room at the ranch, but in Ed's clean-lined Craftsman in Santa Fe...*and why.* She felt her milk let-down and the warm wash of oxytocin hit her bloodstream. Reggie fell blissfully back to sleep for another hour while she took a quick shower, then checked in Ed's refrigerator to see if she could find anything for breakfast. She wanted coffee in the worst way this morning, but while she was nursing, herbal tea would have to do. While the kettle heated, she picked up her phone and called the hospital:

"This is Paige Crawley. I'm calling about a patient, Reggie Barrett, in ICU bed 3. Can you please give me an update on his condition? Until we can locate his next of kin, I'm his emergency contact and the mother of his son."

There's been no change, Ms. Crawley, but that's not necessarily a bad sign. No deterioration in the first twelve to twenty-four hours is considered a positive outcome with head injuries, and we're keeping a close eye on him, the charge nurse explained.

"Thank you. I'll be in later today. I'm going to try reaching out to reach his family this morning."

Alright. We'll see you later, then. Drive safely, the nurse said, ending the call.

Since it was a Saturday, she wasn't able to get in touch with Ed's attorney, Tom Price, who might have every bit of information she needed. The next best thing was to reach out to the other person most likely to have a relationship with Ed: his sister Elizabeth. She searched online to find Elizabeth's married name, because her addled brain couldn't remember the details from her previous internet search. *Something French?*

Oui—Elizabeth Barrett DuBois, it turned out to be. *Google Image search was a useful tool.* Using Ed's desktop computer, Paige searched for an Elizabeth DuBois or an Elizabeth Barrett DuBois in the Palo Alto area, and in nearby San Jose. After half an hour or so, she was relatively sure she had the right person. Then she had to pay a small fee to a people finder service to locate a current phone number. She took a sip of her tea, carefully punched in the number, and waited.

DuBois residence, Chloe speaking, said a teenager's voice.

"Hello, my name is Paige Crawley. I'm a friend of your uncle's, calling from New Mexico. Could I please speak to your mother? It's very important."

My mother's not here right now, but if you'd like to leave your number, I can have her call you, the girl said, politely.

"That would be perfect. I'll give you my cell phone number. Please ask her to call me as soon as possible—it's *urgent* that I speak to her today. Thank you, Chloe."

If she didn't hear back from Ed's sister soon, she'd keep calling back until she could speak to her directly. Hanging up, Paige dialed Harper. "I didn't want you to worry if I don't answer my phone this afternoon. My battery is running low, and I didn't have my phone charger with me when I left for Maggie's." *Just yesterday?*

I'll bring it with me when I come into town. Can you think of anything else you need? Harper asked.

"I guess my pajamas and my toiletries for starters, and an extra nursing bra. Maybe something warm to wear. It's cooler here in Santa Fe than it's been at the ranch."

Got it. Has there been any change in Ed's condition? Harper asked.

"No, no change. I'll call you again after I've been to the hospital. I've reached out to his sister and left a message asking her to call me. Ed's parents are elderly, and I have no idea what kind of shape they're in. No matter what, the accident will come as a shock, so I thought it would be best to let Ed's sister break the news."

I hope you hear from her soon, Paige. I'll try to be in Santa Fe by eleven-thirty, and I'll bring lunch from Maggie's. I can stay as long as you need me to, Harper said.

"But there's so much to do at the ranch," protested Paige. "Are you sure you can spare the time away?"

Absolutely. Caleb's on top of it—and he'll bring in a few guys from his crew, if needed. I want to be there to support you, Paige. You can't take care of a newborn baby and Ed, all by yourself. Let me help you.

"Thanks, it'll be great to have you here. Things are a bit crazy right now," Paige said.

I know they are. You just hang in there, Harper said. *I'll be there by eleven-thirty at the latest.*

"Thanks, Harper. And be careful driving. The traffic on weekends can get gnarly."

After stopping to pick up some more disposable diapers, Paige arrived at St. Vincent's and made her way to the ICU waiting room, carrying Reggie in his car seat with her. She immediately checked in with the nurse at the desk.

"Hello. I'm here to see Reggie Barrett. Has there been any change in his condition?" she asked.

The pretty, young nurse shook her head, "No, not since he got out of recovery last night. If you like, I can see if the hospitalist is free to speak with you."

"Hospitalist?" Paige asked, unfamiliar with that term.

"Dr. Finnegan. He's the resident doctor on the critical care unit who rounds on all the patients and communicates with the specialists involved. It saves a lot of time and provides a better overall quality of care. I'll page him for you."

A few minutes later, the nurse returned. "Dr. Finnegan is with a patient right now, but he'll be doing rounds on Mr. Barrett about eleven-thirty, so you could speak to him then." Glancing at Reggie, she continued, "We have a day care center on-site—it's on the ground floor just to the west of the main entrance. I think they take emergency drop-ins."

"No, I didn't, and thank you for the offer. My son's a pretty good size, but he's actually still a newborn, and my sister will be here soon to help keep an eye on him. Is it alright if I go in to see Mr. Barrett, now?"

"Of course. But if the baby starts to cry, you'll have to bring him out right away. We have a lot of critical patients, and we can't have them disturbed," the nurse said. "That's why we usually don't allow children in the ICU. I can make an exception for a newborn, but not if it proves disruptive."

"I understand. Thank you," said Paige. She picked up Reggie's carrier and walked through the double doors that led to the small ICU where Ed was still sleeping. *And healing*. She much preferred to think of him that way, rather than in a coma.

Still intubated, Ed's ventilator did the work of breathing for him. Paige noted that his heart rate was higher than it had been the night before. His limbs also appeared more swollen, even though the nurses had elevated his fractured leg even higher. His hospital gown had slipped downward, revealing a deep bruise running diagonally across his chest. *But without his seat belt, he wouldn't be here at all.* With the totality of the injuries that he'd suffered in the crash, he was almost unrecognizable. But Ed was still in there, somewhere. *She believed it.*

She spoke to him, quietly. "Good morning, Ed. I hope you slept well." She wanted him to know she was here and that Reggie was, too. She took Reggie out of his car carrier and held him against her chest for a moment, inhaling the sweet, milky fragrance unique to all newborns. Then, she held the baby close to Ed's face, hoping he could smell Reggie's sweet infant scent and know that he needed to come back to them. She gently touched one of Ed's muscular forearms, the only part of him that *didn't* seem to be injured.

She heard a beeping sound, and a nurse came in almost immediately. Paige looked up. "Is everything okay?" she asked. "I hope I didn't disturb anything."

The nurse lowered Ed's leg slightly, glanced at the settings on the IV pump, and then did a head-to-toe sweep with her eyes. "Oh, no. His heart rate is just a little elevated. Don't worry—we're keeping an eye on it."

Paige nodded, staying out of the way. "His body looks a little more swollen than I remember from yesterday. Is that normal?"

"It *can* be—trauma usually triggers an inflammatory cascade. But we're watching it." Then she made a note in the electronic bedside chart and left the room to check on the patient next door.

Paige sat at Ed's bedside as Reggie slept on a while longer. But she knew he'd be waking up soon for another feed, and if he let out a squawk, she'd have to take him to the waiting area. Glancing at the clock on the wall, she hoped the doctor would be here before Reggie awoke. It was almost eleven-thirty, now.

The nurse stuck her head in the door. "You have a visitor, in the waiting room."

"Oh, that must be my sister." She gathered up her purse and the baby carrier and left the room. But it turned out to be Maggie in the waiting room, holding another wicker picnic basket.

"Hey, sweetie, how are you holding up? I brought you some food. Any update on Ed?"

"Oh, Maggie! Thanks for this. I'm waiting to speak to the doctor soon. He said eleven-thirty, and it's nearly that now. I'll know more after I speak to him, but Ed's nurse said there hasn't been much of a change since yesterday. He seems to be getting very good care—when an alarm goes off, they're in there in a flash to check on him."

"Is he breathing on his own yet?" Maggie asked.

"No, he's still intubated, and he hasn't regained consciousness," Paige said, shaking her head. "Ordinarily, that would worry me, but the doctor said they're keeping him heavily sedated."

"Maybe that's a good thing? I think his brain needs some down-time to heal. Anyway, Mariah helped me pack this up for you: blueberry muffins, orange juice, yogurt, some cookies and chips. Just a little something to tide you over. Feeding people is what I do," she said.

"That's so thoughtful, Maggie. Thank you, and please thank Mariah. With the baby, it's so much easier to just stay here than make the trek down to the hospital cafeteria," Paige said.

"The fancy stroller you had at the wedding is probably too big to be practical around the hospital. What if we got you a small portable stroller, one that you wouldn't have to break down and set up?" Maggie asked. "Would that be helpful?"

"I'm not sure," Paige said, her head feeling slightly muddled. *Keeping track of details and making decisions was challenging, when she was overwhelmed and sleep deprived.* "I might have asked Harper to take care of that, but I can't remember. She's on her way here, now."

"Oh, good, then you'll have some company. I can't stay long anyway—I have to get back to the diner. But I wanted to see how Ed was doing."

"I appreciate it so much, Maggie, and I know Ed would, too. But you go on home now. Harper said she'll be here by noon at the latest, and she'll watch Reggie for me. You can call me for an update, anytime. But right now, I don't know any more than I did last night."

"Okay, well, holler if you need anything, anything at all. We all care about you and Ed, and this little fellow," she said, smiling at Reggie's sleeping figure. "You can call me, too, anytime, for anything you need."

After Maggie left, Paige sat and ate a muffin, drank some juice, and ate half a bag of chips. Carbs were good when you were stressed, or at least they helped boost your blood sugar and serotonin, and she could probably use both. Reggie began to whimper and his little bottom lip quivered. Paige pulled him out of the carrier and positioned him. A nursing pro now, he latched on quickly. She leaned her head back and closed her eyes, as she savored a moment of peaceful relaxation. She opened them when she recognized the brisk footsteps of her sister. The familiar sound made her smile. "Hey, Harper, you made good time. I'm glad you're here—I'm supposed to meet with Ed's doctor soon."

"Well, I see you aren't going to starve to death. Maggie and I are going to have to start coordinating our trips," Harper said, taking a seat next to her sister and her multiplying pile of snack foods. "How's the little guy doing?"

"Fine. Doing his job, eating, and growing, and pooping up a storm."

"And how's the big guy doing?" Harper asked, in a softer voice.

"I'm not really sure. I was supposed to talk to the hospitalist at eleven-thirty, but I guess something more pressing came up. He has a *lot* of really sick people to take care of. Maggie arrived about that time, anyway, and I knew I'd have to nurse Reggie. So, it looks like we're still waiting."

Reggie finished nursing and Paige held him gently over her shoulder to burp him. Then she laid him in his baby carrier. As she straightened her clothing, a loud alarm went off, and she caught a surge of activity on the other side of the glass double doors. She watched as two staff wheeled a large red cart down the hallway and three more scrub-clad bodies rushed after it.

CHAPTER TWENTY-SIX

*P*aige stood at the double glass doors, watching the swarm of people surrounding Ed's room. *No, no, no. Not now.* "Can you watch Reggie? I've got to go see what's wrong."

"Sure. Go," Harper told her sister.

Paige pushed through the doors and stood outside the small room, trying to find out what was going on without getting in anyone's way. Through the large windows, she watched as they bared Ed's chest, exposing his ECG pads. Then a nurse splashed his skin with betadine, while another laid out a blue bundle, unwrapping the covering to reveal a shallow plastic tray full of instruments. Taking a long needle from the sterile tray, a doctor inserted it into Ed's chest. He attached a large syringe and pulled back on the plunger, and after ten agonizing seconds, the alarms quieted. A nurse carefully palpated the veins in Ed's neck and nodded her head in the affirmative. The other nurses began returning equipment to the red cart, adjusting Ed's IV rate, and checking his heart monitor.

The doctor pulled off his gloves and tossed them in the waste receptacle. When he noticed Paige standing there, her face no doubt reflecting terror, he said something to the nurse, and she reached a hand up to close the blinds.

"I'm so sorry you had to see that," he said after coming out to talk to her. "I know we'd planned to speak earlier, but then Mr. Barrett, Ed, took a turn for the worse. Why don't you follow me to my office, and we'll talk there?" Without waiting for an answer, he turned and strode down the hall, and Paige followed.

He led her into a small office, and Paige nervously took a seat across the desk. He smiled at her briefly. "I understand you're Mr. Barrett's significant other. I'm Dr. Finnegan, and I'll be supervising Ed's care while he's here in the trauma unit. I'm sure that was a disturbing scene to watch—but the team got to him in good time, and we took care of the problem.

"Ed experienced a serious complication called cardiac tamponade. The nurses reported his elevated heart rate and muffled heart sounds. Then his neck veins grew distended, which is a cardinal sign. If Ed had been conscious and breathing on his own, he'd likely have experienced shortness of breath and chest pain as well. Cardiac tamponade can happen following a blunt chest trauma like the kind Ed suffered, which causes fluid to collect around the heart. It's very serious—even life-threatening. But if you catch the condition early enough, it's treatable. As you saw, I withdrew a significant amount of fluid from the pericardial sac, and then Ed's heart rate began to decrease. Sorry, that's 'doctor speak.' There's a thin membrane that surrounds the heart, and when that cavity fills with fluid, it compresses the heart. Which means less blood can enter the chambers, and the heart has to work even harder. That's what we were seeing with Ed. But he seemed to respond well to the procedure, and we'll have him on one-to-one care for the next twenty-four hours, at least."

"Can this cardiac tamponade reoccur?" Paige asked.

"Yes, unfortunately. It's not uncommon with this kind of severe trauma. But, as Ed's body heals, he'll be less prone to it. And if we need to drain the fluid again, we will," the doctor said. "Now, one of the reasons I wanted to speak with you concerns next of kin. Ideally, since you and Mr. Barrett aren't married, we'll need them to be involved, and the sooner the better—he's not out of the woods, yet. So, have you been able to reach them?"

Paige nodded. "Yes, I've called his sister and left a message asking her to call me. His parents are elderly, and I don't know what state of health they're in. It seemed best that any news be delivered by another family member, rather than a stranger," she said. "If I don't hear back from her within the hour, I'll call again."

"Okay, good. Please let one of the nurses at the front desk know as soon as you make contact—and leave the family's phone number with them. Our social worker can reach out as well. And I'll make sure to call Ed's next of kin with an update," the doctor said.

"Thank you, doctor. I'll let you get back to work."

When Paige returned to the waiting room, Harper looked up expectantly. "Do you think Ed's going to be okay?" she asked.

"Harper, Ed is so far from okay it's not funny. He had some kind of serious event happen—cardiac tamponade, the doctor called it. They had to insert a needle to drain the fluid from around his heart, and now he's on one-to-one care. It's good that they're watching him so closely, but I'm really scared." With her head spinning, she needed to sit down before she ended up on the floor.

"I'm so sorry, Paige. I really hate to bother you at a time like this, but your cell phone rang. I thought it might be important since you've been trying to reach Ed's family. I didn't pick it up, though. I didn't want to add to the confusion."

Paige nodded. "Okay. Just let me catch my breath." She sipped on some juice that Maggie had brought, and after a moment, she picked up the phone and opened the screen. The call had been from Elizabeth DuBois. *Good. This was it—she couldn't back out now, or agonize over whether she'd made the right decision. It had to be done. Ed was critically injured, and he needed his family here with him.*

"Hello, Elizabeth? This is Paige Crawley, a friend of your brother's. Thank you for getting back to me so soon. I'm calling about Ed. I'm very sorry to tell you that he's been seriously injured in a car accident, just outside of Santa Fe. He's in the ICU at Cristus Saint Vincent, here, and the doctors need to speak to his next of kin as soon as possible. I thought it would be best to make contact with you, first. I really hope that was the right thing to do."

Oh, I'm so sorry to hear that! Thank you very much for calling, Paige. And, you're right: my father isn't in the best of health, and my mother would be terribly distraught. If I'll need to come to New Mexico, I'll need some time to make arrangements. I have two teenage daughters, and my husband travels frequently for work. But, please, give my number to whoever is in charge of Ed's care and ask them to call me, right away. I'd like to speak with them as soon as possible, Elizabeth said.

"Of course, I'll do that. I just finished speaking with the doctor in charge of Ed's case. His name is Dr. Finnegan, and he has promised to update you," Paige responded. "But I really think you should come."

I'll do my best. May I ask how you're connected to Ed? Elizabeth asked.

"I'm a good friend, and probably his closest connection in New Mexico, for a variety of reasons," Paige said. At a time like this, hedging seemed better than the alternative—it's complicated. A more in-depth explanation could certainly wait until she met Ed's sister face-to-face. "When do you think you'll be arriving?"

It'll have to be Monday afternoon at the earliest, Elizabeth said. *I'll see about flights and get back to you. And, please, call me Liza.*

"Is someone coming?" asked Harper.

Paige nodded. "Yes, I think so, but probably not until Monday afternoon. His sister Elizabeth, or Liza. I didn't tell her about Reggie. She has plenty to worry about already, and she's got the difficult task of telling her parents about Ed's accident. Her dad isn't in good health, apparently," Paige said, shaking her head. "I really wish Ed had made more of an effort to reconnect with his family, or, at least, his sister. You really need your family at a time like this, don't you?"

Harper reached over and squeezed her sister's hand. "You and Reggie *are* Ed's family. There isn't a piece of paper in the world that could change that."

"I don't want him to die, Harper. No matter what happens with *us*, I want Reggie to have a father. Ed loves Reggie *so* much," she said, holding back tears. "Look," she said. Lifting the oval locket out of her sweater neck, she opened it to reveal the two tiny photographs.

"Oh, my, goodness! Paige, when did Ed give this to you? And why haven't you shown it to me before?"

"He didn't get a chance to give it to me. I found it, accidentally, in his bag of personal effects. It was in a little box that had fallen to the bottom of the bag, along with his keys, which is what I was looking for. I'm not even sure I should be wearing it—but it makes me feel close to Ed."

"Well, I know he would *want* you to have it, and to wear it. No matter what," Harper said.

Too exhausted to speak, Paige could only nod.

"Is there anything else I can do for you while I'm in town? I packed up a few clothes, just the essentials, and most of your undies. They're in a suitcase in the truck."

Paige nodded again and cleared her throat. "Um, I can't remember if we talked about this, but I could really use a small portable stroller for Reggie—one that's the same brand as the car carrier, so I can just attach it when I take him out of the car. I don't know if you'll be able to find one in Santa Fe, or…"

"I'll look in town, first, and if I can't find one, I'll drive to Albuquerque. Either way, you'll have one by tonight. Don't worry about a thing. Ed will be fine. He's as strong, he's getting the best of care, and he's going to fight to come back to you and Reggie. I just know it."

Paige nodded, her tears finally spilling over. "Thanks."

Her sister gave her a quick hug and headed out the door. Looking at the pile of provisions around her, Paige realized she'd accumulated enough food in the last two days to feed the entire ICU staff, but she couldn't eat a bite. She'd see if she could put some of the baked goods in the staff's breakroom—they were taking such good care of Ed, and she didn't want Maggie's generosity, or Harper's, to go to waste.

After a little scavenger hunt via phone, Harper ended up driving to the outskirts of Albuquerque to a big-box store that carried the specific portable stroller Paige needed. She also stocked up on diapers, wipes, and emergency formula—and infant clothing, just in case she hadn't packed enough. Then she headed back up I-25 toward Santa Fe.

Whether or not Paige wanted company, Harper planned to spend the night in town. If Ed improved in the next few days, she'd think about heading home to the ranch—if not, she'd stay as long as she needed to.

She pulled into the scenic rest stop on the rise above Santa Fe to call her sister. "Paige, are you still at the hospital? Or, do you want to meet me back at Ed's house? I can help with Reggie while you lay down for a while, and I'm happy to bring dinner. Okay, see you in half an hour then."

She'd meet Paige at the house. In addition to bringing dinner, she would assemble the stroller and make sure the transfers from car to stroller worked smoothly. Paige didn't need any glitches in the system. Then, she'd bathe Reggie and take him off Paige's hands except for nursing.

Although he was still in critical condition, Ed gradually began to stabilize. Over the next twenty-four hours, he experienced no further incidents of cardiac tamponade, the bruises on his chest began to fade from blue-black, to purple, to greenish yellow, and the swelling in his leg began to decrease. His body was healing. He wasn't breathing on his own, yet, but the doctor said that Ed had shown some response to deep stimulation, which meant that he was still aware on some level.

To Paige, Ed appeared to remain unconscious. But the nurses took the time to explain to Paige that Ed would need to remain sedated while on the ventilator. Although they couldn't yet gauge his cognitive state, fully, his vital stats and neurological signs looked promising.

Liza called Paige with an update: she'd spoken with Dr. Finnegan at length about Ed's condition, and she planned to break the news to her parent's later today. Then, she'd fly directly into Santa Fe that afternoon, arriving shortly after two o'clock. She'd take a taxi to the hospital, and they planned to meet in the ICU waiting area around three.

Harper was staying in town, and she'd offered to stay at the house today and look after Reggie. Paige had pumped enough breast milk to last for two or three feedings; but after that, she'd have to run back to Ed's house to nurse her son.

She wore the locket again today, and in fact, only took it off to shower. *To her, it was priceless.* All thoughts of the ranch, their fledgling business, and the financial challenges she and Harper faced faded into the background. *Ed has to get well, Reggie has to stay well, and we'll all get through this, together.*

At three-fifteen, a tall, slender woman with shoulder-length auburn hair walked through the doors into the ICU waiting room. Paige recognized her from her photo, and stood up to greet her. But the woman strode right past her and straight to the reception desk.

She spoke to the nurse and was immediately escorted back through the inner doors to the ICU beds. *Well, that was that.* Paige sat back down and waited, idly flipping through a magazine called *Brain & Life*—extremely appropriate, given the tense and possibly life-changing circumstances Ed faced.

After forty-five minutes, the woman emerged from the double doors, spoke briefly with the receptionist, then turned and walked toward Paige. "Hello, I'm Liza Barrett DuBois, although I'm not much for formality. Call me Liza. You must be Paige, the woman who I spoke to on the phone. I very much appreciate you taking charge, but I'm here now, and I'll be staying as long as I'm needed. If you have other things to do, I'm happy to keep an eye on my brother."

Oh, boy. Now, 'it's complicated' was unavoidable. "It's nice to meet you, Liza. I'm so glad you were able to come, and I know your being here will mean a lot to Ed. But, if it's alright with you, I'm planning to stay close by. There's…a lot more to tell you. Would you like to grab a cup of coffee in the cafeteria, and maybe we can talk for a few minutes?" Paige asked.

"Sure, that sounds great. I could use a cup of coffee. I spoke at length with Dr. Finnegan, so I'm fairly caught up. But lead the way and I'll follow you," she said, with a tentative smile.

After going through the checkout line, the two women found a small table near the window.

"So," Paige began, "I guess I'll start with this. Your brother and I had a brief relationship last summer, and in March I gave birth to a baby boy. We named him after Ed and your father, but we call him Reggie."

"Wow! My brother and I really *have* been out of touch!" Her brown eyes reflected her surprise, but also, a hint of joy. "Well, Congratulations! Where is your son, now?" Liza asked. "I'd love to meet my new nephew."

"We've been staying with Ed in Santa Fe, part-time. He has a beautiful home, and I know you'll love it. It's not far from the hospital, so you'll be able to come and go easily. Here's a key for you," she said, laying the extra key she'd found on the table between them. "The guest bedroom is already made up and waiting for you. My sister, Harper, who is staying here with me for a few days, has filled the refrigerator and cupboards. So, we're all set."

"That's very thoughtful of you, Paige." Liza smiled, a slightly reserved look in her brown eyes, so like her brother's.

"My sister is watching the baby at the house. But I always carry him with me: Ed had this made for me," she said, opening the locket.

Liza took a long look and her gaze softened. "Oh, he's just beautiful, and I can't wait to meet him. The nurses mentioned that you've been here round-the-clock for days. That can't be easy, with a new baby. Why don't you go back to Ed's house and rest for a while? I promise to call you if anything changes. I'll catch an Uber there later this evening, and we can get better acquainted, then," she said, smiling.

Paige nodded. "Alright, thanks, I'll do that, and you can update me if there are any changes. I'll text you Ed's address right now, in case you don't have it handy." She looked up and met Liza's eyes. "There's one more thing. I think that *you* should have the contact information for Ed's attorney, Tom Price—he handles all of Ed's legal affairs. But…I have every hope that Ed will recover completely." She pushed the attorney's business card across the table to Liza.

Liza nodded in understanding. "Thank you, Paige. I'm sure I have Ed's home address written down somewhere, but it'll be better to have it right in my phone. Thanks again for taking care of my brother." She reached out to touch Paige's hand, briefly. "I'm very grateful."

"Of course. Ed is important to me. I hope he knows that. Oh, before I forget, I wanted to ask about your parents. How did they take the news?" Paige asked, as they left the cafeteria together.

A shadow crossed Liza's face. "It's been really difficult. In my father's eyes, Ed ceased to exist when he left the family business. It's *beyond* disinheriting, it's true estrangement. My mother still cares about Ed, of course—but she's been taking care of my father during his long illness, and that's been her priority. Dad was diagnosed with Parkinson's about four years ago, and unfortunately, his disease has progressed very quickly."

"I'm so sorry," Paige said. "That's such a tough situation."

"Thank you. It's not been easy for my mother, or for me," Liza said, quietly.

Paige found Harper in the kitchen, warming up some Italian food she'd picked up at Piccolino. As kids, back in Virginia, they'd eaten a lot of the familiar comfort food, which was economical for a single mother raising two growing girls, and it was still a mutual favorite. "Mm…that smells heavenly," Paige said.

Harper smiled. "Sit down and take a load off. Reggie is sleeping— I just gave him a bottle, but not *too* much. I figured you'd want to nurse him again before bedtime."

"Thanks, good call, and I appreciate it. Well, I met Liza—she showed up not long after you left. We talked, and I'm glad I called her, and I'm really happy she came. Ed needs his family here. I *shouldn't* be the one, and legally, I *can't* be the one, to make medical decisions for him."

"So, what's she like?" Harper asked, lifting a forkful of angel hair pomodoro.

"She's nice—maybe a little reserved. She has Ed's eyes." Paige smiled, touching her locket. "I showed her a picture of Reggie, and she wants to meet him. By the way, Liza will be staying here with us tonight, and for the foreseeable future. I want to make sure we clean up the kitchen after dinner. You know, it feels a little strange to be playing hostess when this isn't even my house. I know Ed wouldn't mind us being here, but some people might think I'm overstepping. Honestly, I've questioned that, myself. And I don't really know *what* Liza will think."

"Well, what anyone, including Liza, thinks, is out of your control. If I were Ed's sister, I'd be glad that Ed has someone who loves him and cares enough about him to track down his family," Harper said.

"Let's hope so. Gosh, I am wiped out. If you don't mind taking care of the kitchen, I'll open Liza's room up, crack the windows, and turn on the lights. Then I'm going to shower and nurse and sleep for as long as Reggie will let me. Ed seems to be out of the woods now, but it was touch and go there for a while. My body doesn't always handle stress well—at least not *this* level of stress."

"Good, you do that. I'll keep an eye on Reggie, and if Ed's sister arrives, I promise I'll make her feel welcome."

"Thanks," Paige said, giving her sister a little wave before heading up the stairs. She would have given her a hug, but she was afraid that if she did, she wouldn't be able to let go. She'd reached the very end of her reserves.

CHAPTER TWENTY-SEVEN

*L*iza Barrett DuBois drove up to the large Craftsman house and pulled into the wide driveway, parking next to an old truck that had seen better days. *So, this was where Ed had been all these years—not hiding, but building a life I know nothing about,* she thought. She hoped he was happy, but she was a bit taken aback by how little she knew about him. At least he apparently had someone to share his life with. On her first impression, she'd genuinely liked Paige Crawley, and she couldn't wait to meet her infant nephew.

She knocked on the door, and when no one answered, she used her key, stepped into her brother's house, and stood for a moment in the foyer. She heard the distant cry of an infant and the faint sound of running water. Then the baby's cry stopped. She heard muffled footsteps as a young woman wearing faded jeans, a Seahawks sweatshirt, and wool socks descended the wide oak steps.

"Hello, you must be Liza. I'm Harper, Paige's sister, and *this* little fellow is Reggie. He just woke up and he told me, very vocally, that he's hungry." She jiggled the baby a little as he started to fuss, and he quieted. "Paige is in the shower, and she'll be heading to bed with this guy in a few minutes. But I'll be happy to show you to your room. Do you need any help with your suitcases?"

"It's nice to meet you, Harper, and you too, Reggie," Liza said, smiling at the baby. "I can manage, I just have this small carry-on. Lead the way."

"Ed's room is at the end of the hall. Paige and I have the two rooms across from each other, adjacent to the master. And she set this room up for you," Harper said, opening the door to a very nice en suite. "It's on the smaller size, but we thought you'd want your own bathroom. My sister and I are used to sharing. And when you wake up in the morning, you'll see a terrific view of the mountains. The aspens are just starting to turn green."

"Thank you. This all looks very comfortable." She noted the authentic Craftsman details around the windows, and the vintage tiles in the small but well-designed bathroom. The earthy historic colors were well-chosen, and the house suited her brother, or what she remembered of him. She looked at her infant nephew in Paige's sister's arms. His *other* aunt. But *she* was his aunt, too, and she loved babies. "Mind if I have a hold?" Liza asked. "I think I need to get to know my nephew."

"Oh, of course! I'll warn you, he's a solid little chunk. He was just over eleven pounds at birth, and he's a lot heavier than he looks." Harper handed him over, and Liza took him with practiced arms, balancing him over her shoulder. He settled right down, grabbing a chubby fist of her auburn hair in one hand, and popping his other fist into his mouth.

"He's adorable. And I remember that sweet baby scent from my daughters." It captivated her instantly and tugged on her heartstrings. "Would you do me a favor? Can you take a picture of me holding

Reggie? It might come in handy when I have to break the news to my mom and dad that they're grandparents again. At least, my dad has always been vocal about wanting a grandson." She handed her phone to Harper.

"Absolutely!" She snapped a few photos and handed the phone back. "Are you okay holding him while I grab my cell phone, too? It's in my bedroom. I want to take one for Paige, too. She's putting a baby book together for Reggie, and I know she'll want to include you."

"Absolutely. This guy's not going anywhere," Liza said, gently patting his well-padded bottom. Harper was right. *What a solid little chunk!*

Twenty minutes later, when the shower had long stopped running and Paige still hadn't emerged, Harper knocked on her door and opened it. Paige lay face down on the bed, sound asleep, wrapped only in a thick bath towel.

"Paige? Hey, I hate to wake you up, but I know you'll want to give Reggie another feed before you both go down for the night. He's hungry, but if I give him a full bottle, you'll wake up sore in the morning."

"Mm…you're right. But, Harper, I don't think I can move. Can you bring him to me? And can you grab me something to put on? I thought I'd lay down for a minute or two, and I fell asleep."

"Here, try this," Harper said, tossing Paige an oversized t-shirt that was hanging over the back of a chair. It looked like it had recently belonged to Ed. "Liza's here. She's with Reggie now, but I'll go get him, change him, and bring him to you. Do you want his fleece sleeper on him?"

"No, the terrycloth one will do. Reggie's a little heat factory—he'll be fine. Thanks, Harper. I'm really glad you're here," Paige said, in a sleepy voice. "Especially tonight. I thought I was holding myself together, but everything caught up to me all at once, I guess. I'm so glad there are some other adults in the house, because I'm not coping very well."

"I get it. You just take it easy tonight. Liza and I've got this. Get some rest."

Harper returned to Liza's guest room, where she was sitting on the bed, still holding Reggie. "Hey, I need to change this boy and bring him to Paige. She's exhausted, but she still needs to nurse him tonight before bed."

Liza nodded. "I remember those days. I can't imagine managing a newborn, while dealing with a good friend in critical condition. With that much stress, it's no wonder she's out on her feet!" She handed Reggie over, a little reluctantly. "Please, let me know how I can help. Not just with Ed, but with my nephew, too. That's why I'm here—to help."

Harper didn't know exactly what she'd expected from Ed's family, who were apparently the cream of San Francisco Bay Area society, but this wasn't it. Liza seemed to be a very pleasant surprise. Harper was a little relieved—and happy that Paige would have someone pleasant to interact with, instead of unnecessary family drama.

"Come with me," she invited, with a smile. "I'll show you the room they've set up as Reggie's nursery. It's darling. "And while I get him ready for bed, you can tell me more about your family."

⁎

"Oh, this is so cute!" Liza said when she entered the nursery. With Paige's help, they'd painted the walls a soft-green, and installed a crib-level border of desert creatures. The colors were very Santa Fe, but the design was more universal and gender neutral. The sturdy crib was made in a style that fitted the Craftsman house, and outfitted with soft, neutral bedding.

"Yeah, I like it, too. My sister has a real knack for decorating. We've worked together to rehab the Inn we inherited, and it's been a labor of love. Now, tell me about *your* family. Do you have any children?" she asked.

"Yes, I have two daughters, with my husband, Jean-Paul. They're thirteen and coming up on fifteen. We're a close-knit family—and the girls are each other's best friends, for now. We'll see how they deal with each other in a few years. I hear sixteen is the magic number when teenage chaos arrives."

"And your parents? Are they close to your girls?" she asked, butting her nose in where it didn't belong.

"Oh, my mother dotes on the girls, and they love her, too. I think my father would have preferred boys, especially since, well, the situation with Ed hasn't been good for quite a few years. But you get what you get," she said, throwing up her hands. "I'm very happy with Chloe and Halley, and *their* father adores them."

Harper deftly fastened the tabs on Reggie's new diaper and picked him up. He was really going after his fist now, a sign that he'd soon erupt in an ear-splitting cry.

"I'm so glad. My former husband and I didn't have any children together. But I recently married a wonderful man who has a five-year-old daughter. Her mother is in the picture, too, and we all share custody of Ellie. I really love the time we get to spend together. Well, I'd better get this baby to his mama. Would you care for a cup of tea before bed, or are you ready to turn in for the night?"

"Thank you, Harper, but I think I'd better turn in. I want to call and check on my girls, and then I'll shower and get ready for bed. But I'll be up bright and early. I'd like to talk to Paige about setting up a schedule. There's no need for both of us to be at the hospital—I think we should alternate. And I have a feeling Paige could probably use at least one day off to catch up on her rest. But we can talk again in the morning. Thank you for everything. Good night, then." And Liza leaned in to kiss Reggie's cheek. "Sleep well, my darling boy."

"Wow, do I feel better!" said Paige, coming into the kitchen the next morning. Harper and Liza were seated at the breakfast table drinking coffee. She looked at Reggie's two competent aunties and made a spontaneous decision. Approaching them with a cheerful, recently fed, and freshly changed Reggie, she held him out. "Who wants him? I'm going to make myself some breakfast."

Both aunties reached out, but Harper deferred to Liza, who was just getting to know her nephew. "It's your turn. I've had plenty of time with Reggie," Harper said.

"Thanks, Harper. Come here, you. How's my fella doing this morning," Liza asked, in an engaging, high-pitched voice. "Did you have a good night's sleep?" He gurgled something that might have indicated a positive response.

"Can I help you, Paige?" Harper asked. "Caleb swears my cooking's getting better."

"Thanks, but I've got it. I was thinking…if you need to get back to the ranch, Harper, that's fine with me. Liza and I can probably handle things here," she said, smiling at Ed's sister, "and I'll call you with updates on Ed." What a relief that Liza, although a bit reserved, wasn't difficult or unreasonably territorial about her brother. Paige's general impression from the beginning was *I can work with her.*

"Absolutely. I'm here to help—and getting to know Reggie is a wonderful surprise. Speaking of helping, Harper and I think *you* need a day off, Paige. Let me spend the day with Ed, and you can hang out with your baby and get some rest. I promise to call you if anything changes—and then, tomorrow, we can set up an alternating schedule for hospital visits. How does that sound?"

"That sounds really good, actually. I trust you to let me know how Ed's doing—and I think I *do* need a day to rest, and maybe, rehydrate a bit. My milk supply is a little down, and I don't want to mess things up. Nursing has been going pretty well, so far."

"Paige, don't forget, you have a postpartum check-up soon, too, don't you?" Harper said, carrying her breakfast things to the sink.

"Yeah, on Thursday, I think. I promise, I'll check on that today."

"Okay, then, I'm off to the ranch," Harper said, with a hug for her sister and a kiss the baby. "It was nice to meet you, Liza. Hopefully we'll meet again."

CHAPTER TWENTY-EIGHT

$\mathcal{T}$wo full weeks after Ed's accident, his vital signs continued to stabilize. There had been no further reoccurrence of cardiac tamponade, and he'd become increasingly responsive to stimulation, two of the signs the doctors had been waiting for. As next of kin, Liza had signed a release of information allowing Paige to be included in Ed's care. In a conference with both of them, the doctor explained that it was time to consider weaning Ed off the ventilator. If the process went well, he might be extubated as early as the weekend—and that was one step closer toward getting him home. Paige had some thoughts about that.

"How long will the weaning process take?" Liza asked Dr. Finnegan.

"It depends on how Ed responds. We'll try him intermittently off oxygen for a few hours while we monitor his levels. It's a gradual process. But if the weaning process goes well, we hope Ed can come off oxygen completely by Monday, at the latest."

"And then?" Paige asked.

"Depending on his level of consciousness and his ability to participate, we can begin speech therapy, occupational therapy, and physical therapy. With the femur fracture, he'll be off that leg for a while, but after he's able to regain some strength with PT, we can eventually begin working on his transfers. Getting him out of bed is really important for his cardiovascular and respiratory systems—but also for his state of mind. A patient like Ed, who's been through a major trauma, needs to *believe* he can fully recover. Since he's been sedated, we haven't been able to gauge his cognitive state very thoroughly, so please, try not to have high expectations. We're all going to have to be patient with Ed as he begins the rehabilitation process."

Paige nodded, even though the doctor's sense of caution wasn't very comforting, but she'd do everything in her power to help. Unfortunately, Ed's sister couldn't stay in Santa Fe indefinitely—she had a family to look after and elderly parents who needed her. But Paige had been mulling over an idea: she wanted to bring Ed to the ranch, where they'd both have plenty of help and support, including Harper, Caleb, and even Maggie. She hoped Ed would agree to her plan, but if he wasn't able to, she'd need to convince *Liza* that her plan was in Ed's best interest. And Paige was *sure* it was.

"Do you have any idea when Ed might be able to leave the hospital?" Paige asked.

"I really can't say with any certainty at this point," Dr. Finnegan said. "We'll know more after he's been successfully extubated and he's no longer sedated."

"Thank you, that helps," said Paige.

She and Liza had been alternating shifts, and so far, that seemed to be working well—but Ed's sister would have to return to her family soon. Liza had mentioned that, ideally, she wanted to be back in Palo Alto for her daughter Chloe's fifteenth birthday, only a week away. They both had their fingers crossed that Ed could be weaned off the ventilator successfully, and be breathing on his own by the end of the weekend. After that, she hoped that Liza would agree that Ed could come back to the ranch to recuperate. It was the most logical solution she could come up with—so she'd do whatever she had to do to make sure it feasible.

"Liza, let's go grab a cup of coffee. There's something I want to run by you," Paige said.

"Alright, I could use a cup," Liza agreed. "That was a lot of information, all at once. I need a minute to take it all in."

They got their coffee, decaf for Paige, and found a booth on the sunny side of the cafeteria. She was on a mission, and soon, if her plan worked out, she'd be back in Verde Springs. She hadn't been living at the ranch for a full year yet, but already, she missed it so much after only a few weeks away. More importantly, she wanted Ed to have as much support as possible—and she thought she'd come up with a way to make that possible.

"So, about what the doctors said. It's possible that Ed might be able to leave the hospital in a week or two—and I think the best place for him to recuperate is at the ranch."

At Liza's skeptical expression, Paige said, "Please, let me explain. I want Ed to be surrounded by people who love him and care about him. Our ranch in Verde Springs is a beautiful, healing place, and it's already set up as an inn, with many comfortable bedrooms—including a guest room for you, for as long as you'd like to stay with us. My sister lives there, too, with her husband Caleb. I'll be there with Reggie. Ed's good friend Maggie, who runs the local café in town, will help out, too. They're good friends, and she's known Ed longer than almost anybody in New Mexico. I know she'd love to spend more time with him. Liza,

I promise, he'd have someone with him, around the clock. And if any of his Renaissance group friends wanted to come up and visit, they'd be welcome to stay for the weekend in The Coops—we've made them into live/work spaces that we've set up as small studios."

"But what about his therapies?" Liza asked. "Giving Ed the best chance of recovery is what's most important right now."

"I completely agree. I've spoken to the discharge planner earlier, and she assures me she'll be able to arrange for all of Ed's rehabilitation services to be done at the ranch. Christus St. Vincent's has a strong home-health program, and I've already checked with the home-health coordinator. The ranch's location is well within their service radius for nursing care, as well as the therapies Ed will need. And if we have to bring him into town for specific appointments or procedures, we'll have plenty of help to get him here."

"But I don't plan to leave *you* responsible for everything, Paige. Of course, I'd hire professionals, home-care nurses, private care coordinators, whatever Ed needs," Liza said. "Money is no object. I can tap into the family trust, if I have to."

"I appreciate that, and, of course, we'll need to work together on the plan for Ed's rehab. But wouldn't it be best for him to be surrounded by all of the familiar people in his life? Maybe it would even help reorient him.

"My priority these last few weeks has been to be here in Santa Fe, because I wanted to be here with Ed. But the truth is, I can't abandon my business at the ranch forever, and it would be great to have some back-up to help with Reggie. You've been such a great help, Liza, and I really appreciate everything you've done since coming out here—and I know Ed will too. But after you return to Palo Alto, I won't be able to manage here on my own for much longer. I'm sorry, Liza, I just won't." That was putting it mildly—she was approaching emotional and physical exhaustion.

"So, what do you want me to do? Just agree to your plan right off the bat?" Liza asked, her voice tense. "What if it's *not* the right place for my brother? What if this plan is a disaster and it undermines his recovery—and I'm a thousand miles away?"

"I'd *never* suggest anything that might harm Ed—and I'm not expecting you to automatically agree to my plan. What I *would* love is for you to come out and see the set-up for yourself. Please, be our guest at the Inn for a few days. At least, give this idea a chance?" Paige asked. "If being at the ranch makes things *harder* for Ed, we'd change course immediately. And if that happened, I'd make the commitment to stay here at the house in Santa Fe, full time, until Ed has fully recovered—even if it meant I had to hire help. He's Reggie's father, and I really care about him."

After a long moment, Liza said, "I'll consider everything you've suggested—and I'll let you know what I decide. Let's see how Ed does when they try to wean him off the vent. So, when were you planning to leave Santa Fe and head home?"

Paige wanted to continue to be there for Ed, but she thought that the ranch was the best place for Ed to heal—and if her plan was going to work, she'd need a few days to get the house ready for him. "If it's all right with you, I'd like to head straight back to the house to pack up, and then head to the ranch for a few days. I'll come back here for the weekend, though. I want to be here as they wean him off sedation." [did she do this – make the following scenes agree]

Liza nodded. "Yes, of course it is. Take all the time you need. And I'll let you know if there are any changes in Ed's condition."

Liza went to sit with Ed, and Paige returned to the house. She'd left Reggie with Meghan, the lovely young lady she'd met in the bridal shop a few chaotic months ago. Since Harper had returned to the ranch, Meghan been invaluable in helping with the baby's care, often on short notice. Paige owed her a huge debt, beyond paying her a fair wage. When life settled down—whenever that might be—she planned to invite Meghan and a guest to stay at one of the Inn's Coop Studios for a long weekend, complete with a daily gourmet breakfast.

As she packed, Paige felt a welcome lightness in her step, just thinking of returning to her own comfortable room in the old ranch house, surrounded by the companionship of her sister, Caleb, and the friendly folks at Maggie's. She'd even missed the Inn's beautiful spring gardens. Paige realized, suddenly, how *lonely* she'd been in Santa Fe, where she didn't know a soul. After her arrival, Liza had really stepped up, but because of their alternating schedules, they'd rarely had a chance to spend much time together. As much as Paige admired Ed's house and appreciated his impeccable sense of taste, it *wasn't* home, especially when he wasn't there with her. She missed their conversations. She missed watching all of Ed's tender moments with their baby. She missed *him*. But right now, she needed support, and a few days back with the people who loved her would give her that.

As Paige drove into Verde Springs, the stress she'd been under, for weeks, began to fall away almost like a physical weight. She took a few deep breaths of fresh spring air and tried to let it all go. The trees around the town square had finished budding out, and the earlier daffodils and tulips in the flower beds had been replaced by irises in jewel-like colors. All around the square, hedges of lilacs swollen with dark-purple buds waited for the first, truly warm sunny day. As Paige eased Ethel into an empty parking space across from Maggie's, she realized that April had already turned the corner into May.

As she stepped into the comfort of Maggie's, she inhaled the familiar scents of home. "Paige, it's so good to see you!" Mariah said, coming around the counter to wrap her in a warm hug. "And this little guy is getting *so* big. Ed must be doing better, then?" she asked, a note of hope in her voice.

"Yes, he's really progressing! If they're able to wean Ed off the ventilator, and he can breathe on his own, he might be able to leave the hospital soon. I'm hoping to bring him back here, to recover at the ranch."

Overhearing the conversation, Maggie came to join them, resting her forearms on the counter. "I'd be in favor of that, and I'll volunteer to help out as much as I can. Be sure to let us know the details, Paige, and bring Reggie in again soon. I've really missed seeing him—babies change so quickly at this age. And how're you doing, honey?"

"I'm okay. But it's been…a lot. It'll be good to be back home for a few days," Paige said. "To tell you the truth, I really need it. I wanted to thank both of you for all your support. And now, I want to surprise Harper and Caleb with some baked goods, so load me up with brownies, and chocolate chip cookies, and some of that delicious chocolate marble cheesecake my sister is addicted to. Then, I'd better get this guy home to the ranch. Reggie doesn't like being in this car seat for very long."

"You got it, hon. And, Mariah? It's all on the house," said Maggie. "Call it a welcome home present. I'd better get back to the kitchen— we're in the middle of dinner prep."

Mariah accompanied her to the car, carrying pastry boxes and Maggie's to-go bags. Paige fastened Reggie's car seat into the back, and smiled at Mariah. "Thanks so much for this. It helps to have another pair of hands. I'm hoping I'm back for good. So, I'll probably see you soon."

Paige got back in the SUV for the last leg of the trip—nine more miles of winding country roads. *She was almost home.*

Finally, she drove up the ranch's gravel drive between rows of winter-weary lavender just beginning to perk up in the warmer weather. Paige stopped the car for a minute to take a long look at the beautiful, tranquil home she and her sister had created—the place where Ed would heal and become whole again. In the past chaotic year, so full of twists and turns no one could have anticipated, she hadn't only fallen in love with Ed—she'd fallen in love with New Mexico, an unexpected place of renewal and second chances for both she and her sister.

Harper came running out the front door when she heard Paige pulling in. She wrapped her up in a bear hug and said the words Paige most wanted to hear: "Welcome home!"

CHAPTER TWENTY-NINE

"*R*ise and shine, sweetie. I've brought you a welcome home breakfast in bed." Paige heard Harper's knock on the door, seconds before she opened it. "Caleb made everything, so I promise it's good."

"Oh, thanks," said Paige, sitting up, yawning. "This is so nice of you! I woke up earlier to feed Reggie, then I must have fallen back asleep. But I'm glad you woke me—I have a lot to do in a short amount of time. As soon as Ed's off the ventilator and breathing on his own, Liza's going to come check out the set-up, here, and everything has to be ready."

"Well, you won't have to do it alone. Caleb has some work in town this morning, but he promised he'd be back by one-thirty, and he's cleared the afternoon to help you with whatever you need. I'm here, too, and I can help with Reggie, move furniture, or make phone calls—whatever you need me to do, just say the word."

Paige smiled at her sister. "Thanks, Harper. Maybe we can get started right after breakfast? I hope Reggie will have a nice, quiet day—I'm going to need all the free time I can get."

"Hey, I'll *wear* Reggie if I have to. I may not have the desired equipment, but I can keep him temporarily entertained."

"I appreciate it, and I know Ed would, too." Paige said, just before a terrible thought took hold: *what if his head trauma was worse than they expected? What if he didn't remember her, or their last conversation, or why he'd been driving to Verde Spring in the first place, that terrible night? Then, he'd be stuck in a strange place with people he didn't remember, instead of the comfort of his familiar home in Santa Fe. Suddenly, Liza's caution made a lot of sense...*

"What's the matter, Paige? Why do you have that look on your face? Tell me right now," Harper demanded. "You were just fine a minute ago."

"We don't know where Ed is, cognitively. What if he doesn't even recognize me? What if he doesn't even remember Reggie? Lots of people develop periods of amnesia after a serious head trauma like Ed had."

Her sister was momentarily speechless, as she sat on the edge of the bed. "Well...um, I guess we're all operating on a little faith, here, but you can only do what you can do. If Ed's in Santa Fe, you can't be *here*—and *here* is where you need to be right now. The care Ed will get here at the ranch will be no less than he'd get in Santa Fe—the difference is that he'll be surrounded by people who know him and love him. And you and Reggie will have the support *you* need, too. We can do this, Paige."

She nodded. "You're right. We can only try our best, and hope Liza will go along with it. *None* of us can predict what shape Ed will be in when he wakes up—they're still keeping him sedated while he's on the vent.

"Okay, I've made a list: extra-long hospital bed; bedside commode; stand-up pole; ambulance transport; visiting nurse, which the hospital will arrange; and all of Ed's various therapies. We won't even know how intensive they'll need to be until he's off the vent. We *also* don't know how much longer they're going to want to keep him in the hospital after he wakes up. It could be a few more days, or a week, or more..."

"Okay, then, we'll just do our best to get everything ready for him. First off, where are we going to put him?" Harper asked.

Paige nodded her head. "I've thought it all out: our living room is the only real option until he's mobile enough to handle the stairs. But I think it will be perfect. We can dedicate the downstairs bathroom to Ed, and he'll be close enough to wheel out to the breakfast room and the patio, as soon as it's warm enough. We can close the doors for privacy and when Ed wants to rest," Paige said.

"Okay. If you start making calls, I'll go tidy up downstairs and maybe start moving some furniture around. Which way do you want his bed to face?" Harper asked.

"I'd like it to face the garden, if possible. Looking at green plants is healing—I read that in one of the magazines in the hospital. But we'll need to move the sectional out of the way."

"No worries. I've got it. Go on and order Ed the biggest, baddest hospital bed you can find. We're on a mission now."

After a productive five days, Paige returned to Santa Fe. And on Friday, Paige and Liza met at the hospital, where the respiratory therapists on Ed's team began the weaning process. Two hours off the vent, two hours on; then two hours off, one hour on; then three hours off, one hour on. They slowly increased Ed's time off the vent as the day progressed, and by evening, he was breathing on his own, with supplemental oxygen by mask. He was still mildly sedated but he was responding to some simple commands. His doctors were pleased, and Paige and Liza were very optimistic.

Saturday followed a similar routine, gradually weaning Ed off sedation. On Sunday, they worked on transitioning him from the oxygen mask to a simpler nasal cannula. By Monday, Ed was breathing *entirely* on his own, on room air, and his oxygen saturation was in the normal range, even on mild sedation. He'd had a remarkable turnaround, and Paige and Liza were finally able to feel some relief. Ed could still use oxygen by nasal cannula at night, when his oxygenation levels tended to dip, for as long as he needed it. Paige added another item to her list: she'd need to arrange home oxygen delivery.

Tuesday morning, Paige left Reggie at Ed's Santa Fe house with his sitter, Meghan. She wore the locket around her neck and dressed carefully in an outfit she knew Ed had seen her wear before. And she kept her shoulder-length, light, brown hair loose, wanting to look as familiar to him as possible.

She hadn't spent any time alone with Ed since he'd been completely weaned off sedation, which Dr. Finnegan had said occurred sometime late Monday evening, just as he was finishing his rounds. So, this was showtime.

Now that Ed was breathing on his own, he'd been moved to a telemetry step-down room in a unit immediately adjacent to the ICU. He was resting with his eyes closed and his casted leg propped up on a single pillow. *No tubes—no ventilator pumping eerily in and out.* Paige was incredibly grateful to see how very far he had come.

She took a deep breath and entered the quiet room. Approaching the bed, she sat in the adjacent chair and said softly: "Good morning, Ed, it's me." Then she kept her eyes on his face, ever so closely, watching for his reaction.

He opened his eyes and turned his head to look at her. "Paige," was all he said. Then, he cleared his gravelly throat. "Reggie?" he asked.

And all of the pieces in Paige's world began to shift miraculously into place.

"He's fine," she said, quickly reaching for a bedside tissue. "He's getting *so* big, and he really misses his daddy. And I have missed you *so* much," she said, as her tears rolled freely down her cheeks. *Ed had come back to them.*

His voice was still hoarse from being intubated for so many weeks, and he didn't say anything more. But he slowly moved his hand toward the edge of the bed. *Toward her.* She slipped her hand into his, and it was just as warm and comforting as she remembered. He squeezed her hand, and the faintest smile formed on his chapped lips.

And on hers. "Ed, you're going to completely recover from this—I know you will. I'd like to take you back to the ranch and take care of you. You'll see Reggie every day, and Caleb and Harper and Maggie will all help. Is that what *you* want?"

He nodded. "It's perfect," he said, almost in a whisper, but she heard him loud and clear.

The following week, Liza travelled out to the ranch and stayed several nights with them. They'd given her the royal treatment, and after looking over the set-up, she'd agreed that the ground floor room they'd outfitted for Ed would work beautifully. The discharge planner from Christus St. Vincent's had arranged for all of Ed's therapies to continue at the ranch—and they planned to follow up with Dr. Finnegan again in two weeks, in person, at the hospital's outpatient therapy unit.

After seeing Ed through his ordeal and welcoming him back to the land of the living, Liza had flown back to the Bay Area yesterday afternoon, promising that she'd keep in close touch with her brother and with Paige. Later this summer, when her daughters were out of school, they planned to bring the whole DuBois family out for a long visit.

And today, Ed was coming home.

Paige dressed carefully in a rust-colored linen sheath dress and fastened the locket Ed had intended for her around her neck. She wore simple ballet flats and gathered her wavy, shoulder-length hair into a beaded barrette. Wearing slender turquoise earrings for strength and protection, she was as ready as she could be. The gem's energy was one of quiet stillness, yet it held the power of healing, regeneration, and rebirth. And somehow, wearing the beautiful blue-green stones made her feel calm.

Paige had tried to make sure everything was in place and welcoming for Ed's return, and she'd tweaked Reggie's schedule so that he was fed, changed, and in the most mellow mood possible. *But, of course, three-month-old-babies aren't the most reliable.*

Harper popped her head in, buzzing with anticipation: "Do you have everything ready to go? Are you excited? Is there anything I can do?"

Paige shook her head. "Everything's as perfect as we could make it. Thanks for all of the pretty flowers in here. They're a really nice touch, especially since Ed missed almost the entire spring while he was in the hospital. The views out the windows are so beautiful right now. I really hope he loves it here." Hearing the crunch of tires on gravel, she glanced at her sister. "Well, this is it. Wish me luck?"

"You don't need it—you've got this."

Paige walked out to meet the van and waited until the attendants brought Ed out on a stretcher. But then, Ed held up his hand and said something: *he didn't want to be carried into the house.* One of the attendants came back with a wheelchair with an extended leg rest—then the attendants transferred him to the chair and he wheeled himself up the path. Ed smiled up at her, his warm brown eyes full of light, and she met him with a pretty big smile of her own.

"Hey, you. You're looking good! And we're *so* glad you're here," Paige said, leaning in to kiss him on the cheek.

"I'm glad...to be here. Thanks for doing this, Paige. It's...above and beyond," he said.

It was amazing how much Ed's speech had improved over the past week. The gruffness in his voice from his long intubation was nearly gone. And he could put words together just fine, even if took a little longer than it had before his accident. In many ways, he was still healing.

"Well, here it is. You're in the living room, for now, with a view of Harper's gardens, and right next to the breakfast room and the patio. Pretty soon, you'll be getting around here in your wheelchair, and one day very soon, you'll be walking again."

"I'm looking forward to that," Ed said, grinning. "But there's something else I'm looking forward to, even more. After I get settled in that bed, can I see Reggie?"

"Of course, you can! Harper is with him now, up in the nursery. She's just waiting for you to get settled, and she'll bring him down."

"Okay, guys, let's go for it," Ed said. The attendants helped him transfer to the bed, and they stowed the wheelchair in the far corner of the large, airy room.

Paige called up the stairs, and Harper came down holding a much bigger baby than he remembered. He was startled to see how much his son had grown in the six weeks since his accident. Harper handed Reggie off to Paige, who brought him to the bed and laid the baby in his arms. Reggie looked up at him, blinking big, slate-blue eyes that would someday veer toward his own brown, or his mother's gorgeous green. Reggie reached up and touched his face, which was a little stubbly. "Hey, baby boy—do you remember your daddy?" he asked, softly.

Reggie emitted a series of long squeals and squeaks that sounded like the song of a humpback whale, and Ed laughed. "Oh, this feels good. This feels incredibly good. I've missed this. Thank you, Paige. Come sit beside us," he said. "Harper, can you come over here, too?"

"Sure. Welcome home, Ed. I'm really glad you're here," Harper said.

"And I'm happy to be here. Hey…could you take…a picture…of the three of us? Ed asked, haltingly.

"It would be my pleasure," Harper said. She snapped a quick series of photos on her cell phone. Then she slipped quietly out of the room and closed the double doors.

"Paige, can you come around the other side of the bed and sit with me? I want all of us to be together for a few minutes—I've waited a long time for this."

He patted the bed gently and tried not to attach too much weight to the outcome. The next step would be up to this remarkable woman, who'd stood by him throughout his entire recovery. He'd heard it from Dr. Finnegan, from every nurse who'd cared for him, and even from his own sister. And, even though he'd been unable to respond, *he* remembered her being there, too: her voice, her scent, and her quiet, comforting presence in the room with him, for all those weeks.

Paige smiled and sat on the edge of the bed, removed her flats, and swung her legs up to join his. When she turned on her side and rested her head on his shoulder, he put his arm around her and pulled her close. He inhaled the sweet, floral scent he'd always found captivating. The three of them together filled his heart with all the love he never thought he'd find. But he felt it now, and he would never let it go. All of the missteps of the past were behind them now, and everything would work out just fine.

CHAPTER THIRTY

*W*arm July weather brought sunflowers reaching toward the sky. Rosy hollyhocks bloomed against the Inn's golden-hued adobe walls, and banks of snowy shrub roses were in full flower. A month of healing and recovery for Ed had gone by quickly, and after a year that felt much like the 400-meter hurdles at the Summer Olympics, maybe life was finally settling down.

A small crowd had gathered on the shady patio on a warm, early summer evening to celebrate Ed's remarkable recovery. Now able to walk, with the help of a dapper cane, he sat on a wicker chair with his leg up on a hassock. Baby Reggie lay on a striped blanket for tummy time, stretching his legs out, kicking vigorously, and emitting the occasional squeal. Harper and Caleb shared the wicker loveseat, with Ellie snuggled in between them. Birdy and Sunny were there too, sleeping in a shady spot in the garden, content with their life of freedom on the ranch. Maggie dished out chicken enchiladas and green salad, and full plates made the rounds.

Paige looked around at the loving family that she and Harper had miraculously found in such a short time, barely over a year. Something magical had surely happened here, for all of them. *Maybe Aunt Sabina had had a word with the powers that be.* Nothing was beyond belief in The Land of Enchantment. Whenever she managed to have a private word with *La Virgen de Guadalupe,* now watching over them benevolently from her *nicho* above the Inn's front doors, she'd have a lot of thanking to do.

Ed reached out and squeezed her hand. "Paige, why don't you pull up a chair and sit by me?" he asked.

"Okay, I will." The two of them had done a *lot* of talking and a *lot* of smooching and a *lot* of sharing their dreams. He finally understood how much she loved him—not only for the present moment, but for the long haul. *Whatever joys and troubles came their way, they'd get through them together.* No more secrets or hesitation for either of them, and that *surely* qualified as a miracle. In the past few weeks, they had become true partners, something both of them vowed to never take for granted. Reciprocity, mutual trust, and a deep love had built a strong bond that he hoped would last a lifetime.

Ed tapped his iced tea glass with a fork. "Hey, guys. I have something I want to say. First, thank you all so much for helping me get to this point. I couldn't have made it this far without every single one of you—but especially one particular person," he said, looking into her eyes. "Paige, I love that you always wear this locket around your neck," he said, reaching out to touch it. "But I'd like to make a slight adjustment to it. Can you take it off, please?"

With a question in her remarkable green eyes, she unfastened the chain and handed the locket to him.

Ed opened it and removed the two photos, replacing them with one very good photo of all three of them, taken by Harper on the day he'd arrived at the ranch, fragile and still recovering from the accident. He fastened the locket back around Paige's neck. Then, he reached out for her hand and said, "in front of all of our friends and family, I want to ask you a very important question. *Paige Lilliane Crawley*, would you *please* do me the honor of becoming my wife?"

"Of course, I will!" Paige said, leaning across the space between them to pull him close and kiss him. *A really excellent kiss.* "Nothing could make me happier. Thank God, we finally figured this relationship thing out!" she whispered, apparently just loud enough for her sister to overhear.

"I second that," said Harper. "For a while there, I thought we might have to stage an intervention!"

"Water under the bridge, Harper. The best things are worth waiting for." But for the two of them, it had taken more than New Mexico magic to get here. She leaned forward once more to meet Ed's lips again, and seal the deal, once and for all.

The End

Author's Note on Volcanism in New Mexico*

Thousands of faults underlie the landscape of northern New Mexico and most have ruptured in the distant geological past. These faults are largely concentrated along the Rio Grande rift that bisects the Land of Enchantment and our neighbor to the north, Colorado. An example is the well-known Santa Clara fault, near Española, which can be identified by an area of coarse gray sediments juxtaposed against finer rose-colored deposits.

Although past research has characterized the seismic hazard potential in the Rio Grande Rift as moderate compared to other regions of the mountain west, any uptick in seismic activity is reason for concern, given its proximity to large areas of human habitation. Although the probability is statistically low to moderate, the consequence of seismic effects from a quake in the region would likely be significant.

In addition to detectable earth tremors, geologic changes following seismic events can include changes in groundwater level, increases in streamflow in adjacent hydrologic basins, and increases in the concentration of certain ions in natural spring-fed point-sources. Occasionally, we have observed increases in streamflow activity in earthquake-affected areas: **the mechanism of seismic shaking is thought to sometimes rapidly clear clogged fractures overlying pressurized thermal reservoirs.**

Further studies may be necessary to determine the impact of seismic events on the human landscape, even in sparsely populated areas such as northern New Mexico.

With thanks to NMT Seismological Observatory and New Mexico Tech; based on the article "Earthquakes in New Mexico," by Andy Jochems and Dave Love, and adapted for this fictional story.

ABOUT THE AUTHOR

Wendy Cohan writes contemporary women's fiction from her home in Albuquerque, New Mexico. Her trilogy, "The Inn at Verde Springs," debuted with *The Renaissance Sisters* and continues with *Love Child*. Her work has also appeared in *Pittsburgh Magazine*, *Verge Magazine*, *Cricket*, *The Manifest-Station*, and *Be Their Voice: An Anthology for Rescue*. When not writing, she enjoys spending time with her two adult sons and their partners, and hiking in the nearby mountains with her rescue dogs, Birdie and Lola.

ACKNOWLEDGEMENTS

The roadrunners, quail, and whip-tailed lizards that visit my quiet house in Northwest Albuquerque kept me firmly grounded in my New Mexico surroundings and helped make writing The Inn at Verde Springs series possible, but I couldn't have done it alone. I would like to express my heartfelt thanks to Echo Garret and the team at Lucid House Publishing, including editor Brette Sember and graphic designer Jan Sharrow, for their contributions to bringing the Crawley sisters and the characters of Verde Springs to life. Now, book two, *Love Child*, offers Paige Crawley the opportunity to tell *her* unique story. Thank you very much for listening…

Like Harper and Paige in the Inn at Verde Springs series, my older sister and I were born six years apart, and I have relied intensively on our decades-long relationship, quirks and all, to flesh out the unique and special bond that exists between all sisters. Plus, like the Crawley girls, we both like to eat.

As always, I owe a huge debt of gratitude to the dedicated readers who have encouraged me, helped me course-correct, and celebrated my first successes. To Carin Willis, Jennifer Stout, Peggy Delaney, Julie Rall, and most of all, my sister and chief supporter, Kim Kenley, thank you. Without your support, I wouldn't have had the courage to pursue this series through to completion. Although, I admit, book three came as a surprise, even to me—and I can't wait for readers to get their hands on *Gifts and Revelations*, coming in 2024.

I'm grateful for all of the interesting characters who allow me to share their stories—and to the many twists and turns in life that brought me, finally, to the thing I truly love to do most: *write*.

Big ear-scratches of thanks to my pups, Birdie and Lola, who show up in *The Renaissance Sisters,* and *Love Child,* and in my real life, every day. They remind me to get up from my writing desk and take them for a walk—usually at the exact moment when I can't think of what to write next. Every writer needs a dog.

Finally, I would like to express my gratitude to New Mexico, truly, The Land of Enchantment, for giving me a new home and a fresh start, and for opening my eyes its natural wonders, its remarkable history, and its cultural significance. The landscape around me is rich with tales waiting to be told, and I am grateful to be able to share a small part of it with you, dear readers. One last thought, a piece of wisdom from *Love Child*: life is short. If you love someone, tell them often enough that they start to believe it. We can never hear our people say the words "I love you" too often.

THE INN AT VERDE SPRINGS TRILOGY:

Book 1 – The Renaissance Sisters

Book 2 – Love Child

Book 3 – Gifts and Revelations

CPSIA information can be obtained
at www.ICGtesting.com
Printed in the USA
JSHW012001210723
45220JS00004B/83